News from Édouard

News from Édouard

Michel Tremblay

translated by Sheila Fischman

Talonbooks 2000

Talonbooks
#104—3100 Production Way
Burnaby, British Columbia, Canada V5A 4R4

Typeset in Garamond. Printed and bound in Canada by Hignell Printing Ltd.

First Printing: May 2000

Talonbooks are distributed in Canada by General Distribution Services, 325 Humber College Blvd., Toronto, Ontario, Canada M9W 7C3; Tel.: (416) 213-1919; Fax: (416) 213-1917.

Talonbooks are distributed in the U.S.A. by General Distribution Services Inc., 4500 Witmer Industrial Estates, Niagara Falls, New York, U.S.A. 14305-1386; Tel.:1-800-805-1083; Fax:1-800-481-6207.

The publisher gratefully acknowledges the financial support of the Canada Council for the Arts; the Government of Canada through the Book Publishing Industry Development Program; and the Province of British Columbia through the British Columbia Arts Council for our publishing activities.

Des Nouvelles d'Édouard was first published in 1989 by Lémeac Éditeur Inc., Montréal, Québec.

Canadian Cataloguing in Publication Data

Tremblay, Michel, 1942-
[Des nouvelles d'Édouard. English]
News from Édouard

Translation of: Des nouvelles d'Édouard.
ISBN 0-88922-435-8

I. Fischman, Sheila. II. Title.
PS8539.R47D4813 2000   C843'.54   C00-910365-1
PQ3919.2.T73D4813 2000

For Louise-Odile Paquin, Hélène Dessureault, Danièle Lorain,
Lysane Marion, Sophie Lorain and Martin Dignard

*What's the use of telling the story of your life
if you don't make some of it up?*

—The Duchess

Prelude

August 1976

Big Paula-de-Joliette was categorical: the Duchess should stay outside that night. Quite simply. Otherwise Paula, the razorblade swallower, would take some of her props and carve the cheeks of the old human wreck with graffiti so obscene that even the Duchess, who was as vulgar as a pig in pants, would be so ashamed she'd be forced to cover her face with a veil for the rest of her days. Jennifer Jones, her wig stiff with spraynet, her fake fingernails sparkling, had said: "You can't even write your own name, Paula! You won't be able to sign your work!" To which Paula had replied: "Maybe so, but I'm a hell of a carver!" Which was true. Jennifer Jones bore in the crook of her left arm a star-shaped scar that spoke volumes about that particular magician's art. For one brief moment Jennifer had imagined her own scar on the Duchess's forehead or cheek. And she'd smiled. "Maybe it'd dress up her face a little. Poor Duchess, she looks like a whole lot of nothing!" The smell of melted foundation and cheap face powder floated in the ladies' bathroom that served as the dressing room for the artistes who performed at the Coconut Inn. Jennifer sneezed three times; her wig slid onto her forehead and looked, for a few seconds, like the black fur helmets of the Highland Guards. "When are you going to buy yourself some decent powder, Paula! You smell like my aunt Bertha when she came for her Sunday visit and I don't want to be reminded of *that!*" Patiently, Paula checked out her razorblades one by one, carefully looking for the tiniest rust stain, the smallest manufacturing flaw. After all, she'd be putting them in her mouth! "If you paid me more, precious, I could afford to smell like the Queen of England!" Jennifer straightened her wig, patting it delicately. "How do you know what the Queen of England smells like, smart ass?" "She can't afford to smell bad— she's always on!" Jennifer glanced at her friend who was bent lovingly over her props. "Aw, come on, with you the other person's always wrong!" Paula reached out for her cigarette, which was burning down on the edge of the sink. "We've all been taught by the Duchess, Jennifer! We're all trained to have the last word!" Jennifer walked away from the mirror and rearranged some wisps of hair that wouldn't stay put. "And you'd have the gall to carve the skin of the person who taught you everything you know!" Big Paula-de-Joliette sighed. "To quote the Duchess, you can't be and have been!" Jennifer smoothed her left eyebrow with a moistened fingertip. "But you can't *be* without ever having *been*, Sylvain sweetie!" And Jennifer Jones left behind her a wake of excellent powder. Big Paula-de-Joliette tried to sneeze. A heavy beard was beginning to show through her dark pancake. Weekends, when she did three shows, she usually shaved between the two last, but for a while now, she'd been neglecting to do so out of sheer laziness. "Why go to the trouble for a practically empty house? Anyway, this isn't where I'm going to remake my future!" It's true that the Coconut Inn wasn't what you'd call a palace, and the refinement of its noisy and colourful clientele was not what you'd call intact. After all, this was the Main below La Gauchetière and you didn't come to the Coconut Inn to be fancy and refined. You came to drink and to laugh at men dressed as women who swallowed razorblades, swayed their hips as they sang other people's hits, spat fire (Manon-de-Feu was one of the evening's high points), bitched at one another when things weren't going well, bitched even more when they were going too well, spun around in butterfly costumes or undressed in the glaucous lighting, thinking they looked seductive. Big Paula-de-Joliette ran her hand over her cheek. "Too much is too much. I'd better..." But she didn't have time. Already Jennifer, on stage, was teasing B.V.D., the manager of the club, her friend and long-time partner, and announcing her first song—Ginette Reno's latest hit. The bathroom door opened and a customer went in. A real woman, a rare sight at the Coconut Inn. She hesitated for a moment before pushing open the door to the one stall. Paula gathered her things without looking up. "Won't be long, darling, I just have to shave!" She ran her tongue over her lipstick-stained teeth one last time and smiled sadly at her reflection. "Jesus, honey, you look like hell today!"

The third show on Saturday night was the hardest one for the artistes; hardly anybody was listening, cigarette smoke made the air unbreathable, feelings ran high from the alcohol consumed, battles broke out in the middle of a song or a striptease. Jennifer was always apprehensive when this show was getting underway. She liked to sing and wanted people to listen to her, but seeing these red and joyous faces in constant motion, turning away from her, leaning over tables wet with beer, got her down. She had trouble hearing the orchestra, often missed an attack, sometimes got mad—to the great delight of the audience, actually, who liked nothing better than to see Jennifer Jones blow her top on stage. Especially at two a.m. on Saturday. That night though, Jennifer had launched into "Des croissants de soleil" in the right place, the orchestra was playing well, the audience was almost listening, the smoke wasn't burning her throat too badly. This bothered her. It wasn't normal. Something had been hovering over the Coconut Inn since the day before but she hadn't been able to put her finger on it and now she felt she'd been had. She'd always known everything that was going on, where, how, and between whom; she had stoked hatreds, prevented carnage, reconciled sworn enemies and turned blood brothers against one another; she'd found herself at the heart of the unlikeliest problems, had found last-minute solutions to inextricable dramas that were starting to feature revolvers and knives; and so she refused to believe that something could be brewing that she didn't know about. During the final chorus of "Des croissants de soleil," she quickly checked out the audience but didn't see anything special.

B.V.D., all smiles, was going from table to table, patting shoulders, shaking hands. The waiters were wiggling their asses, as usual. At the bar, Sandra, poor dear, was trying to be cute while mixing some mediocre cocktail. At a table in the corner, Tooth Pick was picking his teeth. Really nothing special. Except that it was a Saturday night that felt more like a Wednesday or a Thursday. As she took her bow to the meagre applause, she felt a small pang behind her padded bra. "Maybe they don't like me so much anymore..." Looking up, she saw big Paula-de-Joliette making her way towards Maurice, who always stood next to the cash register, holding a martini. With her hand sheilding her eyes, she shouted into the mike, in the direction of the razorblade swallower: "Hey, Paula, where are you going? Are you so pissed you can't find the stage?" Scattered laughter. Paula shrugged. "For crissake, sing! I don't spy on you when I'm on stage!" A few necks were already craned. When Jennifer Jones and big Paula-de-Joliette went at each other, you had to listen; sometimes outrageous cracks were exchanged, well-kept secrets divulged, discreet affairs unmasked. Bitch City. Jennifer grabbed her mike with both hands. She'd just realized that Paula might be at the heart of this thing that was getting away from her, that was bugging her so badly. She had to make her talk. "When you're on stage, sweetheart, it's so boring nothing *can* happen! There's nobody to spy on, everybody's fast asleep!" No reaction. Jennifer's jaw dropped. Paula had actually turned away! "Answer when I speak to you, you idiot!" Paula didn't even bother to look at her when she replied: "I don't feel like fighting tonight, okay?" She leaned on the bar next to Maurice. From ringside came a murmur of disappointment. Jennifer returned her microphone to its stand. "Go ahead, sigh! What's left if we can't fight! Does it feel like Wednesday to you too?" Shouts, applause. "Okay! Tell me about it! Wake up, for crissake! Doesn't anybody want to push somebody's face in, just for a little atmosphere?" At the bar, Sandra shouted: "Usually on Saturday night you complain that nobody respects your art! So enjoy it! For once we can hear you sing off-key!" Her singer's pride wounded, Jennifer turned to the orchestra. "Let's hear it, guys! 'Le Fer, le marbre et l'acier!' We'll show them!" At the first notes, Sandra rolled her eyes. "When there's nobody to fight with, she fights with that song! And the song always wins!"

"If I see her walk in I don't know what I'll to do her!" The click of her false nails on the metal echoed down to the other end of the bar where Sandra was crooning "Le Fer, le marbre et l'acier," mimicking Jennifer Jones. Maurice set his drink down. "Go do your act, Paula." "You look like you don't believe me! She won't do what she did to me last night, believe me! No sir…" "The Duchess is old and she's tired!" Maurice's voice was soft, nearly emotional. The lamp above the cash register gave him a sort of golden halo that emphasized the fine curve of his nose, his flat forehead, the salt-and-pepper mustache he'd started growing a few weeks before, which had already added several names to his very impressive list of conquests. The Duchess used to say that the whole of the Main was in love with Maurice because of the bastard's profile. Few could resist it. He knew that and he'd always taken advantage of it. The Duchess also said: "If Maurice starts talking profile, close your eyes!" Big Paula-de-Joliette kept hers open, stopped tapping on the counter and put her hand on Maurice's shoulder. "At two a.m. on Saturday night we're all old and tired… and the last thing we need is a hard time from an old bag who pisses us off for laughs!" Maurice knocked back the rest of his martini. "That's all she's got left, Paula, her meanness…Once you understand that you'll understand lots of things…" Suddenly Paula felt a pang as she saw the Duchess again, unsteady on her chair, one hand clutching her beer that was lukewarm because she'd held it for so long, the other fiddling with her gold chain. Real gold, as she pointed out to anyone who'd listen. Paula saw again the nasty eyes, so nasty, the smile, a bitter crease in the midst of the double chin and droopy jowls. The Duchess, who'd once been so funny! Never beautiful, no, but funny! Hilarious! Dear God…Paula realized that little by little, the Duchess had become the very image of what it was that scared everybody, customers and artistes alike, and all the fine folk who came here practically every night to forget about the time that was passing, for nothing. She hated her even more—that living proof of decrepitude, of dejection, of collapse. Within seconds, she understood that she was ready to accept everything, to put up with everything from the Duchess, out of pity for what was liable to happen to herself as well. The revelation was depressing; she knew that till the very end, she would put up with the assaults, the insults, the mockery, the flattery. But until whose end? "Le Fer, le marbre et l'acier" was over. Jennifer Jones had shrieked the final screech, like a scalded cat, that drove everyone crazy, although she was sure that she'd once again attained the summits of vocal art. A serious gloom fell over poor Sylvain Touchette, known with a flagrant lack of imagination as Paula-de-Joliette (he'd been born in Joliette and his middle name was Paul). "If she comes, at least tell her to watch out... it's dangerous, that act of mine." Maurice had a good laugh at that. His beautiful teeth shone. A bubble of saliva formed on his mouth. Just the day before, the Duchess had shouted to the whole world while Paula was removing her brand-new razorblades from her mouth: "She can't cut herself, her mouth's full of dentures!" Maurice wiped his eye with his handkerchief that smelled of Eau Sauvage, the latest rage in the homosexual circles of east-end Montréal. On stage, Jennifer Jones was announcing big Paula-de-Joliette, laying on thick the introduction she'd been delivering every night for months—unique, sensational, incredible—giving it some ironic little emphases that the blade-swallower chose not to notice. Paula crossed the room at the Coconut Inn, standing upright as a queen, head high, arms spread in a caricature of a ballet dancer. She climbed the three steps to the stage, blowing kisses to everyone, and whispered into the ear of Jennifer Jones who was holding out the mike to her: "I know why you think this is Wednesday! The Duchess isn't here to piss us off!" Then they both had the same vision of horror: when the Duchess was gone, on the Main it would always be Wednesday night.

After she'd changed, Jennifer Jones came and sat at Tooth Pick's table. She hadn't touched her head; the makeup and hair were the same but she'd traded her long gown for worn jeans and a canary-yellow T-shirt that read, in phosphorescent letters: SKINNY FOREVER. The effect was rather stupefying. If anyone asked why she never took off her makeup after the show, she replied: "I keep my real face for myself!" Malicious gossips (the Duchess?) maintained that Jennifer Jones didn't have a real face, that she'd been born in pancake and that at her birth, when her mother saw her false eyelashes, she'd exclaimed: "It's a monster! Down below it's a little boy and on top it's a floozy!" Tooth Pick was surprised by Jennifer Jones' visit. He didn't like her, she didn't like him and it suited them both just fine. They avoided each other as much as possible (Tooth Pick's gaze would slip to the floor whenever it inadvertently met Jennifer's) and if they had anything to tell each other, a message from Maurice or some important news, it was always in brief, brisk phrases, between two doors or across the bar. What Jennifer Jones didn't know, however, was that Tooth Pick was one of her biggest fans. As much as he hated her in life with her shouting, her strident laughter, her airs of a backyard star, so he admired her aplomb when she braved the stage: she had no talent, absolutely none, but she charged along with such energy, she murdered the repertoire with such confidence, that when she sang a kind of miracle occurred; nothing she did was any good but her performance had a kind of spellbinding force that undermined your resistance. He came and watched her work nearly every night and *every time* the incomprehensible occurred: as soon as she set foot on the stage, Tooth Pick's reluctance vanished, he wanted to get to his feet and applaud her, and sometimes he even let himself go and cheered her at the end of the show with happy bravos and excited whistling. Jennifer Jones had always assumed that he was making fun of her; he knew that and, feeling protected, he let his excess excitement run its course. Doing Maurice's dirty work, Tooth Pick was a destroyer, an expert at quickly executed third-rate dirty tricks that no one else would have taken on, accommodating when vicious bad faith or double-crossing were involved, and perhaps what he admired most about Jennifer Jones, without knowing it, was precisely the singer's tremendous capacity for destruction: she'd take a song and do a fabulous job of pulverizing it, stamping on it, rendering it formless, and afterwards had the nerve to take a bow as if she'd just given birth to it. In her, he recognized a fragment of himself which he applauded every night with equal pleasure. Heads turned when Jennifer Jones took a seat at the table where Tooth Pick went on picking his teeth. Greta-la-Vieille, a contemporary of the Duchess but in better shape (one day the Duchess had said of her: "Greta-la-Vieille's last makeover dates from the early days of the Renaissance but unfortunately, if you look at her you can see that the dampness has wreaked its havoc and the plaster's starting to peel"), Greta-la-Vieille had leaned across to her neighbour, Bambi, who shared with her namesake only an idiotically innocent expression, to say: "Better stay... I think the shit's about to hit the fan..." Bambi, for once in her life, had a flash of wit: "You think shit, period!" but she didn't get it till a few seconds later when the others at their table were doubled up with laughter, and then she added: "If I'm making jokes tonight, nothing's normal!" Creasing her eyes, Jennifer Jones lit a cigarette. She exhaled a first puff of smoke and then used thumb and forefinger to pluck a shred of tobacco from the tip of her tongue. "The Duchess isn't here tonight..." Tooth Pick looked around with a phony air of surprise. "Well, uh, no... you're right..." Jennifer Jones leaned towards him, even held out one hand to grab his arm, but he dodged in a movement that was not so much abrupt as nervous. "I just remembered, I saw you talking to her last night..." "I talk to the Duchess every night." "But she doesn't always have that look. Did you scare her or something?" Tooth Pick smiled. A surprisingly beautiful smile on his unattractive face. "Answer me!" He stuck another toothpick in his mouth, sucked on it, chewed it. "This is men's business, Jennifer, you'd better stay out of it!" A chuckle from the next table made Jennifer Jones turn around. She barked at Greta-la-Vieille, startling her: "You want to take my picture?" Greta-la-Vieille straightened up on her chair. "I already got one, it's over my toilet and it's full of pins!" Joyous cries greeted this one; Jennifer Jones shrugged. "You're dipping into the Duchess's old stock..." "And you make your living digging into Ginette Reno's old stock!" Tooth Pick had taken advantage of the exchange to get up when Jennifer Jones's back was turned. When she tried to talk to him he was already leaning on the bar next to Maurice. Jennifer Jones ground out her cigarette in the ashtray. "Shit flies attract shit flies!" Greta-la-Vieille looked in Tooth Pick's direction, then returned to the singer. "That didn't fall on deaf ears, darling!" Jennifer Jones reached out towards Greta, grabbed hold of her ecru lace collar. "If you gab it won't be your picture that's full of pins!"

The Duchess was pacing outside the Coconut Inn. A caged she-wolf. Or rather, a she-wolf who was pacing at the door of her cage and couldn't make up her mind to go in. She had brought the Coconut Inn into the world and now the Coconut Inn didn't want her! Even though she'd brought them all into the world— the oldsters like Greta or Miss Saydie Thompson, the youngsters like Bambi, the "intermediates" too: the talentless Jennifer Jones, the tiresome Paula-de-Joliette, the heartless Hosanna, all of them more or less successful replicas of herself, ungrateful kids who'd never even had the guts to send their messages directly, delegating Tooth Pick, the little snake, with his petty insinuations and his petty threats! At the end of their discussion the previous day, the Duchess—though she was the sharpest wit the Main had ever known—couldn't even come up with a crack that would let her make an honourable exit; in the heat of her emotion, real this time, not feigned like when they'd brought her a penis-shaped birthday cake or an indescribably tacky Mother's Day present, she had murmured pitifully, her chin quivering: "You don't get rid of your seventy-year-old mother just like that!" Tooth Pick had laughed, of course, then said softly: "For thirty years you've been giving birth to monsters all over the Main, you shouldn't be surprised when a couple of them rebel!" But those ones! Her favourites, her own reserve, her private coterie, her court! The Duchess patted her hair. A drop of rain? No, it wasn't that. She smiled sadly. "If even the birds on the Main are crapping on my head..." Some kind of hermaphrodite with dirty blond hair and a tottering gait emerged from the Coconut Inn. He seemed surprised to find the Duchess on the sidewalk. "What're you doing there, you old bag? Everybody's looking for you!" The hermaphrodite with dirty blond hair leaned against the grimy little window where Jennifer Jones was turning yellow as she smiled. "Goddamn hormones..." The Duchess came closer so she could prop him up. "You're Raymond, right?" "Reynald! Soon Reynalda! No balls down there, two big ones up here!" The Duchess frowned. Now she was beginning to forget names. There was a time when she could name from memory all the habitués of all the bars on the Main, along with their special features, their sexual preferences, the vices they hid and those they were proud to display. But more and more, the new arrivals who'd been taking over St. Lawrence Boulevard in the past few years were getting away from her. Mother, yes, but grandmother... "Why do you take that stuff? To be a woman? A real one? It's 1976, Reynalda, even women don't want to look like what you want to look like! Read a little, for pete's sake! Learn something! You're out of date before you even exist!" The hermaphrodite pushed the Duchess away feebly. "Fuck off! Tooth Pick and Maurice are right! You try to put crazy things in our heads... You're dangerous, Duchess, you know that?" He walked away, pitiful in jeans that were too tight over legs that were skinny like a frog's and teetering on stiletto heels he wasn't used to yet. The Duchess leaned against the window. "I'm not dangerous to you, you idiot! I'm dangerous for Tooth Pick and Maurice because they're the ones who sell you all the shit you take! Hormones to make you into a phony woman, downers to help you down when you're hysterical, uppers for when you're down and you realize that maybe you don't want your balls cut off!" The Duchess delivered a kick to the brick wall. Maurice too! Even Maurice! She saw again the dangerously handsome teenager who pandered to the whims of everyone on the Plateau Mont-Royal, darling of the girls from Fabre Street and the mature men at the Palace on the corner of Mont-Royal and Fullum. The late forties. The genesis. And then the fifties: their progressive slide towards the Main, Maurice more and more handsome, the Duchess more and more amusing and omnipresent, Thérèse more and more fucked-up, Pierrette more and more drunk, Harelip more and more cringing. And Marcel, a big lost adolescent who dragged his lanky silhouette from bar to bar looking for his sister, whom others drugged by spiking his drinks with a little white powder that made him really crazy—for the hell of it. The Duchess felt down, so down she was bent double. She could feel her numerous stomachs being squeezed together and the taste of pizza, all-dressed, rose in her throat. She swallowed with difficulty and felt the beginnings of the pain that would burn her esophagus. She took out her box of Diovol, snickering: if Hosanna could see her now! "The heartburn will stop but you'll be constipated, poor thing!" The bland taste, like artificially sweetened plaster, turned her stomach. A tear flowed. Cautiously, the hermaphrodite crossed La Gauchetière. Hormones and speed... Another one lost. The Duchess tried to look at herself in the little square window. All she could see were a few tufts of white hair, tousled to give the illusion of a hairdo. "In our day... no... in *my* day you'd put on anything that looked like a dress and imagination did the rest... At least we weren't serious— and we had fun! Dear Lord, what fun we had! Nowadays, they all get cut and think that will change everything, and they're condemned to *never* having any fun again... not down below because there's nothing there, not up above because their heads are stuffed with all the crap you can find on the Main! Jesus, I'm thinking like an old biddy that's way behind the times!" The Duchess had once heard a freshly cut individual who looked vaguely—very vaguely—like Brigitte Bardot say to a new recruit who'd just sailed in from Drummondville or Hull: "The Duchess? She's folklore on the Main! Totally out of date." What a shock! The Duchess had seen herself decked out in a macramé skirt, a homespun shirt, a ceinture fléchée, a hand-woven poncho from

Maria Svatina and Fabienne Thibeault's clogs—and she hadn't even laughed. To the new woman she'd merely said: "At least I've still got the folklore between my legs!" The other didn't catch the allusion and laughed inanely. The Duchess herself wasn't too sure what she'd meant and thought about it a lot later on, till the day when she'd discovered that someone named Édouard was still present in her head and that the Duchess had been just a character part he'd had a lot of fun with over the years. While those who had the operation… Without imagination, nothing was possible. A little boy followed by an imaginary cat crossed his mind, skipping. Then a drunken teenager holding a match close to his mother's hair. As if to escape from this vision that had been haunting her for weeks now, the Duchess pushed open the door of the Coconut Inn. Immediately she spotted Tooth Pick and Maurice who were plotting something over the bar. Big Paula-de-Joliette had just extirpated her string of razor blades from her guts under the mocking gaze of an audience that had seen it all before. Manon-de-Feu would follow her with the eternal burns on her back and her perpetually chapped lips. Folklore… Oh yes!… The Duchess sat next to Tooth Pick on a stool that was a little too high for her. She spoke so quietly that the snake had to come very close to her mouth to hear what she was saying. "I came anyway. And you know what? To tell you the honest truth, I wouldn't really mind dying…"

"You're paranoid, Duchess! What makes you think you're so dangerous we want to get rid of you?" Crowded into what the Duchess called "the ladies' dressing room," they were smoking a joint before going out for one last little drink; big Paula-de-Joliette took long hits and held them in for a long time, widening her eyes like a cat doing its business. Jennifer Jones handled it as if it were a garden-variety Player's, Manon-de-Feu seemed to derive as much pain as pleasure from it, making faces that were hard to interpret. But the Duchess didn't touch it. She claimed to belong to the rubbing-alcohol generation and she'd sip from her glass as soon as a joint made its appearance. When drunk she'd acknowledge her fear: "I tried a few times... it was a downer. It exaggerates the ugliest things about me. It works on my soul like cleansing cream and I hate that." Paula took a last drag before tossing the damp, lipstick-stained butt in the toilet through the half-open door to the stall. "I was fed up with you. You've been pissing me off for weeks, but there's more to the Main than just me!" The Duchess wasn't sure whether this was a relief. "But Tooth Pick..." "Never mind Tooth Pick, Duchess, he's just a little loser..." The Duchess rested her head against the door; suddenly, the air in the bathroom seemed unbreathable. "Losers are dangerous." Jennifer Jones pinched her cheek affectionately. "If losers were dangerous, Duchess, the Main would've been exterminated long ago!" Coughing, the Duchess opened the door. "Excuse me—I'm going to breathe some good old ordinary cigarette smoke..." The other three exchanged a look. Manon-de-Feu spoke in her hoarse voice that was so surprising with her angelic face that had practically no make-up. "I've never seen her like this! We have to do something!" Paula-de-Joliette tapped the dirty sink with her false nails, sighing. "What she needs is a good three or four day drunk..." Jennifer Jones extracted another joint from an old cigarette package. "Maybe so, but not here; when she's bombed you don't want to be around her." She pushed away Paula's hand, which was making more and more noise on the porcelain sink. "Quit doing that! It's a terrible habit! Wherever you are, we can hear your nails on the edge of something or other! It sounds like a spider coming!" Big Paula-de-Joliette tapped even louder, but on the wall of the stall. "Get off my back, you aren't my mother!" Jennifer Jones took a drag, savoured it, let it out, curving her mouth into a pout that the Duchess called her wet hen's asshole. "If I was your mother, sonny boy, I'd be real, real ashamed!" Manon-de-Feu, who'd just come in, burst out laughing. A native of Joliette too, she knew Paula's mother very well and the woman was, in fact, ashamed of her big boy who'd gone wrong. In a broad, dramatic gesture, Paula-de-Joliette pulled off her wig, exposing to the bluish fluorescent light a bald head glistening with sweat. "If I was your mother, Jennifer darling, I'd be so proud of my little girl's career I'd write my memoirs: *My Son, Jennifer Jones...*" The bathroom door opened on the Duchess who was holding a glass of scotch that was already half-empty. "That feels better now, girls!" She went out again, howling "Mes jeunes années" in an ugly falsetto. Jennifer Jones offered the joint to Paula. "And we're off!" Paula took the time to wipe her forehead with the dubious-looking towel hanging next to the sink before she refused the joint. "That's the trouble with pity—it always blows up in your face! Now we'll have to put up with her all night!"

Everything was bathed in a milky light. Voices were filtered through cotton; laughs became murmurs, cries seemed to be coming from across the street. At times the floor would tilt slowly upwards. The Duchess clutched at the table, then let herself slump against a neighbour, staring with a silly grin. She felt she was being observed but instead of feeling insulted, she was smugly satisfied: somebody was looking after her, nothing bad could happen. The Main rehabilitated her. For once, drinking wasn't making her aggressive; instead, she was inclined to gaze tenderly at her progeny. Her children were beautiful, the Coconut Inn was the end of the world, the Main was her kingdom. The last call had come ages ago, the bar was closed, the waiters were up-ending the chairs on the tables so they could sweep the floor. The Duchess could hear things like: "Pretty late...," "Be good till tomorrow...," "Take you home," but her brain absolutely refused to understand what it all meant. Deep in her mind a miserable apartment on Visitation Street was stagnating in a halo of sadness. She felt fine where she was and she'd stay there till the end of time. If she'd spotted Tooth Pick she would have given him a kiss and told him she'd stopped being afraid—of him or of getting old or of dying or of not being funny anymore or of being repudiated by her children. The beneficent scotch masked everything, life had become a show again. A cheap one maybe, but a show all the same. Then, suddenly, just as people around her were getting seriously impatient, she straightened up as if she were having a vision and looked towards the door. Big Paula-de-Joliette, dressed like a biker with a leather helmet and all the rest, got up in turn to support her. The Duchess was saying something that seemed very important but that no one could understand. The others surrounded her, offering encouraging little remarks as they pushed her towards the door. Just before she got there, the Duchess suddenly shook off her torpor, as if she were waking up, and pushed them all away. "You never understand a thing! For ten minutes now I've been trying to tell you I feel like a hotdog! How stupid can you be! Quit trying to send me home to bed, I'm not a child!" She made a dignified exit without thanking anyone. As usual. Big Paula-de-Joliette pulled up the collar of her leather jacket. "If she comes back tomorrow I don't know what I'll do to her!" Jennifer Jones drained the dregs of a beer that was sitting on the bar. "So we're back where we started: what do we do with her now?" A waiter took the glass from him, making a face. "You don't know who was drinking out of that glass!" Jennifer kissed his cheek softly. "You ought to know, no matter who it was I've tasted him! And I'm immune to everything. Even health!"

The Duchess went out at five o'clock. A.M. During the last hour she'd been the only customer at the Montréal Steamer and she wasn't sure if she'd slept, or merely dozed off in the irresistible aroma of frying potatoes. She sat for a long time hunched over her plate, her hands on her thighs which overflowed considerably her favourite high stool, the one near the frying kettle, where she could see everyone entering and leaving. She hadn't noticed the last customers slipping away around four o'clock, giving her a sardonic smile, and she'd sat there simmering in the smell of grease without really noticing. Théo hadn't bothered her too much; he was open all night and it often happened that some hobo or hooker or homeless person would spend part of the night over an empty plate or collapsed at a table in the back. If they smelled too bad Théo would kick them out; if they were funny he'd keep them there to pass the time; if they were good-looking he'd arrange to get them behind the counter. He was one of those profiteers who like to think they're generous. Théo was fond of the Duchess; she always had something nice to say about his steamed hotdogs (after all these years!), she even claimed that they were the only ones on the Main that she could stomach, the others having gone dangerously downhill these past years. She would sail regally into the Montréal Steamer and tell Théo or Marco, his assistant, who was responsible for the chips: "The usual, with a kiss on the dogs as a bonus!" Théo would set down in front of her three steamed hotdogs, all-dressed, a huge serving of fries and a king size Coke—which the Duchess liked to call her appetizers, licking her chops. And then she'd tuck in, surprisingly serious. While in many circumstances the Duchess behaved extravagantly—in the street, at the bar, the theatre, the movies, in the shower, even in bed (which used to exasperate her partners back when she still had any) she became reserved over food, even in company. She'd eat everything with surprising diligence, chewing for a long time, staring at her plate, washing down each mouthful with a little Coke when she was eating cheap, a little wine when she was eating chic. She often said that she never enjoyed solitude as much as when she was eating. For a long time people had thought she was kidding, but eventually they realized that it was the simple truth: even at a party she ate by herself, and they'd finally come to respect this eccentricity (they were quick to make fun of it, but they did respect it). That night, the Duchess had eaten more slowly than usual. She seemed preoccupied. She hadn't even answered Théo's disinterested question: "Aren't you afraid you'll die of acute indigestion? Three hotdogs in the middle of the night?" What was going through the Duchess's mind would have surprised everyone on the Main. For some time now she'd been thinking a lot about Paris. She'd even taken out the diary she'd kept during her trip, where she'd reported daily, or almost, on everything she'd said and done, for her sister-in-law, the fat woman, who'd given it back to her before she died, saying:

"Fifteen years later and it still makes me laugh. And cry. It's helped me through some of the worst times in my life. Hold on to it. Leave it to someone you love. When it's your turn to go there'll still be a reminder of your passage." The fat woman's death had overwhelmed the Duchess for months during which she couldn't even face opening the diary. She'd shoved it into a drawer, gone to Hosanna's place and given him the key: "When I'm dead, open the bottom drawer in my chest and try to have one last laugh to my health. I'm leaving it to you." Hosanna had accused her once again of defeatism, but he'd held onto the key. And the Duchess had forgotten all about it for fifteen years, but over these past few days, she'd felt an urge to go search in the drawer. At first she'd thought that mere curiosity was prompting her, then an absurd thought had slipped into her head: the Duchess had the feeling that she wanted to check on something before—before what? And to check on what? Whether the humiliation had been as bitter as she remembered? And so she'd taken out the navy blue notebook that was all dog-eared, stiff and dusty, but she hadn't touched it. Just seeing it made images of Paris, scents (smells, rather), voices, sounds come back to her and she was overcome by an urge to scream. Nearly thirty years ago already! She was becoming aware not only of the passage of time but even more of her inability to fix anything whatsoever: Paris was far behind her and not ahead of her at all. Before she nodded off over her plate, the Duchess shed a few tears. And when she'd wakened with a start because a fluorescent light had backfired, she murmured: "How do they manage to shit standing up?"

The Main was deserted. The Duchess was surprised till she realized that it was five a.m. She decided to head north on foot, towards St. Catherine Street, before going to bed: the hotdogs were refusing to go down. She checked again to see if her Diovol tablets were still in the purse slung over her shoulder. Maybe she would find a few lost souls with nothing better to do between

Dorchester and St. Catherine: the unavoidable Bambi; Greta-la-Jeune, the other one's son; Rose Latulipe who claimed to be related to Gilles but nobody believed her; Irma-la-Douce, two hundred and forty pounds and as gentle as a troop of tigers in heat. But it was really too late: Mayor Drapeau wanted a beautiful clean city for the summer Olympics that were set to open any day now. There had been an appalling series of raids and the Main of course had been among the first to feel their effect. The Duchess recalled one of her latest quips, which had reduced the entire Main to laughter, even Maurice, though he usually didn't react even when she was hilarious; like everyone else, she'd gone to visit the unfinished stadium and when she first spied the huge concrete doughnut she'd cried out: "Montréal's been so buggered by the mayor she's had to get a concrete asshole!" She crossed La Gauchetière, passing the Coconut Inn again, amazingly bland without its red neon sign and its blinking marquee. She'd spent so many years dreaming in that dump, convinced that some day, something was going to happen! She brushed all that aside and decided to walk in the middle of the street so she'd look carefree even though she didn't feel that way. She crossed Dorchester, trying out a few steps of the Argentinean tango, punctuating it with some well-chosen "pum, pum, pum, parum." Ah, the tango... The night was violet and deep. As all the lights were out on the Main, the Duchess could clearly see the stars turning pale in the east. She stopped outside the Monument National, looking up at the sky. She was about to break into, "Ah! Lève-toi, soleil, fais pâlir les étoiles..." when a faint noise from the parking lot across from the theatre caught her attention. Someone was going "psst, psst" and tapping the hood of a car with a coin. "Another junkie!" The Duchess was about to continue on her way when she heard her own name distinctly. Her real name. Someone was calling her Édouard! She headed for the parking lot with hesitant little steps. Tooth Pick was leaning against a car, a toothpick stuck into his smile. The Duchess crossed the sidewalk, stepped over the metal rail that encircled the parking lot. "What're you doing there at this time of night? Switching to stealing cars?" Tooth Pick's smile stayed frozen. "No. I've been waiting for you,

Édouard…" Something in the Duchess's stomach tightened, then came loose, followed by an ugly gurgling sound. She thought without even understanding what it meant: "It's true, fear speeds up the digestion…" She leaned against the car next to Tooth Pick. "You've got time to kill!" The car sank a little beneath her weight. The silence that followed was so long that the Duchess wondered seriously whether Tooth Pick had fallen asleep. Then she realized that he was waiting for her to talk. Usually, when Tooth Pick was waiting for someone, it implied something very unpleasant, and he must have been used to people pleading, explaining themselves, making him offers… "You say you've been waiting for me but now you aren't saying a word… I can't read your mind, Tooth Pick, I can't guess what you want from me!" Tooth Pick struck a match to stretch out the silence a little more; the notion that he was about to light his toothpick crossed the Duchess's mind and she hid a giggle behind her hand. "What's so funny? Are you still drunk?" The Duchess sighed, then wiped her eye. "I was thinking about something pretty funny: if the cops turn up they'll think I'm soliciting." "You can't solicit at your age! Have you looked at yourself lately?" The reply came so fast that the Duchess couldn't hold it back. Actually, that was a weakness of hers; sometimes she didn't understand the repercussions of her nasty cracks until she'd made them. "And you haven't had a look at yourself either! Only wrecks like me will do deals with wrecks like you!" He was on her in less than a second. He pulled up her short-sleeved sweater and twisted it under her chin. The Duchess choked. The blood rose to her head and her stomach went into cramps. But she still managed to whisper: "If anybody goes by they'll think that you *insist* on kissing me!" Grunting, Tooth Pick let go. The Duchess pulled down her sweater, smoothed it over her belly. Tooth Pick spat out the little wooden stick. Another silence followed. The Duchess was panting. She knew that she couldn't run away and in any case, her pride wouldn't let her. Surprisingly, Tooth Pick was panting a little too. The Duchess thought: "Heavens above, he's nervous!" He seemed to hesitate for a long time before asking her: "You've never liked me, eh Édouard?" The Duchess looked at him with something like compassion in her eyes. "No. Never. All my life I've liked everybody, except pathetic little losers." Tooth Pick took a few steps, kicked at a pebble. "If you knew all the things I've done in my life, Édouard, you wouldn't think I was a loser!" "If I knew all the things you've done in your life Denis Ouimet, I'd probably think you were an even bigger loser! I thought you were a loser when you hung out with my little nephew's gang on Fabre Street, when you were a kid; I thought you were a loser when you followed Maurice after he started raising hell on the Main and today I think you're an even worse loser when you do under the covers what Maurice hasn't got the guts to do on top!" She looked up to the sky which was becoming paler and paler. "And what you're getting ready to do is the most pathetic thing you've ever done. Because it's pointless and it's childish." With his hands in his pockets, Tooth Pick was slowly approaching her. "Because you're the victim?" The Duchess didn't look down. "You want to soil the end of such a beautiful night!" "D'you get that out of a book?" This time it was the Duchess who hurled herself at him but didn't touch him. She was a good head taller and she stood there, bent over his ugly face. "You fucking creep! You're pathetic and you're ignorant! You've got just what you want, eh? You've been waiting to beat me up, now do it! I'll be proud to wear your bruises tonight, I'll say they're from a wild night of sex!" While the Duchess was speaking, Tooth Pick had taken out his knife. Smiling, he showed it to her. "You won't be wearing anything tonight, Édouard!" The Duchess came out with a big laugh that made him jump. "Did you get that out of a book? No, I forgot, you can't read!" The rest happened very quickly. For a few seconds they looked like a pair of lovers: when she felt the blade perforate her stomach, the Duchess tightened her arms around Tooth Pick and seemed to be pressing him against her heart. And Tooth Pick was speaking very softly, as if he were murmuring sweet words. "That's how we deal with nuisances like you, Édouard! You won't be pissing people off anymore! Or sticking your nose into other people's business!" The Duchess was crying as if she were sad about something. Tooth Pick went on. "Something like peace will come back to the Main and we'll be able to do what we have to do without you sneering at us!" He pulled out the knife abruptly. The Duchess opened her arms. "Maurice says hello, Édouard!" She looked him squarely in the eyes. "Maurice said nothing of the kind! Maurice will find out about this when he gets up. And he'll wash his hands of it, as usual! You tell him hello from me!" But Tooth Pick had already headed for Dorchester Street. The Duchess held her stomach in both hands. "Me, die in a parking lot? Never! I intend to die where I reigned!" She raised her head, glimpsed the Monument National and burst out laughing.

Struggling, she went back to the middle of the street. Bending to step over the metal railing, she'd felt dizzy and thought she was falling, but her pride held her up: she had to walk to St. Catherine Street. It didn't occur to her to call for help; she knew she was going to die, she accepted it, but she was determined not to collapse between two cars in the middle of an anonymous parking lot. All her life she'd been carefree; true, she hadn't had many successes, mostly she'd ruined things, but always with superb insolence, as if to say: "Look how well I've accomplished this failure, see how well I've perfected it, how artfully I take it on..." When she was looking for a stage name (every newcomer in her crowd took one, never chosen at random, always drawn from the neophyte's tastes, tics or physical resemblance—real or imagined), she had just finished reading *La Duchesse de Langeais*, which she'd found at once ridiculous and overwhelming, and that mixture of the sublime and the laughable, of fatal wealth and intentional, flamboyant poverty, the road taken from the salons of Paris, where everything was possible except salvation, to the convent in the Balearic Islands where nothing was possible but salvation, had stirred her because she'd realized that the road *she* had to take was precisely the opposite: Montréal may not have been Majorca but nothing was possible there except salvation and so Paris became a goal to achieve rather than a starting point; and so she had chosen the name Duchess of Langeais in the hope that one day she'd end up where the real Duchess had started out. For her, dying in a parking lot meant an out-and-out failure. Even after the bitter humiliations of Paris, she still used the name, Duchess of Langeais (she always said that she wanted to die like the character in Balzac, a barefoot Carmelite, but drinking tea) and she'd made it stick thanks to her eccentricities that were rarely in good taste, and a wit that was often glib but always on target and, most of all, devastating. She'd been the queen of the bitchy remarks on the Main for so many years that she refused to leave it with the memory of a mangled body discovered between two cars: the nasty cracks would come too easily to the imbeciles who would survive her. Her legs were like rubber; cold sweat was running down her face and her back. And no one was coming down the Main. She fell to her knees, her strength vanished. "Come and watch me die, somebody!" She was overcome by dizziness again and a horrible taste filled her mouth. Thinking this was it, she turned her head towards the Monument National. "Help me, you old wreck, don't let me die like a nobody!" The theatre seemed to be illuminated from inside; a greyish, flickering light came through the dirty windows in the neglected doors. The Duchess thought she could make out shadows coming down the main staircase. Without realizing it, she pulled herself to her feet. After a few seconds when she thought she could hear an outdated, repetitious little tune, the doors were flung open as if by the shock of an explosion and a wave of singers, badly dressed and gesticulating awkwardly, spread onto the sidewalk. They sang till they were hoarse a tune straight out of a third-rate operetta that was full of the sweetness of the day and how pleasant it was to stroll down the Champs-Élysées. The Duchess recognized some of her favourite chorus singers, those she'd made fun of during the forties and the fifties: she thought they were just as off-key, just as mediocre, just as corny as they'd been when she and her gang of washed-up queens gave them a standing ovation every time they came on stage. She couldn't help being touched by how ridiculous the situation was and told them: "It's good that you've come to laugh at me while I'm dying, it's only fair..." After one last chorus—

ill-attacked, ill-pursued, ill-concluded—that delighted the Duchess, a couple came on or, rather, came out; they stepped onto the sidewalk of the Main as if it were a garden in the land of smiles or the merry widow's salon, regal, beaming, ridiculous in their prince and princess get-ups, but triumphant all the same because they knew that what would follow would be sublime, because they were brilliant. Pierrette Alarie, Léopold Simoneau. The Duchess had seen them make their début right here, she'd been one of the first to cry genius, she'd followed their career as long as they were in Montréal, lost sight of them when they were swallowed up by the outside world that had praised them to the skies for twenty years in New York, Salzburg, Vienna. Just for her they sang the duet from *The Pearl Fishers*, Pierrette not skimping on the vocal exercises nor Léopold on his famous glissandi. During their final note, which they stretched out to the threshold of apoplexy, Pierrette, with her jutting chin and Léopold with his taut belly, they were beginning to fade away as if the sound that emerged from their mouths was taking away all their vital essence. The Duchess, busy holding in her stomach which was trying to spill over, couldn't applaud them. Or thank them. She had discovered the beauties and the aberrations of the theatre in this hall, she'd made her own début as a fake woman of the world here, and now she was coming here to die all alone, like a barefoot Carmelite. With a pang, she thought: "An unlikely melodrama, the kind I've always liked." Finally she turned towards the still-deserted Main and howled: "The Main's become an operetta set! And we're all a bunch of bad actors! The operetta has come into the street and we've let it!" No reply. "It's intermission. They've all gone to take a leak! The stage is bare..." The light of dawn emphasized the ugliness, the mediocrity of the Main; everything was devoid of colour, of texture, of interest. The Duchess was taking small steps, her eyes glued to St. Catherine Street where, perhaps, something would happen before it was all over. She went past the Midway and the Crystal, which had been renamed and presumably purified but were still dark, smelly dens where teenagers not yet initiated came to provoke or experience their first fondling—elated, hounded, feverish. She had never haunted these spots, though they were very popular, young prey never having interested her. She had often said: "I'll devour beef, but veal makes me sick!" At the corner of St. Lawrence and St. Catherine, she thought to herself that she'd taken this long walk for nothing; there were no more people here than in the parking lot. She turned around twice. Not a soul. She managed a faint smile, more like a grimace. "They're all getting together somewhere else..." Then she thought about Marie Bell whom she'd seen at the Comédie-Canadienne in *Phèdre* in the early sixties: she'd seen her land on her back, dead as a doornail, after her final Alexandrine (one of the most ridiculous things she'd ever seen in her life but that Montréal audiences seemed to think was brilliant), a little like an ironing board you've dropped, and she thought: "I can do that too! It's now or never!" Without giving it any further thought she let herself topple backwards. Her head struck the pavement and she moaned a little. "It hurts like hell if you aren't used to it!" The sky was still white but the stars had come back. She could no longer move; something stifling and warm was rising in her throat. She thought: "The big difference between Marie Bell and the Duchess of Langeais is that after Marie Bell dies, she can still take her bow!" She heard hurried footsteps; someone was bending over her, kneeling. She saw the pale face of a teenager with circles under his eyes who must have been up all night. She couldn't put a name to the face under this dishevelment where already the ravages of drugs could be seen. "What's wrong, Duchess?" She shook her head, grimacing. "*Madame* la Duchesse, you cheeky brat! We don't even know each other!" She raised one hand, felt something move in her abdomen. She wanted to put her fingers on the boy's cheek but he recoiled because of the blood running off them, thick and brownish. "You tell them that even if she's spilled her guts, the Duchess of Langeais didn't shit her pants. She was dignified and poised even in the face of death." Everything toppled. The chorus of imbeciles started up again. This time, Léopold and Pierrette sang themselves hoarse in something that resembled Handel. Then, from the north of the Main, came a strange procession. A compact group of silhouettes marching almost in step, but desperately slow, as if reluctantly. First came a limping old lady, pulling by the hand an overly serious little boy, and around them capered a huge tomcat that was visibly in love. Immediately after them, four women holding knitted garments glided along the pavement, intoning soothing incantations in an archaic language. Next came a fat woman surrounded by a crowd of silent characters: men dressed like women, women disguised as men, a dancer on roller-skates, little girls who were too quiet, a long string of faceless men all with the same physique of a Latin fop, two actresses wearing the costumes that had made them famous; one of them small and wriggling in her navy blue jumper and her battered sailor cap, the other stiff and impassive in her wine-red taffeta gown with an overly-generous low neckline. The procession crossed St. Catherine Street in perfect stillness. Pierrette and Léopold had fallen silent; the chorus too. And when the Duchess's past bent over her, holding a cup of the Carmelites' tea, it was too late. In the movies, the camera would have risen into the air; the audience would have seen the doused neon lights, then the rooftops of the Main which splits the city in two, then St. Catherine herself, so pitiful in the wee small hours of the morning; finally Montréal would have slowly moved away against a sunrise background while the credits rolled. In real life, Édouard had already started to rot.

Scheherazade I

The big navy notebook sat on the coffee table next to the plaster "David" for at least a week before Hosanna decided to touch it. Right after the funeral he'd looked for it at the back of a drawer in the Duchess's dresser but hadn't had the courage to open it, staring at it for hours to the great despair of Cuirette—who couldn't wait to rip open the Duchess's past and laugh about it as the Duchess had asked them to do. The funeral had been grim. Transvestites without wigs or makeup, pale and shivering in the light of nine a.m., so unfamiliar and unflattering: nothing flamboyant about that. Glamour is for the nighttime; by day, this world of illusion takes on a pathetic pallor that brings a lump to your throat. And of the Duchess' family, there was hardly anyone left who still spoke to her. Her sister Albertine had asked to be excused even from the funeral parlour. Pills, people said... As for the rest of them, they were quite simply ashamed of the common grave where one of their own would be buried. Everyone had gone their separate ways after the funeral to go back to bed. And already the perpetual Wednesday night had begun to settle in on the Main. About the Duchess' murder the newspapers had offered a few assumptions, each more far-fetched than the others, especially the one about the innocent youth who'd brought down the goddamn old faggot who'd been forcing his attentions on him, but no one on the Main was fooled and every transvestite from St. Catherine Street to below La Gauchetière was blaming Tooth Pick, who denied everything with a grin that belied his words. Filled with remorse, big Paula-de-Joliette had slashed her wrist with one of her props and was having a hard time recovering. Greta-la-Vieille had tried to take over from the Duchess but she'd been told to forget it because she was so terrible. The Main was in mourning: what had been its soul for the past thirty years had been devastated forever. But a week after the funeral, one night when Cuirette was slumped in front of the TV watching an old Marlon Brando movie badly dubbed into ridiculous French, Hosanna sat down beside him, reached across the coffee table and picked up the Duchess' diary. Cuirette immediately turned the knob and the picture disappeared. "You going to read it out loud?" Hosanna curled up against his boyfriend's shoulder. "Will you have the patience to listen?" "Why not?" "What about Marlon Brando?" "He used to turn me on, but not anymore. And in French he sounds like an old queen..." Hosanna smiled for the first time in a week. "Come to the salon tomorrow, Cuirette. Your hair's greasy again." Cuirette ran his hand through his tresses. "In his movies Marlon Brando always has greasy hair and you never complain about *that!*" "In the movies it shines, it looks good, but in the real world it stinks!" Cuirette stuck his chest out. "I smell like a man!" Hosanna tickled him; Cuirette's chest went flat and his beer belly reappeared, round and pudgy. "You smell like a cave man, it's not the same! Y'know, man invented shampoo two million years ago." Trying to look composed, Cuirette sipped his beer. Hosanna sighed. "Man invented beer too—alas!" "Shut up and read!" Very cautiously, Hosanna opened the blue notebook which smelled of dust and musty paper. "I feel like Scheherazade... If I read for a thousand and one nights, Cuirette, will you make babies with me?" "We've already screwed for a thousand and one nights, Hosanna, and our offspring's pretty feeble..." Hosanna ran his hand over the first page of the diary. "May 1947... Ouch, no kidding... I wasn't even five years old." "You're already making comments! At this rate it'll take two thousand and two nights!" "Hey, look, it starts on a boat..." After glancing at the first page, Cuirette closed his eyes and belched as discreetly as he could. With a lump in his throat, Hosanna started reading. "As I was buying this notebook at the *Liberté*'s chic five-and-dime store..."

Fugue

May-June 1947

Crossing the Atlantic

D ear Sister-in-Law,

When I was buying this notebook at the *Liberté*'s chic five-and-dime store, I saw myself again as a kid at school, sweating and cursing to crank out that week's not very good French composition, my tongue sticking out to show I was concentrating, my fingers stained because I couldn't pick up a pen without getting ink on them. I remember they always gave us some fascinating subject to write about, like: "My Holidays in the Country"—me who'd never set foot outside Montréal and who sneezed till it could break your heart if I saw more than three daisies in a row; or "Autumn's Beauties" in which I absolutely had to avoid the only adjective I knew to describe the extravagance of the trees on Fabre Street in October: multicolored; or "Peace in the Family," when life in our house—between my father's attacks of alcoholic craziness and my mother's acting like a cop in a dress—wasn't what you'd call peaceful. But do you know what? I had to make up a story and doing that developed my imagination! And I made up not just holidays but also an incredible countryside that was a blend of the tropical forests of Jules Verne, whose books I devoured as I lay in my bed eating chocolates (already), and parts of Parc Lafontaine in the bushes around Calixa-Lavallée Street; I'd invent mild sunny autumns that were basically the same as summer but in red and gold, and peace in the family that was exemplary on paper but would have been unbearably boring in real life. And that was how I learned to write more or less correct French. But it was twenty-five years ago and a twenty-five-year-old habit of saying whatever I felt might have tarnished my incomparable style somewhat, and now I wonder how I'm going to bring back the French that I used for inventing instead of describing... We'll see, I guess...

So yes, I decided to keep a diary instead of writing you letters, at least for the part of my trip that I'll be spending on this ship. I can't send you letters in bottles, after all!

You lent me your eyes when I left Montréal, so too bad for you! You're going to have to put up with everything, what I feel as well as what I see!

On paper, it's impossible to be shy and reserved. When I used to talk to you, even though I confided in you more than anyone else, there was always the risk that I'd shock you. I know how understanding you are, but I'd feel too awkward to go as far as I should have. Now though, I don't even know when you'll read this. Maybe never, if I'm too ashamed of what I've written... (See, I'm already censoring myself!)

But I promise one thing, I'm going to write exactly the way I'd talk to you: between you and me it's impossible to be pompous; simplicity and sincerity are enough.

Let me start with our departure from New York.

Against a sunset that could make you swoon, the *Liberté* pulled away from the pier that was awash in confetti and streamers. Actually, we passengers were supposed to fling it all onto the pier, waving bye-bye and blowing kisses to the poor jerks who'd come to see us off, but there's always some clown who does everything backwards: so there I am with two pounds of confetti on my head and I go to my cabin dripping with streamers in every colour of the rainbow. A technicolour mummy! I feel sorry for the poor girl who'll be cleaning the cabin tomorrow morning! And since everybody on board seemed to look pretty much the same, I imagine that we're going to hear some cursing!

I shook myself off as best I could, but it was impossible to get rid of everything: there were still some of those goddamn little paper circles that wouldn't let go... I had to change my clothes.

There were some surprises in store.

The cabin looks like a closet that's been fixed up for a quiet dwarf who doesn't care too much about his comfort. When I open the door, I bang my head on the bed and if I stretch out my arm, my knuckles hit a porthole the size of a soup plate. The girl who sold me my ticket called it a "single"; if you ask me, it's more like a "half": half of me's going to sleep while the other half walks the corridors waiting its turn! And they call it first class: imagine if I'd taken second! They'd've packed me in a suitcase and stuffed it in the bottom of the hold!

Anyway, I never really understood my ticket; the girl said I'd be entitled to eat in first class but that my cabin was between first class and second, though it was considered to be first... She added that it's where they put single people travelling on their own. Maybe she saw it as a disease because it felt as if she was putting me in quarantine. If you ask me, I got screwed yet again and she shipped me off to a part of the boat where nobody wants to be! I had to climb about eighty-two circular staircases and find my way through a maze of crummy-looking corridors and culs-de-sac before I got to the crooked bit of deck I'd been assigned in one corner of the ship, where they'd turned some dog kennels into "spacious and comfortable" (that's what the leaflet calls them) cabins for lonely bachelors who are too embarrassed to stand up for themselves.

And the bathroom... If I told you that compared with it our bathroom on Fabre Street is Versailles, that would give you an idea of its size. You open a cupboard to hang up your clothes and you realize it's the bathroom! You take your shower in something that looks like a battered hot water tank, and as for the toilet ... when I sit on it, my knees are practically rubbing against the bed! There I am with my ass in the bathroom and my knees in the bedroom! You're stout too, you can imagine what it's going to be like to spend a whole week in a closet! With no air either, because the porthole doesn't open! If it's the least bit hot, they're going to find me stewed in my own juice and they'll serve me to the second class for dinner!

I'd left the cabin door open while I did my inspection; I'd seen two poor devils pass by, heads down and shoulders hunched. We exchanged sad little waves. At least I'm not alone in my misery! And maybe we're in a part of the boat where sexy sailors race around all night, screaming hysterically... Okay, so I'm dreaming in technicolour again...

I tried the bed. God almighty, I overflow on three sides!

Later.

I've just had my first meal on board.

My table is as well located as my cabin.

Whenever I go to eat over the next week, I'll have the immense pleasure of being right in the middle of the waiters' ballet: my table is right beside the door to the kitchen and the comings and goings are enough to make you seasick even if you're a good sailor. And speaking of being sick to your stomach, there's one thing that surprises me. Everybody I know had warned me about being seasick and, yes, the dining room was half empty for that first meal, but I felt perfectly fine! Funny, isn't it? I ate with my usual good appetite, that's the least I can say, while the three green cadavers at my table looked at me as if I were a monster straight from hell.

Just before the meal began, the captain (needless to say his table's a good one!) made a little speech, congratulating the passengers who'd been brave enough to come to this first meal on board. Some people were holding their heads in both hands, others were rubbing their bellies, still others wetting their foreheads with their napkins; while me, I'd already downed my tomato juice. And then he tried to persuade them to eat. You should have seen it! Just the word "eat" (in English, by the way: even though it has a French name, on the *Liberté* everything happens *en anglais*, Americans *obligent*), and a dozen people rush to the door, doubled over, while others lean back in their chairs to air out their insides. The captain smiled. Maybe he was thinking that his company wouldn't have to pay so much for food! In the end, he had the nerve to wish everybody *bon appétit*. That was when the swinging door behind me opened and I realized I was in trouble. A flock of waiters started racing through the dining room in every direction and whenever one of them went in or out of the kitchen, I'd feel a hot breath on my back and bits of an amazing commotion would hit me. Let me tell you, that kitchen was no haven of peace on earth! It seems to me they do everything there: raise the animals, kill them, skin them, cook them, serve them—and whatever's left they feed to their dogs (I'm positive I heard barking and I'm sure it wasn't the chef!). There was so much noise from the kitchen, I almost thought the bowling finals were going on! When a waiter went in with a tray-load of dirty dishes I took a look inside. God in Heaven! It was Coney Island!

I realize I've neglected to describe the simple, stylish room where I'll be eating my meals over the next week. Absolutely amazing! First of all, it took me a good fifteen minutes to find it. You can't take anything for granted on this boat! Tomorrow, I think I'll leave a trail of little white pebbles to help me find my way... I finally sorted out all the decks and corridors (strictly by chance, though) and when I finally got to the dining room I just stood there, stunned.

Remember that old silent movie, *Titanic*, that we saw together, where the actors went bug-eyed to express whatever emotion they were supposed to, and we couldn't believe that everything on a boat was so big? Well let me tell you, compared with the one on the *Liberté*, the *Titanic* dining room is an outhouse. It's so big and so rich I nearly didn't go in! I have to say, even though there weren't many people, the ones I saw were very snazzy: tuxes, floor-length dresses, rivers of diamonds, precious stones bigger than bottle stoppers, dozens of fancy perfumes that blended together without making you sick: all that to say we were a long way from the greasy spoons of Plateau Mont-Royal and, for once, I felt very small...

I followed the maître d', standing as straight as I could; I must've looked as relaxed as a man on death row who's on his way to meet the final slipknot. When he showed me to my nobody's table with an ironic little smile, I was as much relieved as disappointed. You know what we're like, don't you? We want to leave our crappy lives behind, but when we see something different, we're too chicken to grab it! Anyway. So I took my seat with silly little smiles at the others at my table (not one woman to have a decent conversation with; just these fat jerks who'll probably spend the week talking about broads and baseball!).

There were enough glasses in front of my plate to open a restaurant! I thought, if I drink from every one of these glasses before the end of the meal, they're going to find me in the kitchen feeling up the help! Short glasses, tall glasses, long ones, bulging ones, more or less ordinary ones (there's always a need for nobodies, right?): an army, I tell you! And me, who's used to drinking my beer from my tomato juice glass, I'll tell you, my eyes were popping out of my head!

When I peered up at the ceiling to admire the chandelier, I saw something amazing: it was only when you looked at the chandelier that you could tell the boat was moving! Maybe because it's hanging there... When you look at it, it seems to be swaying and then all of a sudden you realize it isn't moving, we are! And then I felt a kind of hollow in my stomach and I asked the next person I saw to bring me a glass of tomato juice. It's true I've never travelled, but I've read! The next person in question frowned a little because maybe it wasn't his job, but two minutes later I was wiping my mouth—to the great disgust of my table-mates who forced themselves to look elsewhere.

So after he'd made his speech, the captain (say, is captain what you call him? I know he isn't a pilot—I'll have to buy a Larousse dictionary, if they sell them); anyway, the man in charge tucked into his first course and that was when the fun began. I've rarely had so much trouble holding back the giggles as I did during that meal!

You should have seen the rivers of diamonds flopping around on their necks in rhythm with the retching, the precious stones flying up to the sweaty foreheads, the long dresses jumping up and heading for the exit; the tuxes too, as stiff as long winter underwear when you dry it outside in February, were going in a more or less dignified way towards the door, pretending nothing was wrong. It's something we never think about, but when you get right down to it, rich people's armour is only on the outside!

Twenty minutes later, the captain (or the navigator? the conductor—no, not that!) was practically the only one left at his table and he was smiling like he'd seen it all before.

As for me, I'd just eaten one of the best meals of my life. Aside from the ones you cook, of course. But this one was absolutely different anyway... So complicated you didn't know what you were eating! Mind you, the menu didn't help: when it says things like "The temptation of St. Anthony with balls of rice," or "Salt-meadow dainties with three mustards," or "Chocolate divinities," it's hard to know what to expect. Chocolate, okay, I know what that is, but divinities? I pictured the Blessed Virgin covered with chocolate sauce and I thought, I'll have a hard time putting that in my mouth! The others at the table only spoke English, and because the menu was all in French they were more mixed-up than I was. In any case, I ate everything, purring with pleasure even though I wasn't sure what it was. The chandelier swaying from side to side didn't bother me one little bit. The waiters' ballet fanned my back, which felt good. And eventually I figured out what all the glasses were for: the long thin ones were for white wine, the little pot-bellied ones for red wine, the nobodies for water, as I'd already guessed. I got a little mixed up with the cutlery though: when dessert arrived I had two knives and a fork left. Just try eating chocolate sauce with a fork. (I'd figured out the chocolate sauce, but the divinities turned out to be plain ordinary cream puffs!)

But hang on: when the meal was over, another surprise, a super duper one, was waiting! I'd seen that kind of thing in school, singling somebody out as an example, but in the first class dining room, honestly! That's right, you guessed! At the end of the meal, after the captain wiped his mouth, he stood up and cited as an example the gentleman at table 111 who had such a wonderful appetite! I have to admit, there weren't many people left to applaud me and the ones who did avoided looking at me because I made them sick to their stomachs; still, I nearly died right then and there!

And that was when the seasickness hit! The excitement, I suppose. Everything in my stomach froze, then I felt it moving up and I had to race away from the table.

Throwing up in a toilet bowl the size of a thimble is no joke, believe me!

I'm writing these first episodes in my private diary sitting up in my bed, with an aching back and a prickly sensation in my heart that feels like pain and that I can't explain to myself.

I did everything possible to leave Montréal and it worked, so I ought to be happy... but I'm not, not really. The fatigue and excitement of leaving, I suppose... And I have to tell you, ever since I emptied my stomach this boat feels as if it's moving a lot.

The girl who sold me the ticket (and don't think I've said the last word about her!) had sworn though that these boats don't move... But she also sold me a rat hole when she'd promised me a palace.

I nibbled a couple of chocolate bars, my last souvenir of Montréal. You can probably get chocolate in Europe but it can't be as good as ours.

It's 5:15 a.m. and I haven't slept yet.

I dozed off for an hour or two and then I woke up as usual for what Samarcette calls my four a.m. flood. For a few seconds I didn't know where I was, I couldn't recognize anything—the walls, the door, the ceiling—till finally I thought I was in jail. I don't know why, but I told myself: okay, they've nabbed us, Samarcette and me, they've flung us in jail because to them, we're criminals! But when I switched on the bedside lamp that's screwed to the wall above the bed I told myself there isn't a jail cell in the world that's this small and I remembered that I was in a first class cabin on one of the finest ships in the world...

Needless to say, there was no question of getting back to sleep.

I need more air. Though that shouldn't be a problem out here in the middle of the ocean! There's plenty of air here—in fact that's *all* there is!

I thought about you when you have trouble breathing during our heat waves. The family sometimes thinks you're exaggerating, but I'm beginning to know what it's like. I feel anxious, hot, my heart pounds...

There's a funny sound too that keeps me awake. I don't know if it's the motor of the boat or the machine that grinds up leftovers in the garbage compactor in the kitchen, but it's really getting on my nerves. It's like the rhythm of a train that can't get started; it's struggling so hard you want to go and help it...

Eventually, I nearly did fall asleep but all of a sudden a thought hit me like a slap on the face and it scared me so much that I jumped: in one second, I realized that I was in a metal box surrounded by other metal boxes piled up on top of each other on the deck of a huge piece of scrap that's rusting away in the middle of the ocean! I'm such an idiot! A goddamn fool! How did I end up out in the middle of the ocean like this—me who's too scared to even set foot on the gondola in Parc Lafontaine? Hell's bells! I hate the water so much I don't even own a bathing suit!

In the time it takes to say it, I got up and went out on deck.

My cabin's towards the back of the boat, I think I told you that already; from where I was, I could see the big phosphorescent waves slicing the sea in two, silently. And the sky. I wish you could have seen it! All at once my fear of being cooped up just flew away and it was replaced by a kind of light-headedness because of all the space... I was looking up and I had to grab hold of the railing with both hands. I've never seen a sky like that. In the city, you don't see the sky. You just see little fragments that you look at without really paying attention. But there—I don't even know the words to describe it to you and that makes me furious!

The priests are always telling us we're insignificant; I used to think that they meant in comparison with God, they're always talking about God, but I didn't pay too much attention because I've never been very excited by God. But that's not what it means, not at all. It's absolutely true that we're nothing! And let me tell you, finding that out at the age of forty, all by myself in the middle of the Atlantic Ocean, it was hard to take! I felt so stupid for not understanding it till then! A person thinks they're big because they're obese and take up a lot of room compared with other people, but you take the fattest fat person in the world, stick him in the middle of the ocean cut off from other people, and even if he's the greatest king in the world, out there he's very, very small!

The emptiness of the sky is terrifying even if there are billions of stars in it.

What's the use of being a shoe salesman, who dreams of becoming a transvestite, out there in the middle of that emptiness? My journey and my dreams felt so unimportant, you can't imagine! If my plans work out, I mean if this trip to Europe is successful, how am I supposed to come back to Montréal and sell shoes after everything I'll have seen? I'm not so naïve as to think I could ever make a career of it! Even after what I've seen since leaving Montréal, I wonder how I've managed to spend twenty years crouching at the feet of a bunch of yoyos who don't even know there's a sky above their heads!

I cried, I cried so hard...

I was leaning over the railing and crying like a baby, crushed by the beauty all around me and by the insignificance of my quest.

I went back to my hole. There's no looking back, is there? The boat isn't going to turn around because of my existential dilemma! At least I'm going to get to Le Havre and maybe it *will* be a haven for me...

Meanwhile, I'll try to get some sleep so that tomorrow morning the others won't think I was sick like them...

One last little line before I go to bed. I hope you're going to read this some day. I wish you could read it right now. I need your warmth and your fantastic understanding.

You know what? I'm all alone for the first time in my life! I've always been surrounded by people: at school, at home, at work, with my gang from the Plateau Mont-Royal... I've always been part of a herd but here I'm all alone like a big fat moon in the middle of nothing!

I feel better this morning. When I opened the door of my cell just now I got the sun smack in my face and the wonderful smell of iodine whipped up my blood. As much as I'd felt like a prisoner a minute before, now I felt liberated at the sight of the great open sea, the waves, the peaceful little clouds bumping along in the sky, the sun that rules over everything...

It's funny, the way we're made, don't you think? Last night, I would have cut off an arm to be taken back to the Plateau Mont-Royal—and then all of a sudden I felt this uncontrollable excitement because I was so far away from it! The sky had changed colour and it didn't scare me anymore. All those dark ideas from last night seemed so far away now! I told myself: if what's waiting for you on the other side is crap, at least it'll be different crap! Just try and find another shoe salesman that travels on an ocean liner!

If I hadn't held myself back I'd've jumped up and down with excitement. Good thing I didn't though, because the door of the cabin next to mine opened and one of my companions in misfortune stepped out. When I saw the dejected look on his greenish face I remembered that two-thirds of the *Liberté*'s passengers were probably still sick, and I started laughing and couldn't stop.

My neighbour, a kind of giant as ugly as a monkey's ass scratched with both hands, beckoned to me. I crossed the little deck and introduced myself in French. Mistake. He gawked at me as if I was making up a language while I talked. What'll he do when he gets to France? I hope his family's expecting him!

So I started again, in English this time; he opened his eyes even wider and then he said something that sounded like the noise that comes out of a washing machine. It hummed, it hissed, it broke into a thousand pieces as it was leaving his mouth. He isn't from North America, that's for sure! He's probably come straight from Bogota or Valparaiso or Montevideo or Santa something-or-other...

It was obvious we couldn't say anything to each other, so we just looked and didn't add a word. Believe me, neither one of us looked like a genius! I peeked at his cabin through the half-open door and it looked like hell... He must've been puking his guts out all night! And if he was that sick, he must be from the mountains, not a seaport!

Then all at once I thought he might be mistaking me for a waiter (I'd actually put on my tight black pants with my gorgeous short-sleeved white shirt to make an impression on all the handsome guys I expect to run into if not run away with during this first journey at sea). Maybe he'd just ordered some toast and bacon! To set him straight I planted myself in front of the door to my own cabin, I opened it and then I went inside. Came out a few seconds later, hoping that he'd gotten the picture. He'd done the same thing and I didn't see him again! So either he was ashamed of his gaffe or he thought I was making a pass at him... If I'm the only one on the boat who speaks French, this is going to be a long trip! My English is all right but hell's bells, where I'm going is France! Unless I got on the wrong ship. I could see myself leaning over the railing trying to read the name of the boat... What a jerk I am!

I found my way to the dining room easily enough this morning (I'm not a total idiot after all!); there weren't even as many people as last night. In fact I was the only one at my table. The captain (that's what I'm going to call him; I know who I mean, which is the main thing...) gave me a wave when I came in. My heart was in my throat and I started walking funny...

Have you ever seen such a thing as two poached eggs sitting on a slice of ham sitting on a slice of toast and the whole thing covered with this thick yellow sauce? It's good enough to eat (ha! ha!) but talk about rich...

I sensed that the captain had been observing me while I was eating so I decided to give him a show: the little finger in the air, the hands light and expert, the little nod as I sipped my tea, something like my mother's canary when it was drinking its water... I figured that if he was family, he'd be sure to recognize me from my manners... The strangest ideas came into my head while I was chewing away as if I wasn't thinking about anything: I could see myself set up like a high-class hooker in a big cabin lined with oak or walnut, champagne in a bucket next to the bed and the captain in his undies whispering things in my ear that would send me to hell... Weird, the things we make up, don't you agree? Because if he *is* family like I think, we'll be doing it under a life raft or down in the hold between the dogs that are barking their heads off and the engine room! And then we won't say another word to each other for the rest of the trip! I hope you aren't shocked, but that's the way it is for us just about always: in the dark and swamped by guilt the minute it's over... Is that what it's like for you too? I suppose not, because it's allowed. But for us... all we can hope for is that if God exists, he can't see in the dark.

As you know, with me there's no middle ground: it's either seventh heaven or the third sub-basement!

So there I am, finishing my tea, when the captain approaches my table with great virile strides.

The cup starts shaking in my hand and I have to put it down.

With a big smile he asks:

"Are you American?"

I answer in my finest English:

"No, I am a French Canadian."

His smile gets bigger and he switches to French—obviously happy. He's a Frenchman! My first real Frenchman! In two minutes he manages to say what it would take the rest of us a lifetime... He talked to me about the French Canadians he met at the end of the war (I didn't dare interrupt and tell him I'd stayed home because I had flat feet); how heroic they'd been during the Normandy landing, how his country would be eternally grateful, how it was so commendable for the province of Québec to have remained French after three hundred years, how we had a beautiful accent... You should have seen me! A bird hypnotized by a cat!

He stopped right in the middle of a sentence; I think he thought I wasn't listening... It took a good three seconds before I could get a word out. And then something very strange happened: when I spoke, my voice had changed! I'm not sure what happened but... my *r*'s had moved to another part of my mouth! I'm not sure how to explain it... I wasn't trying to talk like him, may God deliver us as they say in novels, but I couldn't talk like I usually do... He didn't look as if he realized it (what an idiot I am, he'd never heard me before!) and he went on. But I'd stopped listening. I gawked at him as if I was fascinated by what he was saying but I was only thinking about what had just happened. What surprised me most was that it'd happened automatically. Without wanting to, I'd changed the way I speak just because a Frenchman was talking to me! And when he'd finished his monologue and asked me what I did, I told him—still in my new voice and without thinking: "I'm an actor! I'm on my way to France to shoot a film..." So then he got even warmer and I got even more miserable. The eggs congealed in my stomach. I already knew what he was going to say and I wished I could plug my ears. And yes, he told me the last thing I wanted to hear: "I hope we'll have the pleasure of admiring you in one of your starring roles..." or something along those lines.

Disaster! There I am committed to making an ass of myself in front of all the fancy people on an ocean liner! But I tell myself that maybe half an hour from now he'll forget it; after all, it's his job to be nice to people and make them think they're interesting.

But if he doesn't forget... To hell with it. For so long now, the French have been coming over here and telling us whatever they felt like and we've believed every word. Somebody that comes from far away can lie all he wants. There's nobody out in the middle of the Atlantic that's going to tell the first-class passengers on the *Liberté* I'm not an actor! I'll give them "Le Songe d'Athalie," which I recited so often standing on a table at the Palace with a tablecloth around my waist and a hanky on my head!

Anyway, if they're all from Bogota they won't even know what it's about!

I didn't bring anything to read, which was stupid, there's nothing else to do on a boat... Oh, there are games but they don't interest me. Can you see me, stout as I am, standing in the middle of the deck pushing a rubber disc with a broomstick while everybody else looks on? Or swatting at a bird with phony feathers? Honestly! I hate sports with a passion and I'm not about to start playing them in the middle of the ocean!

The passengers have begun to come out of their cabins. There's a good twenty people lying on deck chairs, holding books, old people mostly. I haven't seen any young ones on board, not yet anyway. Children, yes, though they seem to be travelling with their grandparents, not their parents. But maybe old people and children don't get as seasick as people my age...

Two men, as stiff as posts and as red as if they were about to have a stroke, have already ordered drinks. They don't have books. With the rich, apparently it's the women who read, just like with us... Anyway, the two of them stare out to sea as they sip their drinks. Are they going to stay there like that all week? They sit side by side and never say a word to one another. They'll be the last ones I have any fun with!

I've got my diary with me. Good thing, because the store on the ship isn't open yet and without it I wouldn't have anything to do. I don't know why I'm so worried about being bored. I shouldn't be expecting yummy things to happen all the time, this isn't a comic film, it's real life, and real life lasts longer than an hour and a half! Without a slack period now and then, you'd go crazy!

I'm comfortably settled in a deck chair, next to a woman who's reading *Mont-Cinère* by Julien Green. I think, at least she must speak French. We haven't exchanged a word yet but she's had her eye on me ever since I took out my diary and started scribbling in it. Am I going to pass myself off as a writer out of bravado the way I passed myself off as an actor a while ago?

On a boat everything's permitted. You're isolated for a whole week so you can be whoever you want. Especially in first class, where you're supposed to be somebody in any case.

A handsome sailor, very aware of his sexy little pants, just offered me something that sounded like "plade." I should've been careful but I wasn't; I made myself look ridiculous, but so it goes! In my finest English, to impress the woman next to me, I answered: "No thank you, I don't drink in the morning." Apparently a "plade" isn't something you drink because he seemed surprised at my answer and the lady next to me giggled. If we do get to talking I'll have to fix it so she thinks I was kidding... If somebody uses a word you don't understand, you should never pretend that you do, it's dangerous... But what can I say, in my gang I was always the one who used words the others didn't understand! I suppose everybody's an ignoramus to somebody.

These chairs are so comfortable! You feel as if you're a convalescent; you know, like in French movies when the doctor tells the heroine to go to the seashore because she's coughing her lungs out... Those scenes always make me smile. Can you see Dr. Sansregret telling us to go to the seashore whenever we come down with the flu? We'd have to emigrate! It takes four days just to get to the Gaspé!

I don't know if you can ever get tired of looking at the sea. Mind you, I'm not blasé, it's the first time I've seen it. Before, I'd never been past Tadoussac. And the water there was barely salty.

That huge expanse of blue hypnotizes me. I feel like I'm in a dream, limp, with my arms on the arms of the chair, and time passes without my even noticing. I'm beginning to understand why the men haven't brought books. I think I could stay like this, not moving, till I die. Peace. Not the dull kind of peace that's boring, but a peace that almost feels like something to be anxious about. Yes, that's it: I feel at peace and anxious at the same time. As if I'm afraid it will be over too soon or that it won't finish at all. It's a very nice feeling.

I'm going back to my daydreams. I'll tell you parts of them in a while.

Know what? I couldn't even tell you what I've been thinking about for two hours! I woke up as if I'd been asleep but I'm sure my eyes were open all that time. I was thinking about millions of things at once, but not about anything in particular. You were there, I'm sure of that, because you're the only person I know who could appreciate the calm that's come over me since last night, but I'm not sure what you were doing. Maybe nothing, like me. Maybe you were looking at me looking at the sea and smiling.

The woman who's reading *Mont-Cinère* has fallen asleep. Her book dropped onto the deck; I picked it up, being careful not to wake her. Julien Green: I don't think we've read him, have we? Now, I know our taste in literature pretty well stops at the 19th century... No, that's not true, I'm writing whatever comes into my head, you and I love Simenon and you, more than me, Georges Duhamel. And François Mauriac. Anyway. Maybe I'll borrow *Mont-Cinère* when she's finished. Mind you, she's only at page 28 and if she sleeps like this all week she won't get very far.

I'll start it, just for fun...

I didn't realize she'd woken up, so I was a little surprised when she asked:

"Do you like Julien Green?"

She said Grrrrreen rolling the *r* with an Outremont accent you could cut with a knife. In the store, we get loads of pains in the neck from Outremont—the ones that roll their *r*'s while they try on a hundred and twenty-eight pairs of shoes and leave without saying thank you. I'd recognize that accent with my ears plugged!

I pursed my lips into a hen's ass and I asked her:

"Are you from Outremont?"

I realized I was putting on the same accent as I had with the captain. My own *r*'s had dropped into my throat as if I'd swallowed a whisker!

She was startled.

"How could you tell? As far as I know, I don't have 'Outremont' written across my forehead!"

I didn't know what to say. Maybe she doesn't know she's got a typical accent. I couldn't tell her she talks like a nun, even though she does! I let the silence drag on for a little too long. You know me, at awkward moments I turn helpless and somebody has to come and fish me out or I'll sink. Finally, she couldn't take the silence (I'd thought she might have come up with the answer on her own and wanted to move on to something else); she reached for the book and daintily took it from my hands.

"This is the third time I've read *Mont-Cinère*. What a gifted man! To write that at the age of twenty-three! For a first book it's quite stunning!"

She was talking fast, all worked up as if she was describing a hockey game.

"Have you read his diary?"

I didn't even how he'd published one! Can you see me publishing this one that I'm writing for you?

She didn't wait for my answer.

"You know, I'm quite confident that I'll meet him over there..."

She pointed to the horizon as if Paris and Julien Green could be found just beyond the third wave ahead of us.

"He's just finished a new book, *Si j'étais vous*; it's going to be published in a few weeks. I'll be there! I'm sure of it! And I'll tell him how much my friends and I admire him!"

She had straightened up on her deck chair as she spoke; I had the impression she was about to have an epileptic fit.

"And who knows, perhaps he'll agree to pay a visit to our dreary, uncultivated dump."

Outremont an uncultivated dump? What must she think of the rest of Montréal!

She heaved a great sigh as if she was trying to expel some powerful poison that was scalding her insides. Then she leaned back in her deck chair.

"And what do you think of him?"

I was fairly cautious; all I know of Julien Green is the first 37 pages of *Mont-Cinère*! A mother and daughter hate each other enough to commit murder for page after page and nothing happens!

"I think very highly of him, yes indeed, terribly highly."

I emphasized *terribly* to let her know that as far as I was concerned, the discussion was over. That's what you think!

"I assume you're well acquainted with his work?"

I thought if she wants to play the passionate fan I can play along.

"I've read everything, Madame! Absolutely everything! Everything!"

As I was saying the final "everything" I could sense her next question, and a knot formed in my stomach. She leaned across to me like a believer studying the statue of Bernadette Soubirous.

"Which did you like best?"

I had to think fast, right? Funny what can go through your head in a second or two... Titles leaped into my mind though I didn't feel as if I'd summoned them: *Leviathan, The Power and the Glory, Orient Express, Midnight...* but I couldn't remember which ones were by Graham Green and which ones by Julien, I was so worked up. I wanted to impress her but I hadn't read either one of them. For a long time I thought they were the same person. It was you who taught me there were two. So that's what happens when you get your culture from your sister-in-law!

I chose the easy way out, I admit it. Taking no chances, I pointed to *Mont-Cinère* and said with all the self-assurance I could muster:

"That one! It's the best! It's the first, but it's the best! It's all there!"

I was so glad to come up with something, I must have looked like as passionate a fan as her!

She frowned, a look of doubt on her face, and I thought: now I've done it. She was giving me a weird look.

"Oh yes? Do you really think so? But he was so young when he wrote it! It's good, it's very, very good, but the others are so much more... so much more..."

I was relieved to see that she had to search for her words too and I let her get herself untangled on her own, even though I knew that the word she was looking for was probably "mature."

"So much more accomplished!"

How d'you like that? It's true, there are fancier words than "mature!" She held out her hand, just like that, all at once, as if she'd decided to adopt me.

"Antoinette Beaugrand. And yes, I'm from Outremont. You guessed correctly. I'm travelling with my seven-year-old, Lucille, my littlest lamb. I have three other daughters whom I've abandoned to their governess in our home on Davaar Street. But I've brought Lucille because I couldn't bring myself to be apart from her. We're both going to dip our toes in the greatest culture there is."

She pronounced the word "culture" as if it started with a k! I don't know how to describe it exactly… it came out kind of like a sneeze: Kul… tuuuure.

"I only hope my Lucille is sensitive enough to grasp the significance of everything she's going to see, even if she doesn't understand it all. She stayed in the cabin—she's not like her mother, poor child, she's not a good sailor."

I had no desire to hear her sing the praises of her Lucille, so I started getting to my feet. She grabbed my arm to hold me back.

"What about you, what's your name? I heard you tell the *Commandant* just now that you're an actor but I don't think I've seen you on stage… Unless you're from Québec City, or Chicoutimi…"

So on top of everything else she's a spy!

This really isn't my day, is it? My own fault though. If I'd taken a cabin with the other nobodies I wouldn't be here. So I cooked up a story so far-fetched that she had no choice but to believe it: I told her I'd made my career in radio because my somewhat unusual build kept me off the stage. Boyoboy, how do I get out of this one? I told her I'd rather play major parts on radio than minor roles in the theatre. And so then, if you can imagine, she wanted to know what parts I'd done on the radio! I brought out a long string of Lux Radio Theatre plays that you and I listened to together and she seemed to believe me. I think she had me mixed up with Gaston Dauriac! At least till she asked me with a strange little pout:

"Tell me your name again, it's slipped my mind…"

Just try coming up with a theatrical name in two seconds! Gilles Dorais! That's the one I made up. I know, it's a terrible pun; if I were a woman I can imagine myself telling her "Jan

Dark." Strange thing, "Kulture," don't you think? A man goes along thinking he's ignorant and then out of the blue it comes up like a sour stomach.

I don't have to tell you that after all this, I was glad when I could make my getaway!

The bell had just rung. The carillon, rather. Time for luncheon. A new word for me—as you know, we call it dinner. While I was running away like a dog that's ashamed of dirtying the lovely living room carpet, Antoinette Beaugrand shouted:

"We'll see each other at luncheon! Perhaps you'll meet my Lucille!"

For a second I was picturing Antoinette Beaugrand with her lunch pail at the back of the shoe store and I had a good laugh.

I spent part of the rest of the day avoiding Antoinette Beaugrand; I decided I'd done enough fibbing for today.

Luncheon was delicious and I'm glad to tell you that the passengers were starting to get their colour back; one of my table-mates, who wasn't there this morning but who'd forced himself to come out at noon, told me that usually, anybody who doesn't show up on the second day will stay in his cabin all week... I haven't seen my guy from Bogota again. Poor thing...

This meal was a little livelier; I even heard some laughter (rather forced, but still laughter.)

Glancing furtively at Antoinette Beaugrand's table (better located than mine, needless to say), I realized that Lucille, the littlest lamb, is one of those pale, ugly youngsters with her hair braided so tight it looks as if it's going to pop off her head at any moment. She sits there as stiff as a post, sneers at everything, turns up her nose as she picks at her food, and *never* looks directly at her mother. Before I've even met her I hate her like poison!

As expected, the captain (rather, the *Commandant*, according to Antoinette Beaugrand who must have memorized everyone's responsibilities and particularly, his social status), the *Commandant* then, seems to have forgotten my existence now that his table is filling up with rivers of diamonds and other huge precious stones of every colour. I don't think I'll have to go over the text from *Le Songe d'Athalie...*

I ate my first avocado vinaigrette today. What a treat! Rich, creamy, cool... Why don't you and I know about things like that? Monsieur Provost only sells the same damn fruits and the same damn vegetables; is he the one who lacks imagination or are such things really only for the rich? I'd like to eat an avocado now and then, even if I'm not a millionaire. And I'm sure everybody at home would love them too! But oh no, if it isn't peas or potatoes or carrots we'd feel like we were in a foreign country and we wouldn't know what to do with them. I sometimes wonder if we aren't ignorant by choice, because it's easier...

Right after we'd eaten, I came back and shut myself away in my rat cage for fear of seeing the Beaugrands, mother and daughter, trailing me like my shadow. (Antoinette gave me a big wave when I got up from the table but, luckily for me, Lucille hadn't finished her strawberries.)

And I slept like Sleeping Beauty would have slept if she'd been cooped up in a sardine can—the better to preserve her, my dear. As agitated as the night before had been, the two hours I spent in bed this afternoon were calm and restful.

It was when I came out around four o'clock that I started playing hide-and-seek with Antoinette Beaugrand, who was on her own again (she must tie her littlest lamb to the foot of her bed) and definitely in the mood for a passionate conversation about Chapter 24 of *Mont-Cinère*. I pretended I hadn't seen her but that's not always easy to do. The two times I landed face-to-face with her I had to come up with something very urgent to do (take a leak, first of all, but in veiled terms, don't worry, then a book I had to buy.) I was afraid she'd offer to come along and help me choose it but no... Maybe she's not really chasing me and I'm just imagining things...

At the end of the afternoon I went back and collapsed on my deck chair. I started a Simenon I hadn't read before, *Signé Picpus.* It was fun to be back with Maigret, his pipe, his grouchiness, his boring wife, his perpetual flu and the little Paris world that's so fascinating.

Even though I aspire to the title of Duchess and dream about coming home to Montréal more snobbish, more annoying, more chic, more nonchalant and more unbearable than the Frenchwomen themselves (I hope no French woman will ever read this), it's Simenon's world that I want to get to know.

As I told you before I left, I decided to go to Paris without doing any research; whatever I know, I know from the black-and-white movies I've seen and the colourful novels I've read. Very naïvely, I admit, I'm expecting to run into Simone Signoret dressed as Casque d'or or Arletty as Garance… When the French land on our shores they look for Indians and Maria Chapdelaine, so why shouldn't I try to find Zola's Gervaise or Balzac's Lucien de Rubempré! For me, Paris is a fabulous source of folklore I can dip into with both hands. I know I risk disappointment, but I accept that risk, telling myself that whatever happens I'll have fun.

On the eve of my departure, Samarcette said something that really had me worried: "Do you realize you're probably the first French-Canadian shoe salesman to cross the Atlantic at his own expense?" I hadn't thought about it, but he was right! Only intellectuals or rich people come to France to complete their education; the rest of us, the workers, stay home. The only workers to cross the Atlantic up till now were going to fight in the war. Cannon fodder always travels for free. (My God, I'm turning into a philosopher!)

And to think that I owe it all—the ship, the sea, France—to my poor mother who only took one trip in her life, from Duhamel to Montréal, and who bled herself white to put together an inheritance for me because I was her favourite… I know that Gabriel, your husband, and Madeleine, our own littlest lamb, who's so reserved and generous, don't resent it, but maybe some day I'll tell you about the scene Albertine made when she found out that I was going to France with our mother's money. And the worst of it is, I don't blame her! Her own horizons are going to stay very narrow. But I was too selfish to share… I was the one

Mama left her money to and I'm going to do what I want with it! For me it's a chance for salvation, do you understand? Instead of dividing up my inheritance into little snacks for everybody, I'm going to have a banquet just for me. And buy myself some salvation. And if I don't make it, that will be my last hope, but at least I'll have some stories to tell.

But I mustn't give in to these black thoughts... Looking up from my Simenon I saw a sunset that would make up for all the meanness in the world, even mine.

The girl who sold me my ticket (I haven't mentioned her since yesterday) told me there'd be a movie on the boat but I hadn't really paid any attention; I thought it would be like school, that somebody would set up a projector in some room or other (the game room or even the dining room) and they'd show old Laurel and Hardy or Charlie Chaplin movies that I already know by heart. But it wasn't like that at all! You should see the movie theatre here! Red velvet, gilt—the works! It's small but boyoboy, is it ever classy! Makes you feel as if you're at a preview, like a producer. And the programme changes practically every day. Five different movies in one week! And not just anything either: the latest releases!

In Montréal, as you know, we complain about it often enough, we always get movies a good two or three months late, if not more. But it's not like that here. I'll tell you, it doesn't help your inferiority complex to find out that movies come to a boat before they come to your own city!

Tonight, I saw Irene Dunne's latest, *Life With Father*. I cried like a herd of cows caught in a thunderstorm. I can't understand why she hasn't been nominated for an Oscar! You can't imagine how good she is. The theatre was packed, practically all women as a matter of fact, and I want you to know, their hankies were dripping!

And who did I see arriving two minutes before it started? That's right. With Lucille. Luckily for me there were no seats next to me. They sat two rows ahead and I got to see that, in a social situation, Antoinette Beaugrand is very different. She said hello, but barely. At supper she'd been giving me these big smiles again (now that I think of it, that's a social situation too...) but now her mouth barely creased into what could be interpreted as a smile. And I realized that Antoinette hadn't really looked to see if there was a seat next to me. Has she broken the secret of my plebian background? Or had she simply noticed the provocative winks I'd been sending to the *commandant* during dinner? I don't really know how women like her react to flaming queens like me... A liar and a faggot—that's enough to kill her on the spot! Especially because at supper, helped along by my first glass of wine which I'd knocked back in one gulp, I'd dropped some of my polish and my subtlety.

Because I might as well admit it now, I've definitely decided that I've got a crush on the *commandant*. And it seems to be serious because when I saw him come in (he was a little late tonight) in his adorable navy outfit, my heart did a flipflop and I forgot everything: the Caesar salad I'd just finished, the beef Wellington that was coming next, the others at the table who were even duller than they seemed before and Antoinette Beaugrand who must have known something was up if she'd been watching me as closely as I think.

But then again, maybe I'm imagining things; maybe she'd just felt like having a chat this morning and she was only being polite when she said hello in the dining room... Isn't that just like me, to think I'm irresistible... Anyway, the *commandant* seemed to have totally forgotten I existed. Not even one little look in my direction. I'll love him from afar and in silence—as usual!

(Unless he's asked around about me and found out that not only am I not an actor but that I spend ten hours a day on my hands and knees in front of people whose feet don't always smell like flowers...)

After having a good cry for two hours, I came and leaned on the railing, above the lapping of the waves. And I took refuge in my own movie. Music was playing in the grand salon, I could see silhouettes standing out against the windows, two lovers embracing very close to me, the boat barely moving... If I'd had any tears left I'd have shed them, but from joy. My emotions are definitely turbulent since last night. Then, I was on the brink of despair, tonight I'm within an inch of collective hysteria...

I have to say that the scenario I'd put together for myself, inspired by *Life With Father*, is quite thrilling! While I was watching the clouds pass over the moon I made up my mind about something else: no matter what happens in the next few days, a camera is going to travel all over this boat, thousands and thousands of feet of film will be shot—at mealtime, on the decks, in the salons, in that miserable little cabin too; every one of my movements will be recorded, even the most boring, even the most private, and I'll use it all to put together the great immortal masterpiece that I've already entitled quite simply, *The Sea of Desire*, and that I'll project for myself in years to come when I'm feeling blue. Starring: the *commandant* in the role of hero, obviously; myself in the role that would normally have gone to Ingrid Bergman, who was kind enough to withdraw at the last moment; Antoinette Beaugrand as the wicked conspirator (either an escaped member of the SS or a gold-digging white Russian princess, I haven't decided); and Lucille as the dwarf Piéral who's always sticking her nose into things and making nasty cracks (you're right, I stole that one from *L'Éternel Retour*, so what!)

And do you know why I've done that? Quite simply because I have a hard time believing that I am where I am, and an imaginary movie will help me accept it. That's the truth! If I act all week what I have to live through, my state of exaltation won't wear down; but if I simply live it, dark thoughts like the ones last night will bombard me, I'll go back to thinking I'm unworthy of what's happening to me, and I'll get to the other side exhausted and depressed.

You see, I've been used to earning the little that I had; I find it hard to accept the luxury that's coming to me. So I'm going to take shelter in a scenario I can control totally; that way, whatever happens, I'll be able to use it without letting it touch me.

I've re-read what I wrote just now. Isn't it terrible to have such a fixation? Are you like that too? Instead of taking advantage of what's happening we want to hide behind some made-up story to protect ourselves from our inferiority complex. If only you were here, we could take our time and talk this over calmly. But as of now, I intend to learn how to think by myself, though it won't be easy. It strikes me that what I'm writing is terribly confused... and that won't help me understand myself...

Remember what my mother used to say: "It's better to be first in your own little village than second in Paris." Here, on this boat, I don't feel like I'm second, I feel like the last of the last. And that's my problem.

Imagine how it will be when I get to Paris!

Ah, to hell with this stupid scenario! All I have to do is try to face the *commandant*, Antoinette Beaugrand, her littlest lamb, my table-mates, and my good luck at being here and above all, try to *enjoy* it! We'll see...

Second horrible night, but for a very different reason. Since giving it up I'd forgotten my disastrous reaction to garlic. And the Caesar salad last night was swimming in it. Horrors!

For hours and hours I wanted to die, lying there on my back, trying to control my breathing the way you've shown me how to do so often when I'd made a mad dash for all the little pieces of garlic you'd stick in your pork roast or sprinkle over your spaghetti sauce. None of it would go down and I dreamed of seeing you leaning over my cramped little bed, holding out a big spoonful of Fermentol.

But no. I'd forgotten to bring anything to help me with my digestion and I was too proud to try and find someone who could help me. Anyway, where can you go on a boat when nothing will go down, not even a glass of hot water? The infirmary, of course, but I was too embarrassed to admit that I'd made a pig of myself with something I've never been able to digest.

Then there was the breath problem. You know how I'm obsessed with cleanliness... There was no question of breathing my foul breath in a nurse's face, even if it's her job to put up with things like that. You have to respect cleanliness both inside and outside!

So maybe to punish myself for soiling my breath, I put up with everything: the agony of the retching, my guts that feel as if they're clenching and unclenching, the bad taste in my mouth…

Seems to me this trip is getting off to a terrible start. If things keep happening so fast over the months I'm overseas, I'll come back to Montréal looking more like Jeanne Fusier-Gir than Suzy Prim!

The sweat was running off my face and onto my neck and I told myself: "If I have to suffer like this to be beautiful, I'd rather be ugly!"

I'm going to stop writing my diary this morning before I put down some stupid remarks that are just too terrible. I've always thought a person keeps a diary to confide to it the deepest, most sensitive matters: another illusion shattered!

Later.

I can't get to sleep. Just thinking that it will soon be time for the first meal of the day makes my insides heave and I have the sickening taste of garlic in my mouth. Never again! No more garlic, ever!

I have this feeling that I'll be spending the day in my cell… I who bragged about what a good sailor I am, I'd forgotten that my stomach's made of crepe paper!

I'll try to keep busy. I'll read. But when I look at the same thing for too long, I see yellow spots. It's as if my pen is chasing after a yellow disc on the white pages of my diary. Hell's bells! I'm too impatient, I can't relax! A strained stomach stays as hard as cement, everybody knows that!

I know myself, till tomorrow at least I'm going to have breath that could knock down a troop of Italians!

Imagine then that it's not a girl who's house-cleaning my distant corner of first class, it's a cute young man with rather special manners, if you get my drift…

I'd finally dozed off despite my nausea when I heard a key turn in the lock of my prison gate. I was going to call out that I was inside when the door opened on one of the nicest, most cheerful silhouettes.

But I didn't have time to react; before it crossed my mind to assume a sexy pose upon my princely couch, my morning visitor gave a start, grimaced involuntarily and gently shut the door, with a faint apologetic bow.

It took me a good fifteen seconds to realize that my cage probably didn't smell of eucalyptus. Another missed opportunity. If I run into that young Adonis again he'll turn around as if he'd just seen some spoiled meat and he'll be right. Probably he'll never set foot in here again without a gas mask.

I feel dizzy. I haven't even got the strength to take pity on my fate. But what a blah day!

Skip ahead to tomorrow if this is too boring.

I had a strange dream. I was on the back of a whale that was blowing its powerful jet of water right into my face. And I said to myself: "They've cooked some spaghetti sauce for my birthday!" That part is easy to understand: I was suffocating in my own stench of garlic. But then it gets complicated... A table appeared on the whale's back, fully set for a good twenty people. But only two people were sitting there: Antoinette Beaugrand and her littlest lamb. I was trying to take a seat over the spaghetti but Antoinette grabbed the plate, saying: "That's not for you, it's just for the rest of us..." I went all around the table like that, without putting a single forkful of spaghetti in my mouth... I don't understand what it means but I think I ought to, I think it must be very simple to explain. Blocking again, I suppose.

My guts loosened up around the middle of the afternoon. I was reading *Signé Picpus* in small doses, resting after nearly every page, when all at once, with no warning, there was a big commotion inside me. It made a sound like a sink drain being unplugged—very ugly but what a relief!—in my stomach; I turned onto my left side the way I always do when that happens (because of course this has happened before) and in a few minutes everything settled down.

And I slept without waking till evening. I woke up feeling jaunty and refreshed. I was humming when I opened my cabin door. And hungry! Can you believe it? I was absolutely famished!

We gluttons (not to say quite simply pigs!) are all alike, aren't we? A bout of indigestion, no matter how terrible, doesn't cure us of anything! As soon as we feel better we're ready to begin again! Last night's lesson didn't teach me anything; the only thing I care about right now is my hunger pangs, my hollow stomach, my uncontrollable urge to do something stupid again. Maybe even repeat what I've already done! Because do you want to know something else? I think I'd eat garlic again! Do you believe me? Yes? That's good of you because it's hard for me to believe it myself! I picture myself again over my Caesar salad, and I feel just fine, even though a few hours ago I swore by all that's holy that never again would I eat a bite of anything prepared with even a hint of that poison! I'm almost ashamed of myself. But I'm so hungry!

When all's said and done, I've only lost one day. And I feel perfectly capable of making it up.

If supper isn't finished yet I'll slip into my seat as if nothing were amiss. If everybody's already gone to the movie or dancing, I'll raid the kitchen!

And if I have bad breath, tough! I'll stay as far from any humans as possible, that's all! And if I run into Antoinette Beaugrand, I'll breathe right into her face that I come from the dregs of society; it'll make her day. Or her week.

I was feeling high and mighty before I left my cabin but as soon as I set foot on deck I was surprised to find that I was hugging the walls, with my mouth hermetically shut and my neck hunched into my shoulders.

The meal was nearly over. I barely said hello to my table-mates, who were too involved in a fascinating conversation about Mae West to pay any attention to me. The most insufferable of them—a huge American as loud as a loudspeaker on an aircraft carrier and as subtle as a ton of bricks at a debutante ball—was flailing his arms around and puffing on his cigar while maintaining that Mae West is a man: to the annoyance of the three others who are probably wild about her.

It's been twenty years since that theory started making the rounds and they're too embarrassed to check it out! Let them undress her and take a picture of her charms, then they'll know once and for all. In any case, if Mae West were a man, she'd brag about it!

My neighbour on the left, who must have started the discussion because he had his wallet in front of him, open to a signed photo of the bone of contention; he was a long drink of water, dressed to the nines, whom I'd suspected till then of being a priest on a spree, not a slave in chains to the immortal Mae (but you'll tell me that one doesn't necessarily rule out the other), he maintained that Mae West has to be a woman because she doesn't have an Adam's apple. Everybody knows that little bump is a male prerogative. So there they are, bent over the photo, studying their idol's neck (I'm sure it was the first time their eyes had been focussed any higher than her bosom!).

If I hadn't been afraid of stinking them out, I'd've told them that it hardly matters what sex Mae West is; what matters is how it affects them, whether her name is George Baker or Rosalie Levine! I can see the looks on their faces from here! For an American male, to be taken in by a transvestite has to be the worst humiliation! Just think about it! Their virility!

I ate in silence, not responding to the outrageous remarks I was hearing. Tomorrow, I think I'll ask for a different table. I'm sure it's because of them that I'm having digestive problems.

Funny, isn't it, being attracted to men but hating them like that! I've always found it hard to talk to men; I think they're boring, annoying, tiresome, selfish… I wonder what we see in them— aside from what's hanging between their legs and that rarely hangs as much as we'd like it to. But when they're really handsome…

There's times when I think it's the woman in me that I love and the man in them that turns me on.

The cigar-smoker put an end to the discussion in a terribly tactful way: he said that the proof Mae West is a man is, she doesn't give him a hard-on! And *everything* feminine does. There was silence. Among society folks on a classy ocean liner I'm sure that's a term you don't often hear… The priest on a spree put his wallet back in his pocket and the others (the eternal listeners, the inevitable attentive ears, the stupid ones always content to agree, either because they can't give an opinion of their own or because they quite simply don't have one) dived into their rice pudding, which had been pretentiously baptized "La rizière aux perles de Corinthe." This is first class, after all. Where bullshit reigns supreme!

I polished off my soup ("le velouté Crécy" for a plain old carrot soup, really, there's no end to their surprises) when these gentlemen withdrew to the card table to finish their cigars and attack their first liqueur of the evening. They'd have to pay me a bundle to make me set foot in there! The idiotic things that you must hear in just one evening could fill a whole dictionary of stupid remarks, I know it!

I was able to enjoy a peaceful meal then, lingering quietly over the things I like the most.

I must have been a pitiful sight because Antoinette Beaugrand gave me an apologetic look before she left the dining room, dragging her littlest lamb by the hand. As for the *commandant*, he was busy strutting for the important people who adorned his table.

I'm definitely condemned to finish this trip on my own…

You see, two people tried to make contact with me on the first day but I must have disappointed them both because they left me high and dry after just one conversation, as if it had been the worst platitude. Should I have faked it, played the great tragic actor with the *commandant* and sung the praises of Julien Green till I couldn't take any more with the Outremont snob, even if I don't know a thing about him, just to keep them going, make them want to continue a conversation in which they were actually the ones deceived. Is it always up to me to put on a show, to invent a personality for myself, so that others will think I'm interesting?

I'm afraid the answer is yes. After all, I'm the one who's a tourist in their world!

When I got to dessert I was alone in the dining room. A kind of peace made up of the dim light (they'd started dousing the lamps and the chandelier was swaying discreetly) and furtive glides (the waiters maneuvering in silence, probably too tired to play the fool), a rare kind of peace had settled over the huge room. I finished my coffee very slowly, a smile of satisfaction on my lips.

You've often told me, dear sister-in-law, that you'd rather eat after the others so you could enjoy your meal in peace and quiet, without having to worry about Gabriel or the children. You're right. I've just discovered that great pleasure and I'll try to develop it, cultivate it.

But God almighty, not here! I'm not their mother! I didn't come here to avoid them, I bought a first class ticket to see what they're like and to laugh at them if they won't laugh with me! Obviously I'm more comfortable around waiters than socialites, but I'm not going on this trip to surround myself with what I've already got in Montréal! Those socialites would never accept me in their Outremont fief; I've used trickery to slip in among them, to *become* one of them goddammit, and here I am dreaming of taking my meals after everybody else to get some peace and quiet!

Brainless! Coward! Take the plunge and forget about your stupid complexes once and for all!

I even wonder if the garlic wasn't a pretext to huddle away by myself instead of facing up to what I came to face up to.

Tomorrow! Tomorrow, I attack! And watch out: Antoinette Beaugrand will have to polish her erudition, she's going to be doing some skating!

When I re-read this I realized that my style's beginning to change... Which suits me fine. It's coming back to me and I like it. But I mustn't blow my own horn too soon or I'm liable to block.

Today I woke up fresh as a daisy and ready for action. I took a long shower in my hot-water tank, singing my personal version of the "habanera" from *Carmen*; I shaved carefully, with brush, foam, razor, the works (my beard isn't too heavy but now and then I have to do a major clean-up of my chubby cheeks); after that I scalded my face with some lotion that reeked to high heaven but it was all I could find before leaving New York; and finally, I dressed myself in my most elegant spring finery: short-sleeved white cotton shirt, navy slacks and understated jewels: my gold ring, my studs that look like gold and my chain that's trying to look like something that might look like gold. I studied the part of me that the mirror on the back of the closet door had room for: nothing like Gary Cooper, but nothing like Stan Laurel either, so it'll do.

Of course I have no plan of attack. I'll improvise! I tell myself that if I let it show that I'm available, somebody's going to get hooked.

The guy from Bogota emerged from his cabin at the same time I did. He's looking better now, too. The third day of an Atlantic crossing must be the day when people recover. We went from the deck to the dining room together, with him conversing in his language and me saying whatever came into my head in mine.

The water has turned a frightening blue that looks sharp and cold. You almost expect to see ice-cubes floating in it. We aren't at the Gulf Stream yet but it must be coming up at any moment (at least according to my refined table-mates, who switched from Mae West to Joan Crawford this morning). Joan Crawford, by the way, is too mannish for the cigar-sucker and too authoritarian for the priest on a spree; I sense that soon they'll have to make do with some bland-looking actress, June Allyson, say, or Jane Wyman, claiming she's the only possible version of the ideal companion!

Right away I spotted Antoinette and her little Lucille who were nibbling their croissants with the disdainful expression of sated squirrels. I waited patiently till Antoinette looked my way and gave her my best smile, the one for party nights when it's certain that something's going to click. She gave me a pleasant enough look that could have passed for a greeting; I didn't push it and concentrated on the *commandant*.

Who seems to be down in the dumps. I know that particular look very well, from hanging out with the odd neighbourhood Don Juan (Madame Côté's monstrous Maurice, for instance, who can't take no for an answer): somebody must have turned him down and he isn't over it yet... He didn't look my way even once.

I think I'll forget about sex for the rest of the crossing and concentrate on Kulture, which is supposed to be a consolation. Apparently you can't have both at the same time.

Paper and pen casually handled always produce an effect; it's hard to resist them, something I had proof of just now: this morning I was scribbling in my diary, flopped on the same deck chair as yesterday, when Antoinette and her beastly child approached me, dressed up as people who know how to travel: practical *and* becoming.

Lucille was dragging around a doll that was so chic you could dress your little boy for a year with what its clothes must have cost!

Antoinette Beaugrand stopped when she was level with me, her eyes clamped on my notebook.

"Forgive me for this indiscreet question, but I've been burning to ask you since the other day..."

"Go ahead, Madame, no question warrants passing through the flames..."

(Maybe a little stiff as an opener, but it came out by itself.)

"Are you keeping a diary?"

I don't know why or how, but I sensed a kind of contempt at the heart of her curiosity, as if writing in a diary in public as I was doing was somehow inappropriate, even vulgar. She must think that Julien Green goes into hiding to write his, even though he publishes it.

"No, I'm writing an essay..."

At that she started, at once astonished and delighted. She settled in the chair next to mine while Lucille leaned out dangerously over the ocean.

"An essay? About what? Or whom?"

Then, of course, I realized my gaffe. Once again, I'd spoken too soon. I hardly know the word "essay," I'm not even sure exactly what it means, so you can imagine the hoops I went through trying to come up with an answer! I thought fast, I talked fast—and I quickly realized that I'd just made my second mistake.

"I'm trying to prove the influence of the Théâtre National on the artistic life of Montréal."

The up-till-then enticing smile of Antoinette Beaugrand froze on her face like a crushed raspberry.

I'd turned instinctively to what I knew best so as not to lose my composure, but it obviously didn't suit the chic *madame* from Outremont. After a few seconds of silence when I thought that I could actually *hear* her thinking, she brought her hand up to her pearls.

"Ah, I see… What a… what an *astonishing* subject for an essay. I do acknowledge that the Théâtre National may have some importance in east-end Montréal, but to actually see an influence on the artistic life of the city as a whole…"

She was twisting her string of pearls so hard I thought she'd break it. I could already see myself on my hands and knees on the deck, chasing the little spheres as they tried to return to their natal water. I smiled.

I should have known! To Antoinette Beaugrand, east-end Montréal in general and the Théâtre National in particular must represent something like the Belgian Congo or Greenland: a hopeless cultural desert! All she knows about it probably is the offices of Les Amis de l'Art above the toilets in Parc Lafontaine. I could have mentioned the Mountain Playhouse, His Majesty's, at worst the Variétés Lyriques or the Arcade, which is still in the east end—but the Théâtre National!

I decided to take advantage of my faux pas to make her talk. I put my pen inside my notebook and slowly closed my diary, smoothing it with the flat of my hand.

And I attacked (still with those weird r's that made me feel as if I was purring).

"I'm an actor first and foremost, it's true, but a writer has been struggling within me, attempting to come to the surface. I've always written. Inconsequential little things, but they let me keep my hand in. Poems. Musings. Criticisms even, when the great international stars visit us and I'm not satisfied with what I read in the papers. So I must see everything and read everything, you understand…" (That's what's called jumping in the water without a life jacket!)

Antoinette gave me a little nod that relieved me: oozing culture though she did, my act still convinced her! Proof again that well-presented bullshit is always effective!

"In the past ten years, Madame Beaugrand, I've seen everything in Montréal!"

She brought up her hand in a gesture of protest.

"As have I; we're certainly going to get along, you and I!"

I told myself this was going to be harder than I'd thought at first. My bullshit would have to be well documented, because Antoinette Beaugrand wouldn't let anything pass that wasn't strictly accurate.

So in one breath I recited the impressive list of shows I claimed I'd seen: plays, concerts, recitals, operas, operettas, you name it. Good thing I usually read the reviews in *La Presse!* All of it, of course, decked out with comments that were often harsh but fairly amusing as well (not too amusing though; women like her don't really like to laugh, just to coo with a knowing look), sometimes laudatory but offered up in a sententious and erudite tone. (I finally bought myself a Larousse on my way back from the discussion with Antoinette Beaugrand, and "sententious" is the first word I've taken from it.)

Poor Antoinette was drinking in my words while little Lucille was being bored at her side. That child must have been trained to be bored in public because she didn't move a hair while I was pouring my phony erudition onto her mother's head. Antoinette looked as if she was going to take flight, that's how much she liked what I was saying.

For one brief moment I imagined Antoinette slowly levitating above the deck, over the guardrail, suspended several dozen feet above the waves, and underneath her a school of sharks that were looking at her the way first communicants look at the redemptive Host that's offered to them... (One dreams what dreams one can when trying to convince a member of our city's elite that one is cultivated!)

I was talking about John Gielgud, whom I claimed I'd seen recently in *The Importance of Being Earnest* at His Majesty's, when I felt something like a shudder of pleasure stroke my spine. Funny, I felt that before I understood the reason: and by the time I understood why I was shuddering like that, the crisis was nearly over.

I've met so many women like her in theatre lobbies, if you only knew! Wives of doctors, lawyers, businessmen, judges, dressed to the teeth in fur, contemptuous, clinging to their husbands if they've dragged them out to show them off to their friends ("You know my husband, Judge Thing of the Superior Court," "My husband, the leading criminal lawyer Petit-Bonhomme," "My husband Doctor So-and-So,") or swarming together when a group of them meets, exchanging aloud ridiculous statements or remarks that are *always* unkind about the common people around them, especially at matinées where the audience is sometimes too varied for their liking (their hatred is directed simultaneously at students, women on their own, men in pairs—Samarcette and I have put up with our share of caustic looks!—poorly dressed people, children, who shouldn't be allowed inside theatres before they're sixteen, except for concerts of course, old people, who should have the decency to stay at home—except for their own old people who are educated and discreet...) They look down on everything from very high, from a place where a person can't see anything because they're too far away; they judge everything in a tone that won't take any argument; they possess the truth and they proclaim it. Geese in a chicken coop.

And here I was facing one of them, who was drinking in my every word! A fan of Julien Green practically kneeling before me because my imagination was cooking up an incredible brew of fake knowledge and questionable opinions. Me, a shoe salesman she'd probably pissed off more than once, who didn't recognize me because all she'd ever seen of me was the top of my head! I'm well aware that it was easy revenge but the pleasure was tremendous, you can't imagine! I was discovering the delight of conning somebody who's convinced of her own superiority.

But put yourself in my place: she had before her a person who was both an actor and a writer. It didn't matter that she'd never heard of me, I was right there, in the flesh, and *I was talking to her!* If she wasn't so chic she'd have drooled!

I was dominating her! And loving it! I'd decided I was going to make her talk, but there I was carrying on as if someone had cranked me up till my springs nearly broke.

This went on for a good half-hour. A great moment. If it had been in a movie no one would have believed it. Antoinette merely nodded when she agreed with me or frowned when she thought the opposite of what I was saying, and I could sense how happy it made her to be on the receiving end of all this bullshit from a phony initiate. And I understood something very important: as superior and contemptuous as she was in theatre lobbies, she must be small and humble backstage (because women like her hang around backstage between the acts, and let it be known). I could see her gravitating to guest conductors at symphony concerts or to French actors on tour and I thought: "There's always somebody to see us as a nobody!" When that woman sets foot on the soil of France, cradle of Kulture, she'll have a heart attack! She made herself very small in front of me and I'm nothing, but I know how to talk, so think what she'll be like in Paris!

But without realizing it, she burst my balloon (either that or she's a lot smarter than she seems). She shut me up at one point when she said very sweetly:

"That's all fascinating but I still don't understand why you chose the Théâtre National for your book!"

I was out of ideas and out of spit and my vocal cords were on fire (and that's hardly an exaggeration).

I started to make up something so complicated and confused that I wasn't sure how I'd get to the end. I'd start a sentence not knowing where I was going, I'd duck and weave, I'd backtrack, I'd stammer: I must have looked like a goddamn fool.

Then a horrible thought crossed my mind. As I listened to myself think, I realized that I wasn't capable of quite simply telling Antoinette Beaugrand that I thought the people at the Théâtre National were brilliant! That for me, Madame Pétrie and Madame Ouellette were the apotheosis of talent! That I admired not only what they did, but their courage too! And that I loved them.

Earlier, I'd wanted to laugh at Antoinette Beaugrand, but now I wanted to *please* her, to convince her that I was part of her caste so she'd accept me. I was ready to disavow my admiration for my two idols, turn it into condescending and patronizing criticism, for the simple reason that a chic *madame* from Outremont was deigning to listen to me! Instead of praising the subject of my book, I was apologizing for it and consciously emphasizing how important it was. It was my turn to bow down before her and beg for her approval. How disgusting!

My little game could cut either way and I felt myself being hacked to pieces while the situation was getting out of hand because of me.

For the first time in my life I heard myself—I who'd always been so straightforward, so direct—saying the opposite of what I thought, for fear of looking bad. The game of deception that had started off enthusiastically was ending up in a pitiful betrayal. As long as I was inventing it was fun, but now that I was hearing my own lie, I despised myself.

I was saved not by the bell but by the unexpected arrival of the *commandant* who was making his afternoon rounds, bowing to left and right like the King of England. I could have kissed the dear man! The hero out to rescue the damsel in distress. He stopped in front of us, bowed to the ladies (Lucille was behaving with him as if she were 103 years old), kissed Antoinette's hand and turned to me.

I must have been as red and shiny as a boiled crayfish.

"So! Our great actor is paying his respects to his compatriot…"

As if he didn't know what I am and I didn't know what he is!

Antoinette cooed a protest along the lines of "My goodness, *Commandant*," wriggling on her deck chair as if she had a tapeworm, but he cut her off with a hint of severity:

"Captain, Madame. Not *Commandant*. The term is Captain. Captain Simonin, at your service."

The effect would have been less dramatic if he'd slapped her. To correct her in public! And in front of not just any audience: in front of an actor and writer! She changed colour three times in two seconds and stammered apologies nobody could make sense of.

While I beamed. So she can make mistakes too! The grand *bourgeoise* from Outremont who's supposed to know everything—manners, etiquette, people's correct titles—had for three days been calling a captain *commandant* whenever she crossed his path! How disgraceful!

As upright as a freshly-planted fence post, Captain Simonin walked away to greet an old lady in a wheelchair who eats in her cabin but spends her afternoons in the open air, holding a book that she never opens.

A silence as thick as molasses settled in between Antoinette and me. Above all I didn't want to break it: I was relishing it too much.

Antoinette started fiddling with her pearls again while looking out to sea, as if she wished she could lose herself there.

As for me, I told myself that's all very childish when you get right down to it. If she'd laughed it wouldn't been so serious, but you don't teach the very incarnation of Kulture how to laugh.

I've just looked up the difference between *captain* and *commandant* in the Larousse. Honestly!

I've promised myself that if Antoinette makes one more reference to my essay I'll treat her to the most eloquent praise of the Music Hall, which I'm sure she despises, just to finish her off! But it wouldn't change anything, the damage has been done. And

I think I'm a real asshole because I know I'm going to start again the first chance I get. Judas.

Do I have to betray everything like this, to rise above the floor where the shoe salesman plies his trade?

The silence was finally interrupted by the adorable Lucille, who said in a tone as natural as any child who's spent seven years being martyred by Madame Audet: "Mama, might I have my little four o'clock?"

Her little four o'clock? I was wondering what the hell that could be, especially because it was four o'clock on the nose. Then I thought it was probably just her snack. Her "little four o'clock!" God almighty! Does she call supper her "little twenty to six"? Though I'm sure those people don't eat before seven.

Antoinette emerged from her depression to offer a rather chilly goodbye. She'll come down with the flu if she keeps hanging out with me: she's always going from hot to cold! Now she's probably afraid I'll run around the boat telling everybody, especially the other members of her species, that she'd been using the wrong word! Things like that must matter a lot to her!

As for Lucille, she didn't even look at me. Just as well, because I'd've put twelve knots in her braids and hung her around her mother's neck!

The afternoon ended with the score two to one for me: one super-bullshit performance and one betrayal for the chubby Édouard; one humiliation for the classy Antoinette.

You know something? I just remembered that I called the captain by the proper title when I first boarded the ship and it was Antoinette Beaugrand who misled me... That says something, doesn't it? But I mustn't let such things get to me.

Back in my cell, I found an invitation, a lukewarm glass of champagne and a little plate of exotic fruit.

I sampled all the fruit before I opened the invitation. I wanted to test my patience. I've never seen a kiwi disappear so fast! I'd seen one before, in the west end of town, but I'd never actually tasted one. It's an odd kind of fruit. It tastes like all kinds of

things at once but mainly banana, like a banana with juice…
(now don't blush, I wrote that in all innocence!)

While I was chewing the pieces of grapefruit, orange and pineapple (not from a can, imagine!), I was thinking about the orange my mother used to give us at Christmas when we were little, that we'd sometimes keep for a week before we ate it because we knew we wouldn't see another one till the next year… It was terrible: when you think that even now, for us an orange is still the most amazing thing… So there I was, feeling guilty as I sampled the figs, the blue grapes, the dates… A long way from our October apples.

I drained my glass of champagne in one swallow, throwing my head back like a movie actress. Ingrid Bergman. Or Danielle Darrieux. Lukewarm champagne isn't very good. Listen to me, as if I'd been drinking it all my life… Maybe it was just cheap bubbly that I used to drink in Montréal to celebrate something, but at least it was straight from the icebox!

I finally opened the envelope (tore it, actually, I was so anxious to see what was inside). It was for the ball to mark the mid-point of our crossing—tonight! Already! It will be held in the grand ballroom where I haven't yet set foot. But there was something strange at the bottom of the invitation: "Black tie or national costume."

Black tie, I know what that is and I'd bought myself a black tie for this sort of occasion (I may not be very cultivated but I know that the rich enjoy dressing up like penguins when they're on a boat), but national costume… I could see myself decked out in a raccoon coat with a *ceinture fléchée* around my waist, a red tuque and snowshoes, but I had a hunch that wouldn't look too classy… I don't know if a checked shirt and lumberjack pants would qualify as a national costume… I imagine the passengers will opt for black tie. I'm sure not many of them want to remind themselves of where they come from. If I had the guts to do it, I'd wear the black tie—and nothing else—just to see what the rest of them would say… I'd make my grand entrance into the ballroom saying: "Sorry, I didn't bring my national costume, so I decided to wear my black tie…"

That warm champagne gave me a headache; what a wonderful start!

The meal was very lively: everybody was talking about the ball tonight. The captain even promised us a dance band that the company had hired just for tonight and for the ball on the eve of our arrival in France. I wonder what the musicians do the rest of the time. I hope they don't spend their whole lives crossing the Atlantic and working two nights out of six! Not tiring, maybe, but boring as hell! God! Maybe my guy from Bogota plays the trumpet!

Obviously my refined and tactful table-mates spent their time talking about the women who'll be getting all dolled up tonight just to make *them* happy. To make them happy! Is that presumptuous or what? They pointed to the ones they couldn't wait to see and the ones who, in their opinion, ought to stay in their cabins and crochet. Or worse.

Guess what category my pal Antoinette Beaugrand fell into? And look at me being bitchy for no reason, just like them! Tell me, is manliness something you come down with, like a disease? Actually, what they were saying about her was so mean that I nearly came to her defence! I only hope that women say the same kinds of things about men. Those men are supposed to like women! And they're presumably civilized and superior! So money can buy anything except polish. I say that because I haven't got either one: I'm as poor as Job and I've got manners like my uncle Donat, who put milk and sugar in his consommé when I took him to Chez Geracimo last year...

We had something peculiar for supper. It's called a Dover sole *grenobloise*. Sole, that's something I've had before, but this one had lemon and capers and it was as sour as pickles! I cleaned my plate, but you should have seen the face I made! I thought about Gabriel who gets the shivers at the mere sight of a lemon pie in the icebox—he'd have died at that table.

Supper was finished earlier than usual. Apparently the women were in a hurry to change. The men at my table though decided to stay as they were, till I reminded them about their black ties. They had a good laugh at that. They said they'd love to see the guy who'd keep them out of the ball because weren't wearing a black tie... So money buys arrogance too. I won't take any chances myself: my black tie is going to be very visible, and my invitation too. I may be a nobody, but I know it!

Speaking of nobodies, I walked back to my cabin with the guy from Bogota, who's still a total mystery. All I can hope for is that he'll wear his national costume at the ball, which might shed some light on where he's from.

In any event he doesn't seem to have found any fellow countrymen; he stays by himself in his corner, he eats without talking to anybody, then he stares out the windows in the dining room when he's finished. He probably can't even read the menu. It must be strange not to know what you're eating...

Anyway, I told him all kinds of things while we were walking through the maze of corridors, to make him feel less alone. And he did the same. We must've looked like a couple of blockheads. At least he doesn't look at me anymore as if I was a waiter or a sadist who wants to jump him...

I put on my best suit and I look more or less presentable. Judging by the little bit of myself I can see in the mirror of my spacious cabin, that is. The pants fall the way they're supposed to, the sleeves aren't too short (which is so often the case, alas: tailors seem to think that all obese people have short arms!), the tie is as black as it's supposed to be and the silk flower I stuck in my buttonhole gives me a provocative little look that I find quite fetching... Three hundred pounds less and I'd have good reason to be proud of myself (Hee! Hee!).

And now I've got the jitters. My first first-class ball! I thought about Madeleine Renaud in *Carnet de bal*... I could see myself spinning around in the arms of the greatest French actors— except Louis Jouvet, who I think is ugly, pretentious and phony. And I have a hunch that he doesn't smell good, though I couldn't say why. But if I dance tonight it'll be on the arm of Antoinette

Beaugrand, the only person I know on board, and she'll hold herself as straight and stiff as a fence post.

Or else I'll disappear into the wallpaper, sighing in my corner like an ugly girl. But the Duchess of Langeais in me has just rebelled at the idea of disappearing like that. The Duchess of Langeais is going to fix things so she'll have some fun!

Good luck!

Just try having fun with people like that! Does having money force you to be dull, will you tell me? I've been to funerals that were more fun!

In movies, those parties are always wonderful... Beautiful people in beautiful clothes who pause to drink beautiful champagne from beautiful glasses... They make us dream, we're beside ourselves, we think their lives must be filled with exciting moments... And boyoboy, are we ever wrong!

It was fine at first. When I stepped inside, my heart did some flipflops in my chest, for a minute or so I just stood there, rooted to the spot, I was so impressed. Things like that are always the same, impressive at first glance but then when you take a closer look...

The people inside were so chic, I figured I must look like Little Orphan Annie in my ordinary little suit. The men were practically all in tuxedos and the women were decked out in all their finery.

I decide to take a seat in a corner that wasn't too out of the way. I thought things were moving a little too slowly on the dance floor but then I figured I'd probably arrived during the fifteen minutes of slow dances. And it gave me a chance to get a good look at the outfits. The gowns were terribly discreet, cut low but not too low, except in the back, the hairdos were downright depressing (Rita Hayworth would've looked like a mop in the middle of all the fingerwaves) but the jewels... You can't imagine. If the boat had sunk I don't think one of those women would have floated! Diamonds, emeralds, rubies, topazes and gold! Tons of it! There was one woman sitting near the dance floor and she had gold bracelets that started at the wrist and went practically up to the elbow! I wasn't very close to her but whenever she made a move to pick up her champagne glass I could hear them tinkling, and that's the truth!

Twenty minutes later though I was beginning to think that the orchestra (which was very good, by the way) was taking a long time to warm up. Well, it didn't warm up all evening! All evening everybody was elegant, cold, civilized, boring.

Now, when we have a party we'll do just about anything to make sure that our guests have fun, you know that as well as I do: balloons, streamers, swing music, call and answer songs, parlour games, tricks, imitations—you name it!

But those people were languishing as they tried out embarrassed little tango steps, during the slow numbers they danced a mile apart, they thought they were revolutionizing the laws of balance when they awkwardly tried a slow-motion rumba... Really! At the tables, nobody laughed very loud, they took cigarette breaks, they drank heavily but discreetly...

After an hour and half a dozen glasses of champagne, real and chilled, I felt like getting up and singing, "C'est en revenant de Rigaud" to thaw them out!

I was hot, my legs had pins and needles, I wanted something to happen. I felt like I was a prisoner in a wax museum, for pete's sake! There wasn't one person who I could imagine doing his business. They must have been operated on, the whole bunch of them; I'm sure they don't shit or fart or sweat or have bad breath; they must be totally sterilized.

They may be chic but boyoboy, are they ever dull!

In a movie (I always come back to the movies but that's where I've seen most of the rich people I've seen), in a movie you've got the stars in the foreground who speak loudly and behind them you've got the extras who make faces so they don't have to make too much noise... On a real cruise you've just got the extras making faces, and it's all depressing!

Any Hollywood actress would die of boredom after just fifteen minutes with that crowd.

Even the other people at my table were so discreet they were boring, which tells you something. The guy with the cigar was happy to ogle the women but didn't dare to say anything, and the phony priest just stared into space... When you get right down to it, maybe it's only nobodies like me who are impressed by that kind of dullness.

I left early, feeling really blue. Another burst balloon. I tried to tell myself, though: "You're among the high and mighty here, that's what you want to become... to walk around dripping jewels and have men dancing around you..." All I wanted was to be back at the Palace, with Samarcette doing his pirouettes on stage and the Duchess who's murdering "Les Cloches de Corneville"! So tell me, is being able to have fun hereditary?

Unless champagne makes things dull and beer makes things funny.

I leaned against the guardrail and looked at the sky for a while before I went to bed. Even the moon looked as if it was appearing in some dull movie.

Today I made a foray among the poor. I tiptoed off the first-class deck where the usual walkers were beginning their usual exercise (a round of bows to the deck chairs, a stroll on the aft deck, unchanging and unchangeable discussion about the weather, sneaky flight by the men to the games room and the women to the shops that they now know by heart and raid methodically, down to the last nook and cranny of the display cases), and made my way down to second class, which I hoped would be funnier, livelier, more... more real; more like myself, if you want.

And guess what I found? People who dream about going up to first class and act as if they're already there!

The few individuals who saw me emerge on the deck rolled their eyes till they were white enough to scare the mother of an epileptic child. Who was this sick individual, blessed by the gods, who had descended from his ivory tower to mingle with the common herd? Though I'd hoped I looked like a princess slumming it in the less salubrious parts of town, I felt like one of the chosen who turns down his place in heaven and gets booed because people think he's stupid!

It's true that ever since we left New York I've been hearing about second-class passengers who try to sneak into first, I even saw some, dressed up and all the rest, being turned away from the party last night, but I notice that the opposite must be pretty rare: the glorious know how to keep their places, while the nobodies would kill to elevate themselves.

But you know me, I'm as stubborn as a mule; I decided to spend the afternoon there and make a complete tour without a guide.

Surprise number one: there seem to be fewer passengers in second class than in first, as if people who go to Europe almost by definition can afford to travel in luxury. But maybe I'm wrong, maybe second-class passengers spend more time in their cabins...

If a bunch of us decided to go to Europe, we'd have to invent a class just for us, that's for sure!

Is it just in my head or is it possible that the boats are fuller when they're heading for America than when they're coming back?

It's true, I run into more and more foreigners on the streets of Montréal, but I've never heard of one of ours emigrating to Europe, except for some actors like Jean-Louis Roux and intellectuals like Pierre Elliott Trudeau who'll be coming back in any event.

Now don't go thinking I've got anything against foreigners, they don't bother me in the least; it's just something I've observed. Actually, I wonder what the Europeans would say if we decided to emigrate over there en masse... Would the French end up calling us *maudits Canadiens?* I'd never thought of that: when we go over, we're there as visitors; when they come to us, it's to stay!

Anyway. It didn't take long to walk around the second-class deck. The same damn thing as up above, but cruder. The women assume the same poses, but they aren't as natural; the men smoke the same cigars, but they're a little greener. The corridors here don't seem like a barrel of laughs either. And there I was, dreaming about orgies and debauchery!

In fact I wonder if I didn't hate those phony, pretentious people more than the real ones who I can at least laugh at. Because that's what I'm going to do for the mere two days I have left to spend on this old tub: shamelessly make fun of everybody. No more guilt, no more questions, worries, tact. If I don't catch them out, they'll catch me. And if I get caught lying, I'll just laugh even harder! Anyway, they'll be more humiliated at being wrong than I'll be at getting caught.

By the way, here's something I forgot to tell you: I was on my way to supper and I found the exact replica of Antoinette Beaugrand and her littlest lamb, Lucille, on the second-class deck! That's right! I thought I was dreaming when I heard the mother's voice. I positioned myself nearby so I could come into contact with them. They come from—hold onto your hat—they come from Saint-Lambert! Compatriots, if you want, but just as unbearable as the others! What are people from Saint-Lambert going to do in Europe, will you tell me... Madame du Tremblay (if she calls herself *du* Tremblay then three-quarters of French Canadians are nobles!) and her daughter Élisabeth (born the same day as the future Queen of England, poor child) are also going for a bath of "Kulture!" Also with a K. Can it be that Outremont and Saint-Lambert are looking for the same sources?

Now here's something funny: when you travel in second class, do you have the right to visit the same things as those who travel in first, or do you have to be satisfied with cellars, basements and underground passages when you get to Europe? How I *adore* being nasty!

I could see Antoinette Beaugrand and her littlest lamb entering Notre-Dame and heading for the high altar while du Tremblay and her daughter had to turn off and take the stairs down to the catacombs...

We're crazy, aren't we, sometimes when we pretend that we're listening to somebody talk? Because talk is something that du Tremblay's good at! After a half-hour monologue I knew everything there was to know about her: the precise worth, in dollars and cents, of her husband's fortune, the ages of all her children, their shoe sizes and the condition of their teeth, the name of her parish priest (we've got a *monseigneur* too, and we don't think the sun rises and sets on him), the pedigree of her dog and her maid (whom she refers to as her *staff*, emphasizing the word as if she had thirty-two servants), her leisure activities, her family problems (she didn't come right out and say how vulgar her husband is, I guessed that on my own), and most of all, her great admiration for *la France* and *les Français*. And their accent, which she too was trying to imitate (in vain, needless to say).

Just like the other one, I tell you, but less refined. Let's say Nana de Varennes next to Marthe Thierry.

As for Élisabeth, who was a little older than her alter ego, Lucille, she seemed to be terribly ashamed of her mother and jumped whenever she said something silly. Needless to say, she looked as if she had Saint Vitus's dance... She was touching, though, because she was very lovely. With eyes that could take your breath away. The most beautiful eyes I've ever seen! She seems bright and she'll probably suffer a lot on this trip, poor child. Unless she plays deaf.

When Madame *du* asked me for my name, do you know what I told her? I told her my name was Simard and I was in the cement business! Oooh, I love myself when I do things like that!

Leaving second class, which was half-empty and totally insipid, I felt relieved.

I decided not to ask myself anymore questions but there's one that's been running through my mind since I came back to my cabin: if I don't belong in either first class or second, where the hell *do* I fit in?

My dictionary is turning out to be more and more useful and more and more exciting. It's helping me a lot. In fact, I intend to get a French grammar too, if they sell them in the store. Not to develop a style, don't worry, but I won't have to rack my brains and wonder what agrees with what, what takes two *l*'s or just one…

Third conversation on the deck chairs.

This time, all hell broke loose. Because of a third person.

I'd noticed before at the *commandant*'s table this fleshy, conceited old biddy with a high-pitched voice who practically never looked at the other tables. The Princess Clavet-Daudun. And regal she was, to the hilt, but with just a hint of the parvenu that showed in the way she checked to see that everything that she said hit home: at the end of every sentence she'd lean across to the person she'd addressed and let out a very ugly sounding "hmmm?" that she certainly hadn't learned from a private tutor in the family mansion. It was the "hmmm?" of a girl who sold kid gloves, not one who bought them.

Aside from that, the character was perfect. And perfectly disagreeable. She was travelling on her own, boasted about it constantly and drowned it in the champagne that lit up two little flames deep in her eyes that portended nothing good. When the Princess Clavet-Daudun gets angry, her entourage must shake.

Be that as it may, I found this self-proclaimed aristocrat settled into my deck chair and having a lively chat with Antoinette Beaugrand, who was obviously overcome with pride and gratitude. Even if you're from Outremont, a real princess is impressive!

Since I was in the mood to gab and didn't want to finish the afternoon with the card-players and scotch-swillers, I stopped right in front of the two ladies and greeted them politely.

Antoinette Beaugrand seemed very proud to introduce a writer from her country to her new friend who, as she gave me to understand without actually saying so, had herself come and settled on the deck chair to talk with her about our country, which had been a terrible letdown.

"Princess Clavet-Daudun recognized my accent too, can you believe it! Soon I'll actually think I have one! In fact I was rather embarrassed and apologized, but the princess soon reassured me…"

The aforementioned cut her off by tapping her arm. (Was that a noble gesture? Anyway...)

"In point of fact, I find the typical accent of the province of Québec quite enchanting! Hmm?"

When she spoke you felt as if somebody had inadvertently left open the door to a henhouse nearby, letting a turkey escape.

And I heard myself say with my own new accent that came from who knows where:

"You know, Your Highness, not everyone where we come from speaks like Madame Beaugrand... The accent varies with the neighbourhood..."

The princess seemed surprised; Antoinette glared at me. I went on, ignoring her:

"You've been to Montréal then?"

"Yes, I spent three days there. And how frightfully boring it was! That city is an appalling cultural desert. Hmm? Excuse me for being so blunt, but I can understand why the two of you have left. Hmm?"

Madame Beaugrand came out with a sort of little groan of approval and I'd have gladly strangled her.

And that was when the shit hit the fan.

People can do anything to me—laugh at my physique, take pity on my ignorance, make fun of my aspirations, my accent, my way of living and thinking—but let anybody attack my city and I see red! Now it's true that I've left because it's too small, but I want it to be intact when I come home! I don't want people denigrating it even if it's true that it's a cultural desert! I took a deep breath before opening my mouth, otherwise I'd have blown up and they'd have been swabbing the deck till we arrived in Le Havre!

"And how did you spend those three days that were so boring?"

The princess shrugged and gave a hint of a condescending little smile.

"Actually, I was with some friends of Madame Beaugrand, in Upper Outremont..."

I nearly interrupted her, but that would have been too easy.

"…delightful people, actually, who took me all over the city, which I find rather delightful in spite of everything. Hmm? But tourism is all very well in the daytime… and in any case guided tours have never been my specialty… In the evening, at least in the life I lead in Paris, one goes out! Hmm? The ballet, the opera, something… Well, let me tell you, what I saw in Montréal had me stupefied!"

I was seething and it must have shown.

Antoinette Beaugrand of course agreed with everything. After all, she wasn't about to contradict her passport to Paris.

I chased her and I got her: the Princess Clavet-Daudun told me about the unbearable caterwauling of our symphony concerts, of the *appalling* (a word she adores, obviously) amateurishness of our theatre (she saw a production of *L'École des femmes* at the Gésù and claimed it was a horror, though I quite liked it), about the utter desolation of our Musée de Beaux-Arts which in her opinion possesses only one worthwhile painting and hundreds of *appallingly* bad ones and old things that no one else in the world would want. Nothing, absolutely nothing found favour in her eyes. And Antoinette Beaugrand, though she supports Les Amis de l'Art and the symphony concerts and has a subscription to every theatre in Montréal, kept nodding agreement like the worst of the brown-nosers.

And just one little question, which I swear I asked in all innocence, sparked an explosion:

"And during those three days, did you ever go to the east end of Montréal, aside from listening to music at the Plateau?"

Antoinette Beaugrand actually jumped as if someone had jabbed her with a knitting needle through her deck chair. And what emerged from her mouth came so fast that it took me a few seconds to understand. The Princess Clavet-Daudun merely widened her eyes as if her new friend had suddenly started talking Papuan.

"She certainly wouldn't have found art there! Now don't you get started!"

I went on perfectly calmly, which seemed to infuriate her even more. I asked the princess:

"Did you see any typically Canadian shows? Have you heard of Gratien Gélinas? La Poune and Madame Pétrie?"

I thought Antoinette Beaugrand was going to keel over. She was so ashamed she couldn't get a word out.

The princess sensed that something serious was going on before her eyes but she had no idea what.

"Yes, I do believe that I heard something about a Monsieur Gélinas, but my friends the Perriers seemed to consider him rather vulgar. Hmmm?"

I could have scratched her eyes out! But then I thought it wasn't her fault, it was her friends, the Perriers, who'd put that idea in her head. I was just able to say a few words—very feeble compared with what I was thinking:

"That all depends on what you mean by vulgar..."

Madame Beaugrand had had time to get her wits back. After all, her education had prepared her for every possibility—or just about.

"Don't listen to him, Princess, I know the Perriers very well, they're old acquaintances, and they're absolutely right. Let the vulgar stay with their own kind, we love Beauty!"

Then she turned towards me as if I were a hunk of spoiled meat.

"This man may be an actor, but he has some preposterous ideas about the theatre!"

The princess had gone tense.

"An actor? But you introduced him as a writer... In fact I didn't mention literature because of his work, which I haven't had the pleasure of encountering, but if you'd told me he was an actor I wouldn't have assassinated your theatre as I did..."

It's wonderful sight, a Frenchwoman losing her cool... instead of disappearing into her hole she talks... and talks... as if to bury her gaffe under an avalanche of words.

As for me, I couldn't take anymore. *Enough is enough*, as we say in French. I jumped to my feet and I shouted at Madame Beaugrand:

"You asinine idiot! I've never been an actor or a writer in my entire goddamn life! You'd believe anything as long as it's said with an accent from somewhere else! Besides, how do you know that this princess doesn't work at the perfume counter in the Galeries Lafayette? I'm a shoe salesman myself! You've just spent five days with a shoe salesman, you moron!"

And with that I turned to the presumed princess.

"And as for you, if you really want to know, the genuine Montréal accent is the one you're listening to right now, okay? All that woman can do is try and copy yours! Me too, in a way, and believe me I'm ashamed of it! I wouldn't want you to think that everybody talks that way, we aren't all neurotic! *She's* the actress! I'm not surprised you got bored with people like her. If you ever come back to Montréal, take a look around my part of town, *I'll* show you what's worth seeing in my city! I'll show you our real heart instead of our phony head!"

As I walked away I could hear the strident laughter of Princess Clavet-Daudun. "My word, what an actor! Can he change accents like that at will? Yes, what an actor! And can you do that too, Madame Beaugrand?" I also heard a gulp of shame from Antoinette to whom I'd just delivered the coup de grâce.

And I thought to myself once again that we're always somebody else's folklore.

I made the Princess Clavet-Daudun laugh with my real accent, now I only hope that the French will make me laugh with theirs. Trouble is, I'm used to theirs but they aren't used to mine.

Hell's bells!

It's a funny thing, though, high society.

When I walked into the dining room tonight I was still very upset (even though I'd decided yesterday not to let anything get to me anymore), but things seemed to be back to normal for the other two: the princess was waving her arms around at the captain's table and Madame Beaugrand was scolding her littlest lamb whose blouse was sporting a lovely splotch of green soup. The princess waved at me and the *commandant* flashed me a beautiful smile full of healthy, even teeth. Could it be that the Princess Clavet-Daudun is something of a pimp? As for Madame

Beaugrand, she stuck her nose even deeper in her daughter's blouse to avoid looking at me.

So now the French are my allies and my fellow-countrywoman my sworn enemy! It's not what you'd call sticking together, though I'm sure I'd be too grubby for Antoinette to get close to. But that's the way of the world, at least what we know of it.

My table-mates are downright unbearable. It's high time we got to France, before their vulgarity makes me do something I'd regret later on!

At dessert (something that looked like a banana split, but more la-di-da, with the down-to-earth name "barquette de fruits exotiques à la fraîcheur de menthe"), just as they were bringing out their goddamn cigars, the captain asked permission to speak.

First of all, and as usual, he praised our good manners and our public-spiritedness, as if we'd done something special when all we've done for five days is stuff our faces and hang around the deck that's too well kept up to be really interesting; then, all excited, he announced that there was another invitation waiting for us in our cabins, for tomorrow night, that required some explanation.

Did you know that on the last night on these boats, they put on a masquerade ball? I didn't, alas! If I had, I'd have brought a costume to finish off poor Antoinette! I listened to Captain Simonin announce that costumes could be rented on board and, defeatist as always, I figured they wouldn't have anything in my size—and certainly nothing to my liking! I wouldn't want to disguise myself as a pasha or the Easter bunny!

And you know how I love costume parties! I really don't have any luck. I have no idea what I'm going to do but I'm sure as hell going to that party.

Next to me the fake priest asked the cigar-smoker: "Did you bring a costume?" and he replied: "Yeah... I always wear the same one... It's so bo-o-o-ring!" I sincerely hope I'll never become blasé, it's too depressing for other people. He thinks it's boring but he travels the world with a suitcase full of costumes while me, I'm as excited as a débutante and as naked as a worm!

But I'm not too worried, I trust my gift for improvising.

Before she left the dining room, the Princess Clavet-Daudun came over to say hello in person. Antoinette Beaugrand must have choked on her last sip of coffee. I blushed a little myself because I was polishing off the *barquette* of the guy on my left. The princess was very vivacious and oddly enough, she actually managed to say something nice about Montréal. So not all the assholes are to be found in the same pair of pants, eh? Honestly! I mean what if she decides that not only am I quaint, I'm also stupid? I may be a babe in the woods, but there are limits!

In any event, she invited me to play cards with her and some *acquaintances* (she emphasized the word acquaintances so I wouldn't think they were friends of hers) later on, in the games room. I hope she knows "Beggar-your-neighbour" because that's just about the only one I can play. And I hope even more that Antoinette won't be there. But I wouldn't be surprised if Clavet-Daudun was also a troublemaker; in any case, people like her probably have nothing better to do.

There I was wanting to see *Possessed* with Joan Crawford and I may have to act in it!

I'm afraid I'm going to let you down. I wish I could paint a hilarious picture of my evening, with off-beat characters, devastating caricatures of an élite that was blasé to the point of absurdity and rotten to the core, transcribe the way they talk, the way they move, their tics, their smells. But no. I spent part of the evening in front of something resembling an aquarium and the fish that I caught in the act were so dull you couldn't caricature them.

I shaved again (my razor's been scraping dangerously for a while and I'm always afraid I'll slice my jugular, so it takes three times as much attention and time), I got dressed in my best shirt and my brand new suit and I was stunning. A real little man. Dull as dishwater but proper.

By now, I could make my way through the maze of corridors with my eyes shut, so I found the game room very easily.

The boat was pitching a little more than usual; they'd announced heavy winds that were just starting to file their nails on the *Liberté*'s carcass. Two or three strands of my fine hair were out of place; I tried to hold them down with my hand.

The sea was swelling and rising onto the deck in waves of drizzle that got everything wet, so when I reached my destination I was fairly damp myself. I was sure my clothes would start steaming as soon as I entered the room and I pictured the Princess Clavet-Daudun hiding her giggles behind a fan or a handkerchief.

Just before I pushed open the door to the game room a whiff of cigar smoke froze me where I was standing: was my refined table-mate among the princess's guests? Was Her Highness hanging out with the common herd in first class, slumming it in the cigar fumes of Americans on their way to Gay Paree? Was I the only nobody of the evening, or the cherry on a sundae that already had a few?

A big picture window on my left cast a square of light onto the deck that was glistening with rain.

I decided to check on whom I'd be dealing with before I got involved in a card game whose rules and stakes I didn't know.

A good thing I did because the good fairy Boredom had breathed on that party something fierce!

I don't know why, but I more or less assumed that this card game would be a pretext for some fancy society party where we'd sip chilled champagne while chuckling and exchanging gossip as snobbish as it was nasty, like in some French movie with, I don't know, let's say Madeleine Renaud as a countess, Louis Jouvet as a son of a bitch, Raymond Rouleau as a crook, Annie Ducaux as a high-priced hooker and Madeleine Robinson as a striking brunette.

Nope.

Four tables with four places each had the place of honour under a chandelier that was almost too big for the size of the room. Sixteen individuals, nearly motionless and serious as popes blowing bubbles, were devouring their cards with their eyes and declaring slowly, enunciating carefully, as if their lives depended on it. At every table a fifth person was waiting, sitting stiffly on a chair or deceptively relaxed, except at the one farthest from the door, surely the least important one, which was mine. I must have been invited at the last minute as the twentieth because someone else had died of boredom.

I suddenly felt very much like someone's servant. And very humiliated.

All these fine folk were wrapped in dense blue smoke, denser above the table where the princess was drawing with obvious voluptuous pleasure on a cigarillo as thin as a waxed shoe-lace.

Because of its rectangular shape, the window through which I was observing it all made the scene resemble an aquarium that was too brightly lit, especially now that the drizzle was running down the glass and distorting my vision.

I stood planted there in front of the window watching all the big fish in their Sunday best sucking in some air now and then or exchanging multicoloured chips while they assumed blank expressions. There wasn't a sound from the game room. And the wind storm was still blowing at my back.

I was watching one movie and listening to the soundtrack from another.

And nothing I saw tempted me. If those people were enjoying themselves, they weren't letting it show. When *we* play cards, at least the cops come to quiet us down!

What I enjoy smells like something and sounds like something.

At one point the princess got to her feet. I thought I heard her say that she'd just died and that the insipid blond on her left would take over from her. She glanced towards the table where there was one player missing, seemed to note my absence and then turned her head towards the door. I slipped away from the window for fear she'd see me with my nose stuck against it like a puppy in a pet shop that wants to be adopted.

I took a deep breath and a weight was lifted from my heart: we should always check and see what we're getting involved in before we set step into it (which is what I should have told myself before I handed my cheque to the girl who sold me my so-called first class ticket, but anyway…)

You must have sensed something just then because I was calling to you for help so hard I was shaking!

I ended up at the movie theatre, soaking wet, shaking and on the verge of jumping in the water. Joan Crawford and Clark Gable barely brought me comfort for my fate. I cried like a baby over that idiotic woman who sacrifices herself for her husband's career thinking that if it was me, Clark Gable or no Clark Gable, I'd have told him to screw off and continued along my way without looking back!

If we don't reach the other shore soon, they're liable to find a fat man hanging from the dining room chandelier and, classy as they are, they'll have to pretend they don't see me swinging there during the last twenty-four hours of the crossing!

At the worst of the storm, around four-thirty a.m., I asked for death. Again.

I don't know if I can describe to you what I felt, it's still too confused in my mind.

When I woke up I thought I'd fallen out of bed. I tried to hang on but I realized I'd fallen in the other direction—that is, onto the back wall instead of the floor! My feet were practically in the porthole! I figured that the boat was lying on its side, which scared the pants off me. But the boat straightened up almost right away and I landed back in my bed like a sack of potatoes.

You could hear creaking as if the boat was splitting in two, gusts of wind, slamming doors. But no voices. I wondered if maybe I was the only survivor (you know how I can over-dramatize) and I tried to get to my feet. Try and picture it: on both sides, all hell was breaking loose and I finally ended up on my knees next to the shower, my heart in my throat, my brow sweating, close to vomiting (I'm sorry, but I warned you I wouldn't censor anything...)

That was when I asked for death.

I'd rather have died of a stroke then and there than know I was in danger of falling into the icy sea (to hell with the Gulf Stream, I'm sure it's just as cold!) and end up stuck to the ceiling of a cell of a boat that was way too small for me.

I knew deep down that I was exaggerating the danger, but at times like that it's hard to control your imagination.

I finally grabbed hold of my bedside lamp (it was amazing that the electricity was still working) but that didn't calm me down: seeing the cabin pitch from side to side made my nausea even worse.

I curled up on the floor, figuring there was less risk of falling that way, and I prayed.

That's right.

Just in case.

You're a believer, but I'm not really; we've talked a lot about that, you and I. I remember I told you once that even at death's door, I wouldn't have the nerve to call for help after the life I've led... and you see... But I won't ask Him to forgive me and take me into his Beautiful Paradise as if nothing had happened, not me! I've got too much pride to do that. I'll ask Him outright to forget all about me! To let me disappear into the cosmos like dandelion fluff in the grass at Parc Lafontaine. The gorgeous angels with their peacock feather wings don't interest me as much as the devil in the flesh with his tin wings! I wanted to disappear, that's all.

And do you know what? I fell asleep without realizing it, probably lulled by the storm that was calming down. I didn't dream; it was as if I was in a coma.

Waking up at dawn on the floor of a transatlantic cabin, surrounded by vestiges of your own digestive troubles is something I wouldn't wish on anyone.

I got to my feet as best I could and opened the door to let in some air.

The sun was rising innocently, the sea was lapping, calm and friendly, the waves were foaming and everything smelled divine.

I would have thought I'd dreamed it all if I hadn't had to clean up after myself.

At breakfast, joy reigned supreme. We talked about the storm as if it had been a party, laughing about the broken bedside lamps, the suitcases that sprang open by themselves, the sounds like those from a haunted house. You'd think no one but me had been scared.

Which may be true. Maybe I'm the first person in first class who's crossing the ocean for the first time. I'm first at everything, except good deals.

One consolation: when I saw the guy from Bogota walk into the dining room I realized I wasn't alone. He was just as green as me and we exchanged a compassionate look.

My two lady friends aren't speaking to me anymore. Antoinette Beaugrand because of the princess's invitation to me the other night, her Highness because I wasn't at her stupid goddamn card party.

Come on. At least my last day on the boat will be peaceful! Anyhow, I've got something up my sleeve for tonight. I've gone through the whole range of emotions since we left New York, now the others will do the same when I put on my act...

If their masquerade balls are usually as deadly dull as I imagine, believe me, this will be one they'll remember!

Mama often used to say: "When you don't know what to do, do any old thing, make something up, but do *something!*" When I saw the passengers assailing the store that rents costumes I said to myself, she was right: I'll make do with what's already in the cabin instead of trying to unearth something in that ugly old junk. I'd rather just wear the little curtain from the porthole than put on those hideous things that people have been sweating in for generations.

Anyway, I've already got something in mind.

You know me, sticking my nose everywhere like a dog in heat. I did drop into the boutique to see what was going on there. A dense crowd of super-chic ladies and super-aloof gents were groping the costumes with looks of disgust. It's understandable, the smell must be enough to gag a maggot! You could hear nasty cracks in at least twelve languages. Nobodies like me, but rich ones, who didn't know you have to wear a costume on the last night...

As I'd anticipated (even those people are rarely original), gowns in the style of La Pompadour or Joséphine de Beauharnois (as my mother used to call her), Louis XIV outfits and Roman tunics were the first to disappear. ("Let's get dressed up, but let's be royal.") And even if clothes don't make the man, that doesn't stop the man from dressing up! The last to be served (that's right, I waited all that time, I was having more fun than a barrel of monkeys) left, looking pitiful, carrying a Pierrot costume or a shop-worn Harlequin. As for my priest on a spree, he snuck along the wall with a Greek tunic. Well, well…

Neither Antoinette nor the princess showed up. Are they above all that or had they brought their own ceremonial outfits like the cigar-smoker? I'd be surprised if Antoinette Beaugrand travels around with a costume in her suitcase. With the sense of humour she's got—about as much as a cold cup of tea—I'm sure she hasn't dressed up since her wedding! And I'm sure she didn't even know she was doing it then! As for the other one, she'd be the type to discreetly pin a camellia to her waist and think it made all the difference between a real woman of the world and a hooker.

It didn't look good for the costume ball.

Good thing the Duchess of Langeais is around to stir things up!

Afternoon calm, but overwhelming.

I finished *Signé Picpus*. If I don't meet those characters in Paris, I'll have a fit!

A strange thought just occurred to me. You'll laugh. For the first time, I wondered what shoe salesmen in France are like. Funny, isn't it, that I hadn't thought about it before… Princesses, stars, models, yes, sure, I've been dreaming about them all my life, but shoe salesmen like me, who serve all those fine people, what will they be like?

But I suppose the last thing we look for when we go abroad is what we've just left… Though I'm beginning to wonder seriously what I'll have to do to penetrate the high society over there, me with as much education as a calf that's never left its momma!

I suppose I ought to be content with watching, like I've always done at home. In Montréal if you want to see stars you stand outside Radio-Canada, CKAC or CHLP, and you break out in a cold sweat when you see Roger Garceau coming out on the arm of Denyse Saint-Pierre, or Yvette Brind'Amour trotting along between Marjolaine Hébert and Huguette Oligny... But in Paris, where do you go? Does Michèle Morgan walk around between Suzy Prim and Ginette Leclerc when they leave the studio? And if Roger Pigaut shows up with Suzy Delair, does he have to worry about rumours? Where then? Where!

I should've thought about that before.

So I was deep in thought (as they'd say in a novel by Henry Bordeaux) when I heard an embarrassed little voice saying:

"Can I sit here next to you? It's my mother's place."

Antoinette Beaugrand's littlest lamb! All by herself and pink-faced in a mouse-grey frock worthy of an old maid of 99.

I was surprised first of all to see her and then to realize she wasn't talking in the accent she uses around her mother.

"Sure. Take a seat. The deck chairs are for everybody you know..."

She was carrying a *Semaine de Suzette* which she draped over her knees without opening it.

"Will your mother be joining you?"

A little sigh. Of exasperation, maybe.

"No. She's unwell."

I nearly said "Good!" but I bit my tongue in time.

"And what seems to be the trouble?"

(She'd dropped her little Parisian accent but not me! I was rolling my *r*s as much as ever, even to this child for pete's sake!)

"She has a migraine. From reading too much."

Read enough to get a migraine! Do Julien Green and his fellow-writers know how they affect the ladies of Outremont?

I looked at her more attentively. It was obvious right away: she was so tense and feverish, she was shaking. And having a hard time holding back the tears that filled her eyes.

Why was she so upset? Had she been beaten? No, humiliated.

I don't know why, I was attracted by the copy of the *Semaine de Suzette* on her lap. Isn't she a little old to be reading that? And I thought I got a glimpse of a world of lingering childhood, of adolescence postponed with rustling dolls and pitiful stuffed animals. I hope the dance will at least be an outlet for her.

She gave off such distress that it was making me feel uncomfortable. I'd have liked to help her but what can you say to a child from another world who doesn't even ask you outright for your help? What *we* do is take the child in our arms, rock her and give her a kiss, act a little rough with her to make her laugh... but with this one I had the impression that if I touched one hair on her head someone would call "Rape!" and she'd be punished as much as I would.

I realized there was nothing I could do for her and I wanted to scream bloody murder.

God but it's hard to describe that! That must be what it's like to feel helpless.

I turned my head to look out to sea. I felt as if I was betraying her. The same damn waves were creating the same damn spray. Things that are beautiful can also become monotonous.

A few minutes later she said softly:

"Would you mind if I cry?"

And I realized that I could be useful after all.

Lucille Beaugrand unburdened herself of her overflow of exasperation and frustration without a word, with long sobs interrupted by sniffles that weren't very classy and that broke your heart.

Funny, isn't it, it seemed to me I understood her perfectly, but I'll never be absolutely sure.

When I run into her this evening or tomorrow during the landing she'll probably say: "Au revoir, Monsieur!" without even giving me a knowing look, as if I hardly exist, even though she owes me—I'm sure of this—a moment of tremendous relief.

This isn't very clear, I apologize. I'll try to come back to it. For the time being I'm too upset.

Which of those two roles will that little girl be playing in twenty years? Madame Audet's pupil whose speech rings untrue because it's vulgar to be natural, or the rebellious girl who's the only natural one in a world that's false?

My trip is really taking a funny turn. Though I'd gone away to have some fun!

Which is what I'll try and do tonight.

When I'd finished dressing the cabin was turned upside down but I looked fine.

I was wearing pretty well everything in the cabin that wasn't nailed down.

I began by stripping my bed and draping myself in the sheets Roman-style, with one shoulder exposed to the air; then I took the cord from the curtain at the porthole to emphasize the waistline I don't have and I flung the curtain over my head to make a poor man's Nefertiti-style headgear. I held it all in place with three-quarters of a pound of bobbypins; my scalp was bloody but it stayed put.

I looked at myself in the mirror. My get-up lacked character. So then I threw myself into the cabin like a panther with an innocent deer on a night when the moon is full, and I took apart everything that would come apart to create some accessories for myself.

I draped the bedspread over the shoulder that wasn't bare to make it look like a court mantle (a nightmare in orange, white and black, with flowers, big ones; the whole thing soiled by generations of not very meticulous first-class pigs). And then—now listen carefully, you won't believe this—I unscrewed the handles of the taps in the mini-sink to make earrings (I turned the water off first, needless to say), which I attached with little bits of string that I wrapped behind my ears. For a bracelet, I wound a long strip of toilet paper around my wrist and held it in place with an elastic, the edge ruffled to look like a flower; for a necklace, I simply detached the chain in the toilet and fastened it so the brass handle hung down onto my partially bared bosom. Stunning.

I was barefoot because I couldn't think of anything for my feet. After all, I couldn't top off this magnificent creation with my own shiny little pumps: one has taste, after all!

Once again I stepped up to the mirror. I looked supremely ridiculous.

Then I took out my makeup kit. I know I should have started with that but when you improvise you aren't always logical. I painted a face for myself that looked like a silent film star's, sooty and angular. With the face I've got it's a job and a half to carve cheekbones and highlight a chin that's nonexistent because it's buried in lard. Everything was highly emphasized then, almost like a clown face. As I've often said to Samarcette, who I think is too discreet in society: "If you aren't sure of yourself at a party, play the clown, people will think you've got imagination."

Back at the mirror I decided I still needed colour. The only colours I was wearing fell from my left shoulder and looked like a tablecloth on which millions of fat greasy flies have been swatted. And do you know what I did? For writing this edifying work that's addressed to you I'd bought three colours of Waterman ink: Royal Blue, South Sea Blue and Pitch Black. I checked to be sure there was enough left in my pen and then I smeared the rest of the three bottles all over my face.

When one creates one loses the notion of things. I must have created something wild and wonderful because I didn't think even once of the damage I was liable to cause. When I went back to the mirror one last time it looked as if an ink factory had blown up in the cabin. There was ink everywhere and I mean everywhere. Mind you, it's so small that when I take a bath, I end up with water under my pillow!

Very erect in my Nefertiti-Roman costume, I waited till it was dry. Or almost. Momma couldn't wait to make her entrance at the ball.

When it was time to leave I realized I looked like anything except a woman and that had a strange effect on me. But it was no time for grand philosophical questions and I rattled my way out into the corridor.

Now, I've stopped a lot of parties in my life but never like that one!

First, because without knowing it I'd committed an irreparable gaffe by not wearing a mask and then, because high society doesn't seem to think very highly of cross-dressing: all the ladies present were sensibly disguised as ladies and all the gents as gents. And they were nearly all in pairs: the gypsy woman had her gypsy man, the marquise her marquis, the she-monkey her he-monkey, the Pierrot his Columbine and the Mae West her W.C. Fields.

When I made my entrance the party was in full swing (I'd rather be waited for than wait, even when the others aren't actually waiting for me!) and a tango too quick for my liking was in progress. But the couples had started to mingle which made for some rather amazing combinations: Mae West swooning in the arms of a very attentive orangutan, a young bride of a certain age fidgeting around a hunched-over old man in a Pinocchio costume, Snow White (the Disney version, in blue, yellow, red and black) was succumbing, obviously for real, to the advances of a pot-bellied cook decked out in a pitiful mask of a young man with overly red cheeks and holes for eyes.

Yes, they were all wearing masks. I didn't know you were supposed to take the invitation literally and I was quite shamelessly displaying my own handsome face with the features of a dumb lout (remember when Mama used to tell me I had the face of a dumb lout with my eyes close together like a lunatic's when she was mad at me?). I don't need to tell you that a chill spread around me when, regal and haughty, I stepped inside the ballroom which was decorated like an ornament for a millionaire's Christmas tree. In addition to my costume, which they seemed to find rather surprising, my face, which was only made up, seemed to be so shocking it was indecent. Faces turned in my direction but the women's heads leaned across to the men's ears. Laughter burst out, sometimes mocking, sometimes surprised.

I decided to carry on as if everything were normal and waved like King George the Sixth's wife. I plunked myself at one of the numerous bars and delivered a, "Champagne, garçon!" that nearly made the barman jump.

But beneath my phlegmatic appearance, my mind was in an uproar.

Now when there's talk about dressing up I'm as thrilled as a little girl and I do everything I can to be amusing. It seems to me that the words "dressing up" contain their share of the comical and that when you get dressed up, it's mainly to keep from being serious. Not to be incognito! I want people to know that the fat opera singer or the awkward ballerina who's always crashing into the wall as she tries to pirouette is me! Why bother dressing up if nobody notices you?

Wrong, yet again.

Everybody was as serious as a pope and wearing their costume like ceremonial dress. The apes as well as the bluebloods. And me, I looked like the village idiot who didn't get the whole story. I tossed back a second glass of champagne to help me put on a brave face and give me the courage to take on this party that looked as if it was going to be long and, yes, once again, boring as hell.

A shepherdess in a short dress, crook in hand, curly wig, the works, but in whom even a mental case who'd spent the past twenty-eight years in a strait jacket would have recognized Antoinette Beaugrand despite the youthful mask, she was that stiff and unnatural, came up to me and asked in a voice that was nearly scandalized: "I'm prepared to believe that you're an actor, but for the love of God what are you dressed up as?"

I set my empty glass on the bar and proclaimed: "As a first-class toilet, Madame Beaugrand!"

And that was when I decided to have myself a wild old time!

And wild it was, believe me!

I grabbed the first marquise who came along and we were off to the races.

You know me, when there's dancing nobody can stop me. I love to dance—and I'm pretty damn good! After I chose my dancing partner I went straight to the middle of the dance floor where I was sure everybody could see me, and I tackled everything—waltz, tango, polka, overcharged and swaggering.

A few women wouldn't dance with me because I was wearing a dress, but the ones who did weren't sorry. I spun them around more energetically than the old rags who'd come before me; I dipped them to the floor; I pitched them in the air. I had the right step, the right rhythm, the right breath—and next to me all the other dancers looked like amateurs.

After ten or twelve dances I found *the* partner: a tubby little woman who was going home after a year-long stay with her sister in Connecticut and had been missing the Saturday night dances in her neighbourhood, the 14th arrondissement in Paris. She quickly took off her mask because she was too hot and we danced together for the rest of the evening under the stunned looks of the other passengers whose main concern had become trying to avoid us in our glides, figures and arabesques. My partner knew the secrets of all the South American dances and when she saw that I was having trouble, she took over and led without it showing.

Between two dances, while we were towelling ourselves dry, I asked her why I hadn't seen her all week; she confessed that she was travelling in second class and had managed to sneak in because of her magnificent Japanese costume, a real one, inherited from another sister who travelled a lot. She had however made some changes to this *real* Japanese costume: the skirt was slit to the thigh to facilitate movement and the top had obviously been modified to emphasize her bosom.

She was a very good dancer but she also smelled very strong.

After a couple of hours of frantic rapture I finally begged for mercy and Étiennette pushed me towards the tables that were becoming surrounded by winded dancers and dead-drunk drinkers.

It was then that I noticed something rather surprising: in the corners of the ballroom, where as it happened the light was very subdued, some strange things were going on. While Étiennette and I were wearing ourselves out, couples had come undone, others had formed and withdrawn to areas that were more discreet. I don't need to draw you a picture but I'll tell you, the costumes didn't match at all! Mae West had dropped W.C. Fields and Pierrot had long since shed his Columbine. New couples that were odd and combinations that were sometimes downright weird were snuggled up together in the dim light, and we could hear some unmistakable little moans. But all done with exquisite manners, with a cleanliness even that was almost shocking.

And I understood the reason for the masks. As long as they could pretend not to recognize each other, everything was permitted. The other night, at the first ball, they'd merely carried on with their usual respectable habits but tonight, thanks to the false anonymity, they could give in to their baser instincts. While maintaining a certain distinction. They knew about good manners, after all!

When it was over, in the first rays of dawn, every Jack had found his Jill and everything went back to normal thanks to that marvelous thing that's probably called collective amnesia. A beautiful pretentious painting entitled "Honour Saved by a Mask."

Now I've seen orgies, real ones, with asses swaying in every direction and climaxes that blasted your eardrums, but none of them shocked me like this one, though it was neat and tidy and, in particular, very well-dressed. You could have knocked me over with a feather more than once these past five days; God knows where it's all going to end up!

Étiennette taught me that this was the reason for masked balls and carnivals: to allow people, disguised and under the cover of a party, to do things they'd be ashamed to do in broad daylight. And I sensed from her misty eyes that she wouldn't have minded the two of us joining in with this amorous feast to the languorous accents of the orchestra now condemned to play music that was nearly dirty. Poor girl. Surely my costume wouldn't have made her think that...

I looked around for the captain. He was at the head table (again!), conversing calmly with the Princess Clavet-Daudun and, of course, Antoinette Beaugrand. He didn't look as if he was courting them. The three of them were simply talking as if everything were normal. Deaf and blind to what was going on around them.

That was when I decided to deliver my final punch. I left Étiennette and headed for the trio from hell, declaiming very loudly "Le Songe d'Athalie," which I'd committed to memory after seeing Sarah Bernhardt bellow it in Dominion Square one windy day when I was a teenager.

Ripples formed amid the debauchery; wet mouths turned towards me, gasps were interrupted, spasms repressed. Antoinette Beaugrand had stopped fiddling with her pearls for a few seconds, only to start up again more than ever when she recognized me. I made my way very slowly to the head table, arms flung up like a bad tragic actress, my voice drawn out and disgracefully modulated, nasal and nasty, and my back arched. An obese sleepwalker.

It's very hard to keep an orgy going, no matter how antiseptic, to the music of Racine; they were listening to me with impatience I could touch, it was so thick. A malicious joy was making me feel queasy. I say malicious because when you get right down to it I had no reason for doing what I was doing. But I was getting such pleasure from it! After all, am I not simply an envious person who who'd rather piss people off than go unnoticed in a world where he doesn't belong? Probably. But nobody gives a good goddamn.

Because along with the satisfaction of disturbing everybody I got another reward, much keener, much more significant: I believe I caught a little knowing look from the captain out of the corner of my eye and that thrilled me.

There was some polite applause when I'd finished my gurgling and my lamentations, but the fun had fallen off and the party was beginning to flag. The beautiful costumes had been mishandled, you might say, and everything looked like the morning after the night before.

The Princess Clavet-Daudun had the gall to congratulate me when we both knew that I'd been excruciating, and my fellow countrywoman pretended that I wasn't there.

And the captain did something that finished off the two ladies: rising, he bowed and kissed my hand, saying: "A great Athalie always merits a bow."

Rather than discreetly savour my victory (which really isn't my style) I rushed towards the stage, grabbed hold of the mike and intoned in the most vulgar voice I could find the subtle call and answer song that Albertine's late husband used to shove down our throats at every family get-together, "C'est en revenant de Rigaud," without skimping on the snorts, the smacking lips, and the imitation farts and burps.

The Duchess of Langeais had given way to Édouard and I realized that, as of this moment, the two would be inextricably entwined, for better and for worse, a love match if there ever was one, unfailing passion, happiness guaranteed or your money refunded.

When I'd finished with my sound effects I resumed my dignified expression and before I left, in an embarrassed silence, I bellowed: "*Un peu moins de respect, et plus de confiance. Tous ces présents, messieurs, irritent mon dépit: Je vois mes honneurs croître, et tomber mon crédit.*"

What can I say, I'm an erudite shoe salesman!

I spent a good part of the night struggling with my guilt. We aren't in the habit of doing brave deeds and when we *do* do one we regret it almost right away, because of other people's opinion: what will the neighbours say, what will the family think... it's enough to make you think we only care about what other people think of us!

And yet I sincerely think that what I did yesterday was brave, because I upset that stuffy bunch, I put a little life into a funeral disguised as a cruise, I shocked, I embarrassed, I offended the constipated... but I'm also well aware that in a while, when we land, my cheeks will be red and my eyes will be glued to the toes of my shoes.

Every time I was overcome by a wave of guilt, I tried to fight it; I told myself it was ridiculous to feel ashamed over having fun—because I *did* have fun, a lot of it—instead of wasting my

114

time in a corner, drinking warm champagne and watching the most uninteresting couples in creation since Adam and Eve whirl across the dance floor. But my discomfort hung on because something deep inside me was telling me I'd been wrong, because I was the only person who'd had any fun! Can't you picture it? That's us, isn't it? Be a doormat, let others walk all over you!

I'm too sure that the other passengers in first class are superior to me to really enjoy it when I disturb them or laugh at them. I'm like the child who has a fit because he knows he's wrong: I howl, my nose runs, I kick wherever I can —and right afterwards I want to ask their forgiveness. I absolutely have to toughen up or I won't escape. I'm sure that everybody slept very well last night, except me!

Once again I haven't got the words to describe how I feel and on top of that, I tell myself that if I did have them, it would mean I had more education than I've got, I'd belong to another caste, and I most definitely wouldn't have the same problems! Either you're ignorant and you can't express your dissatisfaction in words or you're educated and you haven't got the same dissatisfactions! Does that mean that our dissatisfactions can't be expressed? Even though it seems to me that what I've written so far is relatively clear...

Dammit all anyway, I wish you were here!

Do you know what hell is? It's being an upstart who knows he's an upstart and just feels like going back in his hole because he knows he'll never be accepted by the social class he longs for.

And heaven is probably being an upstart who doesn't know it.

France. I've finally seen the coast of France.

They announced it a good hour ago but a fog bank was hiding it. I craned my neck, I got up on tiptoe; if I hadn't controlled myself I'd have climbed up on the guard-rail and been the first one to cry "Land ho!" I was excited, I was hot, I was cold...

Then all of a sudden I spied some chimneys. At first I thought it was another boat but then houses, factories, wharves emerged from the fog, the sun was casting its beautiful golden rays over everything and I realized that France, *France*, was appearing to me!

I shouted "Hurray!" as if I'd just scored a goal—me who hates hockey with a passion! I clapped my hands and jumped up and down. I hadn't scored a goal but I had reached one!

And something very wonderful happened: I knew that once again I'd behaved like a nobody but I didn't care! I was the only one of all the passengers to show my excitement and I was actually quite proud of it, not ashamed. And I sensed that I wasn't going to feel guilty!

When I cried out for the last time, it was a brave cry, a deliberate one, a cry of deliverance; Antoinette Beaugrand looked at me and I was surprised to see jealousy in her eyes! I felt like telling her: "Shout along, you silly fool, if that's what you want, it feels so good!" And I let out a third "Hurray!" watching her. But she turned away. Tough.

Lucille, so vulnerable yesterday, so pitiful, was back in character, that of an educated little turkey: she climbed up on the first rung of the guard-rail and said in the voice of the pupil who comes first in diction: "How beautiful it is, Mama, how beautiful! Look at the lovely homes!" when you couldn't see a house yet. To hell with her too!

We sailed into Le Havre under a dazzling sky. The tugboats came and pulled us very slowly into port. I was as excited as a young bride on her way to the church: I was simultaneously eager and scared. In the port, people waved at us. Relatives, friends who'd come to meet passengers. I pictured you, because you think they talk so funny, dressed up as a Frenchwoman, and I laughed!

In a few minutes I'll be setting foot on French soil. I'll tell you how it felt when I get to the hotel where I'm going to spend the night.

The motors have just stopped. The boat isn't moving now. I think I feel sick to my stomach.

Insert

Scheherazade II

"I don't believe it! You actually stayed awake!" Cuirette seemed downright insulted. "When you read me dumb articles in English from *People* magazine or gossip from *Échos-Vedettes*, I fall asleep because they're dull; *that* was interesting." Hosanna stretched like a cat that's been motionless for eighteen hours straight, his mouth open in a yawn he didn't even try to hide. "What's the time?" "Twenty past four." Hosanna set the manuscript on the coffee table on which was displayed the same old plaster "David" that had been missing an arm since the famous night when Cuirette had admitted that he'd picked up "a little something" during an orgy at Jennifer Jones's. "Hey, I have to work tomorrow! My mother's coming to the salon at nine a.m." Cuirette scratched his belly the way he always did when he was tired. "You can do her tomorrow afternoon, there's less chance to screw it up like you did last time..." In the bathroom, Hosanna was already downing his two Valiums before brushing his teeth. "I've got other clients, Cuirette! If all I had was my mother I'd be on welfare like you! Over thirty, desperate case." Cuirette, impervious to his boyfriend's darts, was leafing through Édouard's diary. "When'll you read me the rest? I'm dying to hear it!" He heard some gargling to the tune of "Sur la mer calmée" from *Madama Butterfly*, then, "Tomorrow night, darling, like the other queen who was afraid of getting killed!" A silly little laugh. "You're so harmless, Cuirette, the idea that you might be dangerous makes me laugh!" Slowly, Cuirette peeled off his clothes, dropping his shoes onto the hardwood floor, his leather belt buckle clinking. Hosanna often said: "When the metal rings, the bull's out of his things!" Cuirette was placidly picking his nose. "Do you think it's true, all that stuff the Duchess talks about?" Hosanna came back into the living room-bedroom dressed in a sexy dressing gown of almond green nylon, a vestige of the time when he still saw himself as Elizabeth Taylor. "Of course not, jerk! You know what she was like! Tell her some bit of news and she'd turn it into a global disaster! She could've been seasick in her cabin all five days!" Moving automatically, they shifted the coffee table. Then Cuirette opened the hide-a-bed, cursing, as usual. Hosanna sighed, pouting. "I won't be able to sleep now, I'm too tired." Cuirette hopped into the bed, shivering in the sheets as if he'd just dived into an icy lake. He picked up the Duchess's diary again. "I'll read the second part if you want. I looked at it, it's shorter..." Hosanna lit up what was supposed to be one last cigarette. "You mean you know how?" A few seconds later he was howling: "Don't tickle! Don't tickle me! You know that gives me a fit and it could kill me!" And so the second part of Édouard's diary wasn't read that night, since Cuirette and Hosanna's tickling sessions always led to something that was more serious and too exhausting for them to concentrate afterwards on reading even one word.

Crossing France

A nd now that my train is speeding towards Paris, here's the true story of my arrival in Le Havre.

I'd been expecting a white city battered by the waves, and sailboats, medieval houses with thatched roofs, women with arms akimbo selling still-wriggling fish, and loud-mouthed men with cigarettes clamped between their teeth and fresh bread under their arms.

Not exactly.

Even though we've heard about the war, read the papers, seen the movies or listened to descriptions by people who were there, nothing can show the horror of it like a city that's been destroyed as though it's been wiped off the map.

Le Havre is a construction site.

As the boat approached the city and then began to sail along the seawall that holds back the ocean, the sight that was unfolding before us, so clear in the afternoon sun, nearly took away any urge to disembark. The war's been over for two years now but the city is still dead. No, that's not true: the construction sites that cover it seem to want to be crying out, through steam-shovels, cranes, drills and hammers, that life is still possible, even after the worst calamities.

I'll tell you, it was the furthest thing from our romantic ideas about France! Once we were off the boat, past the customs shed that smelled of dampness and dust, the gloomy sight of the wharves, even though they were crammed with noisy people crying and waving their arms, kissing and patting each other, already had me extremely depressed. I couldn't describe exactly what I was feeling. I hadn't been expecting a red carpet or a brass band, but something was missing. Even though I was surrounded by all kinds of happy reunions and I could hear shouts of joy, sobs, names called out like cries of relief. But what I'd glimpsed from high up on my first-class deck and was circling these momentarily joyous wharves—this city that was exhausting itself in attempts to be reborn—kept me from enjoying my arrival as much as I should have. What was missing was any certainty that I'd find the France I had imagined.

Was it guilt because I wasn't there three years ago to help push back the horror that had prevailed for too long? What could I do? Nature had endowed me with flat feet; ever since my tender youth I've been cultivating a nearly indecent portliness and in any case, they wouldn't have wanted a pariah like me. False duchesses don't experience genuine landings.

A shriek in the loudspeaker, the sound of crumpling paper, a woman's voice: "Passengers in transit for Paris are requested to make their way to the Vauban Basin."

The Princess Clavet-Daudun strolled past me, followed by a porter pushing a trolley piled high with something like a hundred and eighty-two suitcases. "Come along dear man, you mustn't miss the train!" Dear man? The train? I started mincing along beside her, my heavy suitcase bumping against my legs. "What do you mean, the train? What train?" The princess slowed down a little. "You mustn't spend even one night in this hole! Such a depressing town! In any event the cost of the train from Le Havre to Paris is included in your ticket." I set down my suitcase in a puddle of oil and took out my ticket. The princess continued on her way, moving through the jubilant crowd with a certain grace all the same.

The date and time for the train did indeed appear on my ticket: Sunday, June 1, 1947 at 17:17. Now I suppose I have to get used to telling time like that! What does that mean anyway, 17:17? Seven p.m.? It's just three now, so I've got four hours to wait.. No, it isn't seven p.m.. If 12 means noon then five hours more means... it means five p.m.! Looks like I'll be doing a lot of mental arithmetic.

So all I saw of Le Havre was its construction sites from the deck of the *Liberté* and from the window of my compartment on the train.

At the Vauban Basin, ten men came rushing up to carry my suitcase. If the circumstances had been different I'd have boasted, but I knew they were only doing it to earn a little money and that embarrassed me. In their eyes I also saw hostility and even something like contempt, as if carrying my valise was their way of mocking me. I tried to make them see that I'm strong but they talked louder, pushed me, insisted... Finally, I surrendered my poor suitcase (a blue metal monster) to the hands of a swarthy little guy, not very clean, who was practically running ahead of me. I could see myself criss-crossing France without a change of clothes because he'd stolen my luggage so I tagged along behind my porter.

The railway station was near the Vauban Basin but the Vauban Basin was a good ways away from the boat... I never could have carted my metal case over such a distance but the skinny little guy did it without putting it down even once.

As soon as I'd left the harbour area, the noise of the city hit me and nearly knocked me out. People were screaming at taxis, porters were arguing with their clients, there was a smell of exhaust fumes, buses were tearing along... I was nearly dizzy. But I had to keep racing behind my porter who never once turned around to make sure I was there.

At the foot of the stone steps a white limousine was waiting. I thought, that's it, the Princess is going to blow me a kiss... but guess who I saw diving into it after he'd given me a friendly handshake? My guy from Bogota! A white Packard, after I'd written him off as some poor jerk like me! Maybe he's a movie star travelling incognito! Don't tell me I'd been hanging out for days with a famous actor and hadn't recognized him! Maybe he was Tyrone Power, pretending he didn't speak English or French! Or Gary Cooper! No, it must've been somebody with a banana plantation or a cigar factory, or someone from the SS sneaking back into Europe! Even though his accommodations were no better than mine!

Still on the heels of my porter, I crossed a big avenue called Boulevard de Strasbourg. I couldn't make head or tail of the traffic lights and I nearly got run over twice, with plenty of insults on top of it.

At the corner of the boulevard and the Cours Chevalier de la Barre, I got my first real sight of France: a huge café with a red awning where a peaceful crowd was sipping some kind of beverage. I stopped for a minute to take a good look. That's what I'd come here to find. It reassured me a little. And I didn't look around again till we'd arrived at the SNCF station.

I spent a long time in the dictionary trying to find a word to describe the free-for-all that was waiting for us at the station. And I just found it. Pandemonium. Did you know that Pandemonium is supposed to be the capital of Hell? That little town must have a huge population! But I'm getting away from my story.

Remember barely ten days ago, when you came with me to the Windsor Station in Montréal and how big we thought the crowd was? It felt like Eaton's at Christmas-time. Well let me tell you, that was the Gobi desert compared with the station at Le Havre! Trains seem to be a lot more important in French peoples' lives than they are in ours. A noisy crowd, not very well-mannered, were pushing and shoving on the platforms, people were racing around in every direction, a woman's voice was announcing arrivals and departures, whistles kept slicing the air... I was getting pretty worked-up myself because I couldn't make any sense of the departure list when my porter stops. "Are you going to Paris?" I answered in the closest I could come to his accent: "Yes, indeed!" And I showed him my ticket... "Ah! Monsieur is travelling in first class! Monsieur is a bourgeois!" It felt weird to be called that: back home I'm the lowest of the low. "Monsieur doesn't mingle with the riffraff!" If he only knew that the riffraff is my specialty! He headed straight for platform A and stopped at the first-class car right in the middle of the train, fancier than the others of course and shiny as a new penny. The porter didn't even take his cigarette out to his mouth to tell me: "Fifty francs!" as if it was an order.

And that was when I realized that I didn't have any French money!

You can't imagine the trouble I had changing my Canadian money. In the kiosks at the station they looked at me as if I'd just printed it myself; at the bank they whispered and pointed to the picture of King George VI as if he were an extra-terrestrial. Somebody asked me if I was English and I showed him the word "Canada" written in big letters on the bill. Gee whiz, can't they read? They're used to seeing English books because of the English people who cross the Channel, but English money isn't the same as ours... So they stuck their noses into some big fat books, they figured out what my money was worth—and do you know what? I realized that I'm a millionaire! Me! The two thousand dollars I'd hidden in my suitcase and on my gorgeous alabaster body is worth a little more than a million francs! Which means that in Andrex's movies where the whole town of Marseille was killing each other over a million francs, they were doing it for a miserable few thousand Canadian dollars. It was all very well for you and me to not take them seriously, with their black shirts and their white ties, though mind you, two thousand bucks is a lot of money—but not enough to wipe out a whole city with their guns and fists!

I changed a hundred dollars, which brought me the astronomical sum of fifty thousand francs and change... Suddenly I felt very rich and I offered a hundred francs to the porter who'd been following behind with my suitcase and was visibly weakening, poor guy. Then we started racing towards the train even though we were an hour and a half early. The porter was sweating like a pig and I could hear him breathing, the breathing of a heavy smoker. He must cough his lungs out when he gets up in the morning. And his arms must've grown two inches longer this afternoon!

Back in my compartment, I found Antoinette Beaugrand and her littlest lamb sitting at the table over what they called "a tiny bite," snapping the consonants as if they were sucking sour candy.

It would be hard to exaggerate how funny people can be: after last night's scandal and my "Hurrays" a while ago, I'd have expected at least some hostility, if not outright animosity from them, but no, they barely rolled their eyes when they saw me coming on board. Coming on board? Did my week on a ship mix up my vocabulary? In any case, they're sitting across from me while I write these pages. They're reading with fine concentration, the littlest lamb a young people's magazine called *Fripounet et Marisette*—and Antoinette—you guessed it—the divine Julien. But not *Mont-Cinère. Léviathan.* It must be either very sad or very daring because she's staring in disbelief.

Our train couldn't be more typical: old, clattering, noisy, and quite odd because you go directly into the compartment from the platform: you open the door, climb two steps, sort of like our streetcars, and there you are facing the velvet-covered seats, worn-out and very hard but fairly comfortable anyway. I'd have liked to behave like a French actress and wave my hanky out the door. But a very serious gentleman in a cap and uniform came to punch our tickets and look at our papers while he joked about the oh-so-funny accent of us French Canadians. Antoinette blanched. I blushed. I felt like telling him that his accent was just as funny to us, but he wouldn't have got it. As of now I have to accept the fact that I'm in the minority here, that I'm the one with an accent. It won't be easy because on Mont-Royal Street we used to have a good laugh whenever we heard somebody with a French accent... But I'm talking as if all that was in the past, as if you didn't exist anymore, when I'm writing to you, for you. It's strange to think that while I'm over here everything's going on as usual back home. Sometimes I feel as if everybody has travelled with me, as if where I am is the only place that exists. I don't mean to be pretentious, it's just that it's new to me. I've got so used to being with the same people ever since I was born that it feels as if I haven't left them. But that must be true for anybody who's travelling for the first time. What about you, can you imagine that I'm here in France, on a train between Le Havre and Paris, and that the cows I see aren't even the same size as ours?

Some of the towns we pass through, even some of the villages, have been affected by the war. I don't have time to list everything I see, we're travelling too fast, but images of devastated farms or of whole sections of walls that have collapsed show up often between two clumps of trees, just long enough to make me feel uncomfortable. It's as if the bomb had just burst, as if the dust has barely had enough time to settle, and I keep expecting to see a Red Cross ambulance materialize. I often lean across towards the window, turning my head to follow a particularly interesting sight, which seems to get on Antoinette's nerves, making her sigh with exasperation. I move around too much for her liking. She must have told her daughter to keep still and here I am squirming like a child who's never been on a train before.

Names, weird and sometimes even downright funny, file past on the little train stations we go by with a deafening roar, and at the level crossings where practically no one ever watches us: Eprétot, Houquetot, Nointot, Beuzeville-la-Grande, Bolbec, Bollevielle, Foucart, Yvetot, Pavilly. Not many saints in the landscape, not like our town names!

Nature seems very different too: leaves have grown everywhere while back home at the beginning of June they're still young and fragile. Not many maple or fir trees but lots of oaks and tall beeches that seem to whip the sky as we go past.

All the houses in the small towns and the godforsaken little villages have the same kind of slate roofs, worn down by bad weather and burnt by the sun. When the town is remote and the scars left by the war aren't too apparent, it's so beautiful it takes your breath away. I feel disoriented, as if I were dreaming that I'm on a train in France. A sense of unreality that upsets me. I don't know if the French are as surprised at our flat roofs and our forests of half-dead fir trees.

The two Beaugrands don't pay much attention to these wonders that disappear as fast as they come into view; the bucolic landscape and the little back roads must not be part of their "Kulture." Unless they're painted on a canvas that isn't dry yet.

They've just announced Rouen, our first stop since Le Havre. I feel a little hungry (I could eat two our three steamed hotdogs with fries but I think I'd better forget about that for a while) and I wouldn't mind picking up some postcards. I'm sure Rouen's famous for something!

Later. I'm so winded my heart's in my mouth! I must be as red as a lobster trying to crawl out of its pot. And hot! I hope I at least don't smell bad... There's nothing in this world that I hate more than people who smell of sweat. But I'm alone in my compartment now so it doesn't matter.

Was I supposed to know that in France trains only stop at the stations for two or three minutes? I figured I'd have a good fifteen minutes or half an hour. I heard that same damn woman's voice (she travels fast, that one!) say something, but with the creaking of the metal wheels all I could understand was the word "minutes"...

Dammit all, I didn't even have time to pick up a sandwich!

The stations are built very funny here. You've got two or three platforms parallel to the station but you aren't allowed to cross the tracks, so you have to go into a tunnel to get to where you're going. So I followed the travellers who were getting off at Rouen. I even helped a little old lady who was bent over so far she probably never saw the colour of the sky and who kept thanking me for carrying her suitcase till I wanted to smack her. That held me up, needless to say. When I get to the main platform I see a sign that says "Restaurant." I abandon my little old lady who thanks me, congratulates me, thanks me, blesses me, thanks me—and head for the restaurant, my mouth already watering at the prospect of my first sandwich made with real French bread.

In the movies, bread seems to be terribly important, so I've always figured it must be the best in the world.

I'm pushing the iron gate when I hear that same goddamn voice saying blandly: "The train for Paris will depart Platform C in thirty seconds. Travellers are requested to close their doors." The blood dropped from my face so fast, I thought my feet had swollen! I lost precious seconds wondering if I'd heard right, then I heard the doors of the train clang shut.

I turned back towards the train. Lucille Beaugrand was waving bye-bye through the open window, a sardonic smile on her lips. The station master called out *"En voiture!"* like in the movies; the train disappeared in the smoke and your humble servant thought his last moment had come. I only had a few thousand francs on me, not even one piece of ID, and I could already see all my francs flying to Paris without me, where some nobody would find it and spend it on hookers. On the edge of my consciousness I even got a glimpse of Antoinette Beaugrand herself trying on a simple, little two-piece suit from Balmain or Dior, and that made my energy come back.

To hell with the tunnel! How I did it I'll never know but there I was next to the train just as it was starting to pull away. (If a train had gone past on track A or B just then, your beloved brother-in-law would be covering the gravel with a lovely pinkish hue.) The station master waved his arms and shouted that it was too late but I grabbed a door handle with both hands and pulled with a strength born of desperation. All that while I was running—and you know how I've always thought of running—as a disease that affects a child of an awkward age who has energy to burn and who's been forbidden to masturbate if he doesn't want to go deaf. I landed at the feet of six terrified individuals, two of them yelling their lungs out, who probably thought I was a highway robber.

I apologized, at least I think I did, and set off to look for my compartment, which wasn't nearly as easy as you might think. As I told you earlier, the first-class compartment was in the middle of the train and I had no idea where I'd boarded. I checked out the corridors cluttered with suitcases, cages of rabbits and hens, and lucky folks who were biting into wonderful sandwiches that crackled under their teeth. Hell's bells!

I arrived at my compartment sheepish and panting. Antoinette and Lucille hid their joy behind what they were reading—which they were holding much too close to their eyes to be able to see anything at all. I sat down, wiped my face, and said to them blandly: "I hope the smell won't bother you too much, I dirtied my drawers!" Two minutes later I had the compartment to myself. Antoinette must be throwing up in the first class toilet! Boyoboy, sometimes I really do love myself! I put my feet up on the seat across from me to tell you about my adventure.

Do you think all of that really happened? So what, it doesn't matter, as long as I've made you smile…

I'm hungry. I'm thirsty. I'm hot. And I don't dare leave my compartment for fear that something disastrous might happen.

The train took a long swerve towards the right just now and I got a look at the locomotive spewing black smoke. A few travellers in the first car were waving at those in the last one. I went to the window too. I was in the exact centre of the arc of the circle formed by the train. It felt as if we were travelling around an imaginary world at the heart of which lay Paris, that monster I know nothing about but that I'm naïve enough to think I'm going to conquer.

The closer I get to my goal the sillier I think I am. Why should Paris pay any attention to me? The city probably won't even notice I'm there. I can always tell myself that I'll take what I can from her, but I know perfectly well that the crumbs she'll give me to peck at will be nothing compared with the banquet she reserves for the others, the real ones, those who've prepared themselves, those who are worthy of her. Yes, the Beaugrands and their like. I can laugh at them all I want, but I still envy them. They belong. I don't.

Oh oh, my complexes are back.

Instead of savoring every passing moment, appreciating the delightful absurdity of it, I'm giving in to melancholy. Again. It's because the fear that's been tormenting me ever since I realized that Paris is just a few dozen kilometres away is uncontrollable. All I've got for making my entrance is an address and a letter of introduction to a concierge on rue Doudeauville. A tiny apartment, sublet through someone else, is waiting for me in the heart of Montmartre, yet I'd gladly give away my million francs to be at a table in the Palace with my girlfriends, doing my famous imitation of Germaine Giroux in *Madame Sans-Gêne*. I'd like to reverse engines, dismantle the mechanism that keeps leading us towards the future, and go back to hide in the heart of Montréal like a cat under a gallery. And swear that I'll never come out.

What an idiotic idea! You dumb ox! Go back to what? To twenty years of crouching at the feet of the well-to-do on St. Catherine Street and the others who'd like to join them? All followed by wonderful twilight years spent sitting around in a bar on the Main all day long, going over the same ludicrous memories, massacring the same old tunes from childish operettas? Burst out sobbing in the middle of "J'ai fait trois fois le tour du monde" because I've never been any further than Niagara Falls or the Percé rock?

Help me. Please!

I've just seen a huge blue billboard with five white letters screaming: PARIS.

The train has begun to slow down. Houses, narrow, tall and grey, are streaming past overhead. A woman is shaking a rag out her window. My first Parisienne won't have been Gaby Morlay warbling down the Champs-Élysées, on the arm of Pierre Fresnay, or Michèle Morgan strolling languidly along the banks of the Seine. I console myself by thinking that the housewife would be more likely to end up as the heroine in a novel by Simenon.

Slowly we enter a vast metal shed. It must be the Gare Saint-Lazare. I'm shaking from head to foot. I must look like a bowl of Jello that hasn't set.

Put your hand on my arm, put your other one on my shoulder; whisper an encouraging word and give me a push, gentle but firm.

Thank you.

I'll close this notebook now and ask you to meet me at 36 rue Doudeauville, in the 18th arrondissement. I have no idea where that is but I've been told that it's a nice neighbourhood compared with some others. The next time I open this notebook I'll be either settled in or totally lost.

Insert

Scheherazade III

"So what now? Do I go on reading or do you want to sleep? The sun's coming up..." Cuirette fluffed up his pillow, sipped some beer, scratched his crotch. "Go on... You've haven't even been reading for an hour... And I want to know what happens in Paris!" Hosanna slipped on the reading glasses that made him look like an old maid librarian, which Cuirette, who'd always hated libraries, found hilarious. "I don't know if I'll make it to the end though... That's just like you, asking me to read at four a.m. after a night in the bars..." "You could've said no!" "Then I'd've had to put up with you reading! I'd rather make the sacrifice!" Cuirette sat up in the bed. "If you're looking for trouble, you'll get it!" "No, thanks, I found plenty when I met you!" They both remembered at the same time that it was one of the Duchess's favourite cracks, a retort she'd made to Samarcette in front of everybody on the verge of one of their numerous break-ups, and she'd used it so many times afterwards that towards the end they'd all say it in chorus—transvestites, waiters, customers—applauding thunderously afterwards as they'd have done after a purple passage at the theatre. Sighing, Hosanna opened the blue notebook again. "Let's go back to the source... Look, there's an old letter folded in four..." Cuirette grabbed it, held it out at arm's length. "I'm reading this one! I can't believe you won't let me read a letter!" Hosanna rolled his eyes. "Try and put a little more heart in it than when you read Jacques Beauchamps' column from *Le Journal de Montréal*..."

Letter from the fat woman
to her brother-in-law Édouard

M ontréal, 27 May 1947

My dear Édouard,

I just read in the paper that you can send letters by airplane now and they only take three or four days to reach their destination. I thought you'd like to find a letter from Montréal in your mailbox when you arrive in Paris, that it would help you feel less lost if you do feel lost; but knowing you like I do, and how easily you fit in everywhere, Paris will have to get up pretty early if she wants to make an impression on you!

The other day when we took you to Windsor Station, I didn't really have time to talk to you. Emotion, the crowd too that was making such a racket, like a zoo going crazy, and especially Albertine, with her crying jag that was more like hysterics than sadness because you were going away—all that kept us from telling each other what we really felt. Seeing you go away upset me terribly because I had the impression I was losing a cohort, an ally.

I already miss you a lot, even though we hadn't been seeing that much of each other before you left. Just knowing that you aren't somewhere in Montréal, making fun of yourself or laughing at your customers or making them or your friends laugh, leaves a big gap in my life. I've never really felt your absences because they were punctuated with quick visits, unexpected phone calls, funny little notes (I had such a good laugh that time when you sent me a postcard from Dorion Street as if you were on vacation at the other end of the world), but this absence weighs on me because it's the first one that's real! I know it will be a while before I hear from you but I can't help worrying. Because I also know that setting out on this adventure that you decided on so quickly, without really thinking it over, is the most important decision you've ever made.

I often try to picture where you are, what you're doing or seeing, but you know me, I have trouble inventing things. It's easy for me to embellish what I know or what I read or see at the movies; I can picture myself in places I dream about or having impossible adventures, but I can't shift someone I know into a real journey, on a real boat, with the ocean all around and millions of glittering stars; I'd be more likely to see Harry Baur acting your part, or Albert Duquesne.

So as I wait to hear from you I feel both excited and worried. Yes, worried. I'm afraid things won't go the way you want them to, that settling into Paris will be harder than you think. So when there isn't much going on, when you're feeling either low or excited, think about me, think that we're both travelling, that I've lent you my eyes and I want to know *everything!* Look, smell, touch, listen, taste, record everything, store every emotion, hoard your thoughts and your criticisms, whether they're negative or positive; when you come back you'll give me an epic account that we'll stretch out as long as we can and then reinvent it when it's over.

Here, everything is in a rut. If I describe our daily adventures to you they'd be far from epic, believe me. Our two families put up with each other as best they can and the sparks that are given off haven't generated anything interesting for a long time now. It's not that I don't love my husband, my children, my sister-in-law and her children, they're my whole life, but there are times when I look at them a little too coldly for my liking; I don't understand what that means and I don't want to think about it too much. Your going away, maybe, the fact that I know that a member of the family has really left Fabre Street and gone in search of adventure, real adventure, and that it isn't me, fills me with longing. Not jealousy. Longing.

It's glorious here, at the end of May, more like early September (and you know how much I love September) with the scent of lilacs and lily-of-the-valley added on. In the yard next door, where nobody lives but where Marcel spends his days, the lilacs have never been so beautiful and the lily-of-the-valley has taken over the whole lawn.

But the house is so dreary that not even books can help me feel less depressed. Or the movies. Besides, going to the movies without you isn't any fun.

There's one thing that worries me though, that frightens me even, more and more: it's Marcel. We talked it over before you left and we'd decided to let him do as he liked because in any case his education is his mother's business more than ours; but the gulf between Albertine and Marcel is getting so much deeper day by day, I'm afraid that it will end badly.

I don't know if it's from bravado or because he's slowly slipping into insanity, but Marcel spends hours at the dining room table, moving his fingers along the edge as if he were playing the piano. He'll look ecstatic, as if he's listening to something divine; sometimes he'll even burst into sobs and cry out to his imaginary cat that music is his only consolation. His mother looks at him and doesn't say a word but I can feel the tension rising and I know that the day when she does blow up we'll feel very sorry for poor Marcel. My youngest also seems hypnotized by whatever his cousin is up to. But I get the impression that unlike his aunt he *wants* to hear what Marcel is playing and that exasperates me. I've tried to talk to him about it but it didn't really help. All he said was that he likes to watch Marcel because he's different.

You understand, the dining room is the heart of this house, it's impossible to avoid it and whenever anyone goes there, Gabriel, Richard, Philippe, Albertine, Thérèse, they're terribly upset by this sight that none of us can do anything about. It creates an uneasiness in the household that's hard to put up with and everyone feels the effects.

Gabriel has finally said something about moving. But do we have the right to abandon Albertine and her two children to the hell that's in store for them if we leave? On the other hand, it could be that the survival of our own nest is at stake!

As you can see, life here isn't a barrel of laughs. Appreciate yours and enjoy it all you can, because even the worst disappointments will have the great virtue of being new!

Now don't tell anybody, but I think I could put up with some worse trials and tribulation than what I've known if someone told me that they'd be totally different and *new*. My little problems are always the same and I can't stand that.

Say hello to the Eiffel Tower for me. And give Notre Dame a kiss. Hug Montmartre, where you'll be living, which I picture as being a little like a movie set with costumed movie stars and extras going back and forth.

If you should run into Pierre Fresnay, throw yourself at his feet for me. But keep your hands off!

Love,

Your devoted sister-in-law.

P.S. If you see any Chénard "Tulipe noire," please buy me a bottle, I'm sure that it costs less than here.

Crossing Paris

My only consolation in all the hysteria of my arrival was your letter which was waiting for me with the concierge, that I read sitting on my metal suitcase in the dark entrance of 36 rue goddamn Doudeauville.

When I got off the train I was thirsty, I was hungry—and I had to go. I apologize for mentioning nature's call like that but it was very powerful and it became much more important than such things do back home.

I figured that if I had something to eat before I got into the taxi that would take me to Montmartre, I could relieve myself at the same time. So I spot a huge restaurant, the Café de la Gare, which is packed and noisy (it was eight p.m.), and I go inside after a quick look at the menu where I hardly understand a thing (remember, French money is still a total mystery to me, even though I know I just have to divide everything by five hundred).

I had to go so badly I was squirming in my seat. A handsome waiter in a sexy white apron came and asked what I wanted. I wanted something quick so I asked for the cheapest thing on the menu: an *assiette anglaise*. Here I am in France, land of gastronomy, and my first meal is going to be an English plate! Anyway. He asks what I want to drink, I say coffee because I don't imagine you can find Coke in every café. And then, before he goes away, I lean over and murmur:

"The toilet, please..."

He looks at me bug-eyed.

"I beg your pardon?"

I think it's safe to say that he hasn't understood so I repeat it, trying to sound as much like him as I can.

"*Les toilettes, s'il vous plaît.*"

He jumps as if I've just insulted him.

"Ah! Monsieur wants the *vay say!* You should have said so! In the basement, Monsieur. Straight ahead!"

The *vay say?* Have you ever heard of that? I got an even bigger surprise when I headed for the stairs to the basement: it wasn't *vay say*, it was W.C.! (I just checked in my dictionary: that stands for Water Closet! English again!)

But as they say in adventure novels, there were more trials in store for our hero. At the bottom of the spiral staircase was a lady sitting on a straight-back chair behind a table with a plate that had a few coins sitting in it... I thought to myself, the beggars in France are lucky they can ply their trade inside where it's warm (even if the heat was a little dubious) and I walked into the men's room. There was a row of urinals, most of them occupied (the toilets here seem to be as well-used as ours—more about that later) and about fifteen stalls with wooden doors that have seen better days, as if some customers had had to fight their way in or out. I plunk my suitcase on the floor and pull open a door. And what I saw paralyzed me. The toilet bowl had been pulled out! There was just a hole in the floor! I think: "The toilets in Paris look a lot worse than ours... What'll I do if I have to come back? I'll never shit in Paris again..." I open another door: same thing. You won't believe me but I checked out every one before I realized that's how they're made! And then my heart did a flipflop. I was seeing myself for months having to squat down to do my business—me who has trouble bending his legs! But maybe it's just like that in restaurants... I'll never believe that everybody in France shits standing up!

What can I tell you, that's the way it is... I got undressed (I didn't want to go in my pants or risk dragging them through it...), I bent over a little, supporting myself on either side...

Remember just a few weeks ago, when we were on the balcony on Fabre Street, imagining my arrival in Paris, how wonderful it was going to be, how poetic? It was a sunny day, the birds were singing, there was a wonderful smell of spring, we could practically hear the whole city singing, "Sous les ponts de Paris" in chorus and blowing kisses like in a bad production at the Monument National...

Forget it!

Because when I'd finished and was looking around for the toilet paper I understood why Madame Pétrie, when she heard I was going to France, patted my arm and whispered: "Let me tell you just one thing, little boy... Take along toilet paper because they aren't very good about it over there."

I had to sacrifice my brand new white undies that I'd paid a fortune for at Morgan's.

And that wasn't all! I made the mistake of pulling the chain before I moved my feet off the two little porcelain rectangles... You guessed, both legs wet halfway up... Good thing I'd undressed or I'd have gone out with my slacks cruddy up to the knees, ashamed as a two-year-old who's dirtied his pants...

Try putting your socks on over wet feet! And your shoes!

I left there so furious I couldn't help shouting at the guys at the urinals (probably the same ones) who were looking at each other's dicks: "Better find another place, it stinks like hell in there!" But they must have thought I was a Turk or a Yugoslav.

I was about to go back up the stairs when the lady sitting behind the little table yells at me: "*Service!*" in a voice so nasal she probably doesn't need her mouth for talking. I turned towards her and then it dawned on me (if I keep understanding too late like that, its going to be a wonderful trip!): she's a lady you pay because she keeps an eye on the toilets—*and she sells toilet paper!* I felt pretty ashamed of myself. She probably thought I'd wiped myself with my fingers!

Back at my table, I see a few slices of salami and a couple of pieces of baloney next to a pile of dwarf potatoes, all yellow and oily. The sight of it turned my stomach and I thought to myself, Okay, there's a limit to everything. So I walked out without touching my plate—or paying! I'd rather go hungry!

I made my way to the door where there were supposed to be taxis, feeling furious, humiliated, and floating in my pants.

And then all at once, after I'd walked past a beautiful stone archway that in my rotten mood I'd hardly noticed, Paris leaped up at me.

Paris! At last!

You can't imagine it.

The life, the movement, the light, the colours! I could have sat and watched for hours, as if it were a show! My hunger, my fury, my fatigue, all flew away and I had to get a grip on myself to keep from crying like a baby.

The women, mostly bare-headed but some in wonderful hats, travellers most likely, were walking along with a nonchalance we never see back home, purses under their arms, often smiling and, to my eyes anyway, very elegant. The men were good-looking too, but they were drab in their grey or beige fedoras, they seemed busy too, and walked along at a good clip. Busses sped by, car horns sounding sharper than ours echoed off the stone walls, the red of the café awnings and the white of the neon signs gleamed under the sky that was a blue I've never seen before, nearly white, transparent, but palpable—and so present I was amazed. The Place Gabriel-Péri isn't all that big but you could see a huge expanse of sky there and my head was drawn up to it.

I stood there at the top of the stone steps, not moving, holding my suitcase, and feasting my eyes on my first beautiful view of Paris, hoping that back home, where it was three p.m.—you'd stop whatever you were doing and cry with joy.

I wish I could have stopped one of those busy men I met, one of those women hurrying along, and clap my hands and tell them: "Look, here I am! I've just arrived from far away, from the other end of the world, and I'm so glad to be here! Have you seen the colour of the sky? Have you seen how beautiful everything is here? How everything fits together, like in a stage set? But probably they'd have laughed at me: they were born in it; they probably don't see it anymore.

To hell with taxis, I decided to walk for a while, even though my suitcase was getting heavier and heavier. I must have looked like the world's biggest idiot because people were pointing at me and sneering. They must have thought I was a hick who'd come to the capital for a good time. Which was true, as a matter of fact. I'll tell you, the Duchess of Langeais was a long ways away! There was just little Édouard, with his big eyes and his silly grin, strolling down the rue de Rome without looking at the traffic, thrilled, moved, on the verge of fainting. Passersby must've thought I was having a vision!

A sense of unreality came over me right in the middle of the rue de Rome; all at once I felt like a spectator, as if I were in a movie, I could almost smell the coke and popcorn. It's hard to describe… It wasn't me who was walking, there was a stage set moving along on either side of me by itself and disappearing behind my back. I felt as if I was surrounded by something fragile and that with just one gust of wind everything would be destroyed and disappear forever. I held my breath for fear of causing a disaster.

But at the corner of rue de Provence I was suddenly brought back to reality: a lady, all dolled up in her Sunday best, grabs hold of my sleeve, and comes out with a: "Want some fun, big boy?" that surprised me so much, I broke into a run.

My first French hooker! The minute I got off the train! I suppose it's normal around a railway station… But right out loud like that, on the street… Back home she'd be stoned to death! Then I realized that the rue de Provence was full of them. Leaning against the wall or walking back and forth, many of them beautiful, some of them well past their prime, but all of them absorbed in what they were doing: some whistled at me, some blew kisses, some shouted; they cooed in my ear and stroked my neck… I was pink with embarrassment and pleasure. Finally, some human contact!

But after five minutes at the corner of rue de Mogador, I got a cramp in the fleshy part of my right arm and I reminded myself that I didn't have to walk around the whole city on the first night, carrying a suitcase and too tired to really understand what was happening.

The sky had darkened a little but it was still very light. When I saw the first star appear, I wished so hard, I'm sure the passersby could hear it! I put down my suitcase. Water was coming out of a gutter and bubbling away. Another thing that's different from back home. The gutters here run in reverse.

I was outside a café that wasn't too busy. I took a seat at a little table sitting right out on the sidewalk and ordered two sandwiches, one with *rillettes* (that's what they call *cretons*) and one with ham and cheese. And were they ever good! The inside of the bread was soft, the crust nice and crusty... I ate so fast, I was out of breath when I'd finished. Let me tell you, there's times when eating really does you good! I don't know if it was a joke, but the waiter said when he came back for my plate: "Enjoy them, they could be your last!" I guess he thought I was desperate man because I'd eaten so fast! I downed a coffee that tasted like the juice in a pipe, but it got my system revved up.

When I stood up it was dark. Just the thought that I was going to have to lift my suitcase gave me the shivers. When I looked for a taxi one was coming along. I raised my arm.

I was too exhausted to disguise my accent. As soon as I'd opened my mouth the driver, who had an accent you could cut with a knife, started laughing.

"You're Canadian?"

"Yes. You can tell?"

"And how! I know Canada very well, you see. I've got a sister who moved there years ago. To Saint-Boniface. Do you know her?"

"I'm from Montréal myself..."

He wasn't listening.

"Madame Debout's her name. Tall brunette, a little on the heavy side. Her husband teaches French over there... You don't recognize the name?"

"You see, Saint-Boniface is nearly as far from Montréal as Paris!"

The man laughed so hard I thought he was going to drive us inside the Église de la Trinité instead of around it.

"You Canadians are such jokers! Talk to me, go ahead, say something, your accent's hilarious!"

After the day I'd had I was in no mood to play the clown on the back seat of a taxi. But he was so insistent I said whatever came into my head while I gazed out the window.

Every street sign, every square we passed, reminded me of a book I'd read, a movie we'd seen; I was moved to tears but instead of giving in to it, I was playing the comic uncle at a family party to amuse my taxi driver!

I know I should have told him to get lost but I'm not there yet.

We drove up rue Pigalle (do you realize what that meant for me?); we crossed Place Pigalle with its boring little fountain, after we'd driven past the window of Chez Moune, the most famous cabaret for women in the world; out of the corner of my eye, I caught a glimpse of the Moulin-Rouge on my left as we were making our way to Place Blanche; we drove along boulevard Rochechouart, then onto boulevard Barbès (remember the movie by Marcel Carné that we saw together at the Saint-Denis, where you saw the Barbès-Rochechouart Station? Well I saw it in the flesh!) I was expecting we'd climb higher up than that in Montmartre but it seemed like we were going around it without getting too close. Now and then I'd spot the Sacré-Coeur, all white, at the top of the Butte Montmartre, but never for long enough to get a good look.

I'd just started a dirty story to the great delight of my driver when we turned right onto rue Poulet and drove past a butcher shop that sold horsemeat. They sell horsemeat here! Openly, right on the street! Remember the time Gabriel brought home a horsemeat steak he'd hidden under his coat? He'd bought it from a guy at the tavern, who'd told him it was more tender than beef and nobody in the house would touch it. You and Albertine didn't even want to cook it! Finally, Mama ate the whole thing, saying we didn't have the right to let good meat go to waste. When I saw the horse's head surrounded by its white neon light at the corner of rue Poulet and rue Doudeauville, I found myself missing Mama so badly that I couldn't speak. I stopped right in the middle of my story. It was the first time that's happened to me since she died. I realized that I'd never see my mother again while I was driving past a horse-butcher shop in the middle of Paris.

Believe me, I didn't feel like playing the comic uncle anymore!

If my calculations were correct, it cost next to nothing to come here by taxi. I gave what I thought was a big tip to the driver, who reminded me one last time how funny my accent was. I was sick and tired of hearing that and, like an idiot, I told him:

"Back home, if we laughed every time we heard a Frenchman talk, they'd think we were hysterical!"

And that was when I realized he didn't understand a word I'd said, he was just laughing at the sounds I was making!

I spent a few minutes looking at the house where I'll be living. Not what you'd call a castle. The whole street actually has a rundown look that disappointed me. The façades have been neglected and they're all greyish and peeling; the shutters haven't seen a fresh coat of paint for generations. There's just the paint on the front door that looks fresh and bright.

The door is huge, big enough for carriages to drive through in the old days, with a little gate cut into it which I pushed, but in vain. Locked! At ten-thirty p.m.! There was a big bell button on my right but I was afraid I'd wake somebody up. But since I had to see the concierge in any case to get the key to the apartment, I finally did it. There was a little electric buzz and the door opened all by itself.

Inside, it was pitch black. I heard a door creak, then a woman yelled:

"What is it?"

I stood there frozen for a few seconds and finally murmured:

"It's me. I've arrived from Canada."

It seems like nothing here is simple.

The concierge, suspicious, listened to my story with a frown, a doubtful look twisting the bottom part of her face. She read my letter of introduction warily, looked me up and down as if I were a side of beef and finally disappeared into her lodge, which had a funny smell (soup made from cabbage or leeks), after a: "One moment" that was tinged with disapproval.

I hadn't wakened her though, she was fully dressed; she even had a kind of bandanna tied around her neck, as if she was hiding dirty or uncombed hair, or dark roots.

She came back with a big key and a letter. She held out the key. "I won't go up with you, my legs are giving me trouble, and anyway you'll find it by yourself."

Then the letter.

"This came for you yesterday. It's from Canada. From Montréal. A lady who lives on rue Fabre…"

For a moment I thought she was going to recite your whole letter by heart!

Too excited to wait till I was in my apartment to read it, I sat down on my suitcase and tore open the envelope. Almost at that very moment the light went out. The concierge pressed the same button she'd pressed before when she opened her door.

"You'll have trouble reading, Monsieur, the *minuterie* goes off every sixty seconds."

Minuterie? Another mystery. I thought I understood that it's an electrical system that gives you just enough time to get up to your apartment and then turns off automatically. If you're between floors, tough luck, you just find your way in the dark! What a bunch of cheapskates!

I shifted my metal suitcase closer to the yellowish porcelain button and I read your letter, pressing the button every sixty seconds.

And all that time the concierge stood there in the doorway of her lodge as if she were reading your letter in my eyes.

When I'd finished, moved, overwhelmed really, I pressed the pages to my heart, trying hard not to cry.

She must have thought… Anyway, it softened her a little because she looked almost compassionate when she said:

"You can't stay here, it's forbidden. Go on up. It's the fourth floor on the right, first door on your left. There's a *minuterie* on every floor."

Your letter made me forget the setbacks I'd suffered that day and I felt lighter. I climbed resolutely up the first staircase but a very characteristic, very unpleasant smell slowed me down when I got to the second floor. In the bend of the second staircase, above a door that wasn't properly closed, I saw those two damn letters sloppily painted, practically smeared: W.C. I held my breath and kept climbing. There was another toilet between the next two floors that didn't stink so badly. I had a horrible thought when I got to the fourth floor but I chased it away, otherwise I'd have came racing back down.

When I got to the door of what had to be my apartment I realized that the key didn't even go into the lock, which was much too small. I fiddled with it a little but all that did was make a shrill, ugly sound of metal on metal. Then a woman's voice inside the apartment murmured:

"Is that you, Maurice?"

I stood there bewildered and silent.

Now the voice sounded worried.

"Who is it? Please, answer."

I took a deep breath, thinking that if they'd rented me an apartment that was already occupied I was going to kill somebody, the concierge most likely, who'd had the nerve to feel the envelope with your letter in it a little too closely for my liking, and I said in my fancypants French accent that I haven't quite got the hang of:

"Am I not on the fourth floor?"

"No, Madame, you are not, you're on the third! Count your staircases! Or use your eyes, there's a sign on every floor! How thoughtless, disturbing people at this hour of the night! Can't you read? I've never heard such a thing! Honestly! It's impossible to sleep in peace!"

Actually I had counted three staircases but I couldn't tell her that, she didn't shut up long enough. Then I remembered that I'd seen *rez-de-chaussée* on a sign next to the concierge's lodge. On top of everything else I had another floor to climb!

For you and me, the fourth floor is the fourth floor, not the fifth! Why complicate your life with a *rez-de-chaussée*? It's a lot simpler to start counting at one, not zero, if you ask me!

Anyway. I climbed up the fourth set of stairs and I found the third W.C. (And where do the people on the *rez-de-chaussée* go to the toilet? At the concierge's? Is that why she cooks so much soup, to hide the smell?)

You guessed it, that's what scared me: if there was no toilet in my apartment I was sure I'd have a fit of collective hysteria. My numerous personalities would all rebel at the same time and rue Doudeauville would witness its first riot in the Québécois language!

The key slipped easily into the lock. I found the light switch on the right as she'd told me.

Surprise. The apartment is actually very nice. One room with two big windows. One end is the bedroom, the other the dining room with a tiny kitchen, very cute, with its own window that must look out on the inside courtyard. In one corner near the table, a black marble fireplace with a huge mirror above it, speckled but you can recognize yourself all the same. Immediately to the right of the front door, a gigantic wooden armoire that must be where you keep your clothes. Three lamps with pink silk shades shed a soft amber light.

But no toilet or bathroom!

I felt like getting down on all fours and pounding the floor with my fists!

I was so depressed that everything I'd just thought was pretty looked ugly. I would have traded everything around me for a dank and dirty maid's room with a tub and a toilet!

I left the apartment and glanced at the door to the W.C. between the third and fourth floors, after pressing the goddamn *minuterie*, of course. But I didn't have the heart to go down and see what state it was in.

Will I have to stand in a corner to do my business the whole time I'm here?

If you only knew how sick and tired I am of talking about that! Already! Twice in the same evening! But it's one of the most important functions in a man's life and I can't understand why all the human beings who live in this house go along with leaving their own apartment, climbing up or down half a floor that's probably freezing cold in winter and stifling in summer, to relieve themselves on top of the... the... business of their neighbour across the landing!

Back home, even the poorest of the poor have a toilet!

Do you know what I did? I ran to the kitchen to see if I had running water! Whew! But I noticed there's no icebox! How will I keep my eggs fresh? And my milk? And my coke? If they've got coke here.

I felt so low when I went to bed... But the bed is comfortable. I like the bolster and the pillows that are twice the size of ours.

It's four a.m. My hand is numb from writing so much. I stop for five minutes every now and then and listen to the sounds of Paris through the open window. A woman was walking up rue Doudeauville just now and you could hear her high heels click against the pavement. I'll have to hold on to details like that if I don't want to go nuts.

What a day!

I decided to try and forget all that for a few hours, to sleep as long as I can, to get my strength back before I tackle head-on my real, everyday life in Paris.

I'm afraid to take stock of this day. The high points were too exciting but the unpleasant surprises were too many and too big for me just to brush them aside, and they're interfering with my enthusiasm.

I don't want this trip to be spoiled by physiological problems! But how will I manage that, for crying out loud?

I know I mustn't expect to find the same things here as at home, I kept telling myself that all week on board the *Liberté*, but if a change of scene is too dramatic, isn't it liable to drown everything else?

We'll see.

The sky is beginning to get light.

And I'm hungry already!

I woke up with a craving for bacon—and a full bladder. I put aside the first to concentrate on the second, which needed my urgent attention. I draped myself in my gorgeous floor-length Nile green flowered silk dressing gown; I cracked open the apartment door and took a timid look around before venturing outside.

Not a soul.

There was a good smell of coffee that was comforting.

Just as I was about to close the door behind me I thought about my key. Can't you see me, stuck on the staircase and looking like Ginette Leclerc before she puts on her makeup?

I'll spare you my visit to the powder room, I'll just tell you that wiping yourself with newspaper cut into little pieces that are stuck on a rusty nail is not the pleasantest thing in the world, or the most hygienic. I'm sure that smearing rust around your nether parts must lead to diseases. And a horrible colour.

And the smell! A pigsty during a heatwave. As for the filth, let's just say it was discreet since luckily, there was practically no light in this damp and peeling corner of the staircase. But imagining filth might be worse than seeing it, especially for somebody with an imagination like your humble servant's.

Relieved all the same (and I swear this is the last time I'll bring that up!), I went back up to my place, my silk a little rumpled and my stomach feeling queasy.

But when I opened the door I was amazed by the light, which I hadn't noticed when I woke up, too absorbed in my needs. The apartment faced south and the sun, already high, was pouring in the two windows I'd left open all night. It brightened my new home and cheered me up after the horrors of the hallway. A hubbub was rising from the street, something else I hadn't noticed before. I went to the window, adjusting my dressing-gown.

People were running in every direction, yelling at each other as they lined up at the doors of the stores (though the war's been over for two years!), men were racing around in a panic, swearing like they swear over here; women were crying, children on their way to school were being pushed and shoved. I thought to myself that Parisians seem to wake up agitated and before I got dressed, I looked up to the right.

Beauty!

Leaning out like that, over the rusty wrought-iron railing, just before I landed five storeys down (four for the French,) I could catch a glimpse of the Sacré-Coeur bell-tower, a long white needle, nearly obscene, that stood out with amazing precision against the very clear blue of the sky. I felt a pang then and it sank in for maybe the first time that I really was in Paris.

In a few seconds all my travel plans, the steps I'd taken to realize them, my crossing on the *Liberté*, my arrival here went through my mind and I felt giddy. Leaning out above the street as I was, at an amazing height for a Montréaler used to two- or three-storey houses, I felt as if I were dreaming about something that was so beautiful it seemed risky. I knew that I wasn't going to wake up in my bed on Dorion Street, that I was really there, suspended dangerously above a street in Montmartre, but I couldn't believe it! As I do whenever I feel the slightest bit uneasy (as you know because you married one of her sons, my mother's teachings are indelible), I shut my eyes and took some deep breaths. My ears were buzzing and my eyes were damp.

But it was the gurgling of my guts that brought me back to reality. I hadn't eaten for more than twelve hours, an absolute record in my not all that brief existence.

Before closing the window—I was curious, after all—I had a good look at the houses across the street, to see if I might catch some handsome, scantily clad Frenchman doing morning gymnastics and singing Jean Sablon's latest hit.

Another theatre set. But old, dilapidated, bare. If the house-fronts were cleaned they could be very beautiful, even impressive, I think, with the combination of cut stone and cement. But everything's a dirty grey streaked with soot and even in the bright sunlight, it's depressing. The contrast was really too great between the life in the street and the prevailing desolation above it.

But Paris is an old city, while we in North America haven't had time to get dirty yet!

My craving for bacon was becoming more and more urgent so I dressed quickly (sexy—I hope—pants and a short-sleeved shirt), took my key and raced down the stairs, looking away when I got to any suspect corners.

The concierge was washing the flagstones in the entrance. It smelled of too much disinfectant, the camouflage of odours not a total success. She pushed back a lock of hair before asking:

"Well now, did our Canadian have a good night's sleep?"

I pursed my lips and told her:

"Fahn-tahstic!"

And I looked like a lunatic.

I know this will happen often in the weeks to come but I hope that my shame won't be so bitter as it wears down.

I tug at the front door, but it won't open. Trying to be casual I look to see if there's a key in the lock. Nothing. I pull again. Still nothing. I'm about to take out my apartment key and try it in the lock when I hear a little laugh behind me. The concierge comes up, shows me a bell exactly like the one on the street side and tells me in a superior tone that's absolutely humiliating:

"You have to press on this, Monsieur! Don't you have doors in your country?"

I felt like yelling at her: "In my country we ring the bell when we get to the door, not when we're leaving!" But I held my tongue: they live here, they're entitled to do what they want.

Can you imagine though? Back home on Fabre Street, if you had to press a button every time you leave the house we'd have all gone deaf years ago! Albertine would be tied to her bed in a straitjacket and her two children nailed to the wall with a dagger!

But, *autres pays, autres moeurs*. We read that somewhere, remember, and it struck us. I didn't know though that there are even other ways of opening and closing doors!

I felt as if I was joining a parade that I couldn't make head nor tail of. Groups of people walked by, gesticulating, solid and serious, sometimes with heads bowed as if facing an altar or, on the contrary, standing tall and cackling like starving hens. I heard bits of conversation, the odd word here and there, and I realized that they were all talking about the same thing but I couldn't figure out what. An elderly lady, all bent over and walking with a cane, looked my way and said: "Well, I never!" while a gent laced into a grey suit replied, even though she wasn't speaking to him: "It's unacceptable, Madame, unacceptable!"

I told myself: "Oh boy, I've landed in the middle of a riot— either that or they've just declared World War Three to celebrate my arrival in Paris!"

Exactly across from the building I'd just left there was a kind of corner grocery store with a few crates of potatoes sitting on the doorstep and some bags of onions and other vegetables I didn't recognize piled up in pyramids. Exactly what I was looking for; surely I'd find what I needed to put together the breakfast of a lifetime.

I crossed rue Doudeauville, weaving through Parisians driven crazy by some mysterious malady and stood at the end of the line made up almost exclusively of housewives holding string bags.

The lady ahead of me, venerable and chubby, stiff and corseted, immediately shouted at me:

"This is inconceivable, you'd think it was three or four years ago! I've spent too much time standing in lines, Monsieur, I've deprived myself quite enough, I have no intention of starting again! I have all the tickets I need, and I intend to have them respected!"

She could have been speaking Serbo-Croatian for all I understood. She must have been expecting some sign of agreement from me, or some hostile protest, because she leaned over to me, with her eyes very dark and probing. She smelled funny. A mixture of strong perfume and sweat. I just smiled and she must have taken me for a moron or some foreigner who didn't speak French, because she turned away with a shrug, muttering between her teeth: "I swear, you don't always know who you're talking to, isn't that the truth..."

The comings and goings went on. Some individuals were hurrying along with a loaf of bread under their arm like in the movies, and I looked at them tenderly.

A man about my age walked by, telling the woman who'd just spoken to me: "I got one! I got one!" and brandishing a skinny loaf of bread that was all burnt.

That made me even more uncomfortable. I like bread as much as the next person but I don't go crazy when I buy it! This was bugging me. I felt as if I was on the verge of understanding something that I didn't want to face up to. I looked over towards rue Ernestine. (The name of the street after it was Léon, can you believe it?) The line outside the corner bakery was much longer and a lot more agitated. There was some problem with the bread...

I decided that instead of going to buy myself a fresh loaf of bread I'd head for the grocery store and get one already sliced and make toast. Besides, I was too hungry to stand in another line.

I could already see myself sitting over four slices of beautiful golden toast, two fried eggs and some good crisp bacon...

The grocery store smelled wonderful. A mixture of different kinds of paté (there were three or four sitting in china plates, plump and glistening, making me drool), cheap lavender soap, spices, ground coffee...

After protesting the situation one last time, describing it now as indefensible, the lady ahead of me bought a box of crackers and a bottle of water. I thought her parties must be pretty dull, which made me laugh. She glared at me. "It's no laughing matter, Monsieur, I'll have you know!" She paid with coins that were worn thin, that I couldn't make any sense of, and the grocer, a swarthy guy who can't have been from Paris because he had a weird accent, looked at me as if I was disturbing him.

"Monsieur?"

Trying hard for my own Parisian accent I told him:

"I'd like a dozen eggs, please!

"I don't do eggs."

I didn't dare to tell him that I wasn't asking him to do them, just to sell them, I was too afraid that he'd bite me!

"Okay then, a quart of milk..."

"A *what?*"

"Milk."

"For milk you go to the *crémerie.*"

I stood there stunned for barely a second but even that got Blackie's back up (I'd decided to call him that because everything about him—hair, eyes, mustache, even his skin, a little—was black). He let fly:

"And after that?"

"Butter."

"But I just told you to go to the *crémerie*, Monsieur! See here, I can't waste anymore time, move along... Next!"

Panicking, I looked around.

The dish of *rillettes* was sitting next to the cash register, with a price by the kilo stuck into it. I figured it was pointless to ask for bacon because I couldn't see any. Better to ask for something I was sure he had. I'm afraid I jostled the woman behind me who fortunately was looking for her shopping list.

"Some *rillettes*, then."

Now Blackie was giving me a really dirty look.

"How much?"

Dear God, I hadn't thought about that!

"A kilo!"

"Are you joking? A kilo of *rillettes?*"

I thought it wasn't enough.

"Okay, give me two kilos."

When I saw him cut off a block of *rillettes* that could have fed two armies of soldiers who'd been famished for two years, I could feel my stomach turn at the mere thought of seeing that huge pile of pork and pork fat drying out on my little table. Then I remembered that I don't even have an icebox and I started to shiver.

But when I asked him for a loaf of sliced bread I thought Blackie was going to kill me.

"See here, that's quite enough out of you! I haven't got time to fool around this morning! Bread is at the bakery, dairy products at the *crémerie* and lunatics in the asylum! Where do you come from? Next thing I know, you'll be asking for meat!"

You can imagine how relieved I was that I hadn't mentioned bacon! But actually, *rillettes* are meat—try and make sense out of that...

I left with my block of *rillettes*, a package of crackers and a bottle of water. I hadn't taken any chances, I bought the same thing as the tubby little woman.

At the *crémerie* the smell was so strong I walked right past it. But I need my glass of milk every day and my bit of cheese at bedtime... I don't even dare to wonder if they've got cheddar cheese over here. And I have trouble seeing myself in a store that smells like sour milk that's been left on the kitchen table overnight in July...

When I got to the bakery I felt very discouraged. The only thing that was keeping me on my feet was the thought that I'd soon be tasting some of that divine French bread I've been hearing about all my life and that I barely got a taste of last night.

But a long poster in the window of the bakery, which I had plenty of time to read while I stood in line, nearly floored me. Too much is too much!

BAKERS' STRIKE

For June second and third, the daily bread ration has been reduced to 150 grams in Seine and in Seine-Étiennette-Oise.

It can be acquired by the obligatory remittance of "M" tickets that are neither crossed nor circled for "M" cards; of crossed "J" tickets for "J3" cards; of uncrossed "D" tickets for "J2" cards; of uncircled "G" tickets for "J1" cards.

Labourers will receive 75 grams in return for a crossed "M" ticket for "M" cards.

For the "E" ration no change will be introduced.

Greek, absolutely Greek!

I cut out an article for you from the newspaper I bought on my way home that says more or less the same thing.

I was so depressed I had to lean against the store window. I realized that all the people who were lining up like me were carrying a booklet with different coloured coupons in it, something like the rationing coupons we had back home during the war.

No bread, no butter, no milk, no bacon.

Have you ever eaten *rillettes* on crackers with mineral water first thing in the morning? I cried so hard I was worn out when I finished. One of the main things I'd come for was the food!

What in God's name am I going to do?

Anyway, let me tell you, those *rillettes* ended up in the corner of the staircase between the fourth and fifth floors!

I feel like an old floozy who's just lost her final illusion. Drained. Dry. Worn-out. And for so little, really. Where do we get the chronic lack of courage that you find in practically every member of our family? There's just Thérèse who seems to want to charge into life; and even so it's in the wrong direction. At the first setback we give up and launch into endless lamentations, doing everything in our power to make others pity us by baring our hearts in public.

But here I haven't got an audience. For the first time in my life I'm unable to put on my act, and you can't imagine how frustrating that is.

Back home, I'd be able to laugh at what's just happened because somebody would think I was funny while I was telling it, miming it, exaggerating it! I can't do that here, I'm alone in a world where I don't understand even the simplest mechanisms and everything strikes me as hostile. I've only had one quick outing and yet I wish I could tell myself I'll never again lay eyes on that nasty grocer, all those comings and goings, too hysterical for so early in the morning, these people who have to stand in line at three or four different stores every morning just to put together a breakfast, and most of all that poster I couldn't believe I was reading, it was so absolutely absurd!

It seems to me that I ought to carry on in spite of these meaningless everyday problems (I'll just eat in restaurants), but I can't. It's as if there's a barrier, some major impediment to my coming to live here. All I feel like doing is shutting myself inside my apartment without a bathroom and dying of gloom! Though I've gone through periods infinitely harder and I've met human beings much meaner than the ones whose paths I barely crossed this morning. I try to tell myself that I didn't cross the Atlantic just to die of shame after my first letdown, not in a million years!

And yet if I'd had the train schedule for Le Havre I'm sure I would have taken the first one that was leaving this afternoon and that tomorrow morning I'd have been on board the *Liberté* or any other old tub that was sailing to America.

You see, it's all because my reasons for coming here are so totally unconnected to what's been happening to me since I got off the train last night. And I don't have the patience to wait for everything to get back to normal or to fall into place.

On one hand, there are the novels and movies that have given me such an idealized notion of Paris; I'd never realized that those people have an everyday life just as we do, but so different that at first it seems incomprehensible and ridiculous. I came here to live my life in a theatre set, without thinking that backstage, human beings continue to function and do things you never see in movies or novels. I knew all that, I'm an intelligent man, it's just that I'd never really taken it in! Either that or I hadn't read as much as I should. Or looked at the movies carefully enough. Or I hadn't understood a thing.

In movies, the French have always seemed like nice people, or cultivated, or funny. Grouchy, sure, but with a touch of humour at the corner of their mouths. What I liked was to see myself in them, even though we're so different. But what I found this morning was people who were in a rotten mood from the minute they got up, with excellent reasons for it and not a hint of humour at the corner of their mouths because that's real life, and when they leave my field of vision they won't be touching up their makeup and waiting for the next shot.

I'd dreamed of being welcomed to rue Doudeauville with open arms, by characters created by Simenon: how naïve I was! It took me twenty years to put together a bunch of friends on Mont-Royal Street, and there I was thinking I'd find one here ready-made, without having to look, as if they'd been waiting for me like the Messiah! But rue Doudeauville wasn't waiting for me at all. It's got other things to do. It's not even interested in me. Nope, it doesn't give a damn about the shoe salesman from Montréal who's come to the old country to show how smart he is because his mother left him some money!

I'm ashamed of it, but I think that deep down I figured rue Doudeauville would adapt to me, while in fact I'm less than nothing here, and it's me who has to adapt—if I stick around, of course—I have to adjust to every absurdity, to the slightest meaningless situation in this life that I'd come here to spy on as a visitor, but that I'll have to submit to because I'll have to live it. Or so I say, yet as soon as I find myself in the presence of a Frenchman, my accent changes. I change my accent, yes, but I also have to change my way of living from A to Z...

And after all, how can you take seriously a neighbourhood where the streets have names like Ernestine and Léon? (I've finally made myself smile; all is not lost.)

As for the other aspect of my trip; as for my true quest... I've hardly brought it up so far because it's still not very clear in my own mind. And if I really think about it, this trip is turning out to be more like an escape than a quest...

I know what I've run away from: being suffocated in an ignorant city where everything is material for a scandal; the boredom it secretes from day to day that finally drives crazy even mild-mannered fatsoes like me; the inevitable lack of room for pariahs who are too much alike and end up being together too often, and hating each other because they influence each other too much. But what I've come here in search of is still very nebulous. I left Montréal howling that I'd come back a woman of the world to the core; I explained to Samarcette, who looked at me incredulously, that I was coming to Paris so that once and for all I would merit the title Duchess of Langeais which, when you get right down to it, is of no interest to anyone but me, and I could very well have taken it on without crossing the Atlantic because in any case, you and I are the only ones who actually know who Antoinette de Navarreins, Duchess of Langeais and barefoot Carmelite were; to you, I've often talked about my frustration at not being able to go on stage since I have no talent and about how badly I want to have some talent in life, to become a star of the everyday, a walking madness, instead of being nothing but a barnyard buffoon. Those were words that intoxicated me, that I ended up believing because I'd repeated them so often without grasping their significance. And that inheritance from Mama that hit me like a justification, as if from the grave she was trying to help me make this absurd dream of mine come true, that I could never have attained without her. So I had the means to go away before I understood *why* I wanted to.

Now, I'd like to be able to consider this flight as a pleasure trip, a well-earned vacation, but that's exactly the problem: I haven't earned it, I've never done anything in my life, and I'm not enjoying it all that much because everything scares me! Why travel so far when you're so unprepared?

I just thought about Antoinette Beaugrand and her Lucille. Are they lying in their hotel room being depressed, like me, because they feel that Paris is hostile to them? I'm sure they aren't! They must be strolling along the Seine, going into raptures over the barges and the beautiful bridges or snooping around on rue Saint-Honoré and pretending they were born there, or quietly visiting Notre-Dame because *their* education has prepared them for it, goddamnit! And for sure they haven't ended up deep in the 18th arrondissement, in an apartment without a bathroom or an icebox! They may actually be shadowing Julien Green while I haven't even figured out how to open doors! I came here on a whim, without thinking, while they've just done it because they deserved it! One more reason to be furious with myself for being a jerk!

There's a weight on my heart that's making it hard to breathe. I feel as if this city is too big for me, as if I'll never be able to master it. And that makes me furious too! Because it's yet another defeat. The most bitter, most shameful of defeats. I'm talking about this city as though it's been making me suffer for years when all I've done is cross a street that's disrupted by a bakers' strike! If I was able to carve out a little place for myself on the *Liberté*, why do I feel that I can't do it here? Because the *Liberté* was a closed world, harmless and unreal, but here the cages are open and the guns are ready to fire?

Mama was right: we're wishy-washy in our family. And one of these days our congenital wishy-washiness is going to do us in.

It was hunger that finally got me out of my hole. Like a rat. But—and this is going to amaze you—a rat in a good mood!

I'd fallen asleep, exhausted by my tears and my dejection, across the blue silk bedspread with the yellow and pink flowers, threadbare from being sat on by generations of backsides eager to go off to work or exhausted from drudgery.

At first I didn't know where I was. The light is so much more present up here where I am than it is in my *rez-de-chaussée* on Dorion Street where one ray of sunlight can easily be seen as a curiosity. I knew that I was acquainted with this place but I couldn't put a name to it. I looked at the big armoire, the table, the chairs, the fireplace, and I thought: "When I figure out where all this is, I don't know if I'll be disappointed or glad..." Mainly, I was relieved because it could have been worse. I looked at my watch. Twenty to six. I thought, it gets bright early here and then the taste of *rillettes* came back to me and I realized it was six p.m.. I'd slept through the afternoon. And I was hungry. Hungrier than ever. I'd had my last real meal on board the *Liberté*, when I'd bolted a double portion of eggs Benedict because they'd just announced that France was finally coming into sight through the fog, which was lifting.

I could have used a nice hot bath.

Good luck!

Surprisingly resigned (already?) I went to the kitchen. I wanted to heat some water to wash myself, parish by parish, with a washcloth I'd found in the armoire. The little gas stove wasn't working! Strike a match, turn the key: nothing. Strike another match, turn the key again... Right then I felt like opening the window and flinging everything in the apartment into the inner courtyard, then throw myself after it as an offering to the gods of human stupidity. I actually did open the window to breathe some air before I exploded.

And guess what! All over the inner courtyard, from every kitchen window, were hanging bags, boxes, string bags where my neighbours kept their perishable food. Maybe they don't have iceboxes, but they're ingenious, these Parisians! I saw eggs, bottles of milk, cheese, pieces of meat wrapped in waxed paper... Ingenious, but imagine the smell in mid-August!

The sun was still beating down on the rooftops, which were turning a beautiful colour somewhere between gold and ochre. The inner courtyard, already dim, became almost blue. I could smell fried onions and simmering meat. Through the open windows I could make out parts of living rooms, corners of kitchens, turns in stairways. Everywhere, there were flowers were growing in pots. Somewhere, a radio had been turned on. Lucienne Boyer was singing.

A rush of warmth rose from my belly, more powerful than hunger, so overwhelming that it gave me goose-pimples. I had to lean against the wrought-iron railing. A moment of unbearable happiness had me bent in two. I don't know why I was so happy when everything was going so badly; the strangeness of what I was seeing, maybe; after all, my window on Dorion Street that looks right onto the sidewalk gives me an unobstructed view of passing cars and the neighbours across the street who laugh at me all day long; either that or this vision resembles too closely the notion I had of Paris before I came here: clichés are always reassuring. Still, I caught myself singing along with Lucienne Boyer despite the hunger pangs and the rather dubious smell that I was starting to give off. (You know how we are: cleanliness above all! Mama used to say: "We may not be rich, but we're clean!" I think I've even heard you say the same thing... So what I had to do before anything else was wash...)

When I turned around to run myself a glass of water, the first thing I saw was the key for the gas, in a corner of the kitchen above the stove. And a second later I knew that I was going to be able to master this apartment, to learn its secrets, overcome its inconveniences: all I needed to do was to understand and sort out every detail, one by one, instead of panicking over the whole situation which, of course, seemed to me insurmountable.

Five minutes later the water was boiling and for the first time in his life, your beloved brother-in-law was standing naked in the middle of a kitchen. No shower or bath has ever felt so good. It took ten times as long as it does at home but time is something I had plenty of! What right did I have to complain, I asked myself, when instead of having to go out and sell shoes in a phony-chic store on St. Catherine Street, I had nothing better to do, before I went out and stuffed myself like a pig, than to wash my private parts *in the middle of Paris!*

When I'd finished my ablutions there was water all over the kitchen and do you know what? I didn't give a damn! I left it to dry, assuming that other Parisians must do the same. I dabbed a drop of alluring scent behind my ears, took one last look at the roofs that were changing more and more, I closed the kitchen window and went to open my suitcase.

And now I'm all set to go out and I look good enough to eat; I feel like a young bridegroom. *À nous deux, Paris! À nous trois,* actually, because you're coming along with me.

I went into the first restaurant I spotted, immediately on the left after leaving the building. I don't know anything about Arab food but I was too hungry to look for anything else. It was closed. That surprised me, it was already ten to seven. Then the thought that every restaurant in Paris might be closed because of the bakers' strike went through my mind and I began feeling gloomy again.

I practically ran across rue Stephenson. A restaurant—French-looking, this time, with its bright red awning and gold-coloured letters that read: "Chez Carco"—stood at the corner. I pushed the door without looking at the menu, just to check whether it was open. The door was unlocked but it was very dark inside... I made my way to the middle of the little room that smelled very good and, not seeing anyone, took a seat at a table in a corner at the back. From the kitchen came the sound of conversation. Of a run-in, rather. Someone was calling someone else a stupid bastard, an idiot and a lousy lay. I thought I'd landed in the middle of a family quarrel and I was about to get up and leave when a *monsieur* all dressed in black, his hair so slick you had to wonder if he'd washed it in the past two years, with bushy eyebrows and a jerky walk, came into the room. When he spotted me, he jumped.

"What do you think you're doing here?"

His tone was so abrupt that I was practically mute with embarrassment. I swallowed, then said:

"It was open..."

"But it's closed! It isn't seven o'clock! You know perfectly well we don't open till seven!"

Charming way to greet customers.

To gain time, I looked at my watch.

"It's ten to seven, practically five to..."

"Exactly! What did I tell you? Now leave! You can come back at seven o'clock!"

"But can't I stay till then? I could look at the menu..."

He gawked at me while I was tripping over my words.

"Where are you from, with an accent like that? Are you Belgian or what?"

I don't know if that was an insult but that's how I took it. I jumped up and yelled at him:

"Kiss my ass, you son-of-a-bitch! If you don't want people coming to your goddamn restaurant, keep it shut! Put a padlock on the door till seven o'clock if you're too big an idiot to open it before!"

He pulled himself up on tiptoe (I forgot to mention he was about four foot two) and pointed to the exit.

"We don't serve Arabs here, Monsieur!"

First a Belgian, now an Arab! Honestly!

As I walked past him I eyed him up and down with my most contemptuous expression.

"Tell me, shrimp, when people come up to your door do they have to show their passports?"

He obviously hadn't understood a word. He simply repeated: "Get out, Monsieur, get out..." more and more steamed up and red as a beet.

So there I am, standing on rue Doudeauville at five to seven, livid with rage and my stomach doing somersaults. On the corner across the street stood another restaurant. I felt like dragging myself there on my knees, pounding on the door, pleading, promising heaven and earth, even offering my beautiful alabaster body if only they'd deign to give me a crumb of bread and even—yuck, just thinking about it turns my stomach—a morsel of *rillettes*. That happens when you're hungry, right?

On the door of the restaurant was a little white sign with red and blue lettering: "Open at seven p.m." I plunked myself outside the door and waited, patiently, thinking:

"What the hell is it about this crazy country, where you can't get your supper before seven o'clock? I've never heard of such a thing! How do the French keep from gnawing at their fists if they don't eat at five-thirty like everybody else? But maybe it's like that everywhere. Maybe it's because of the strike... The bread is late...

I was thinking that bread had a lot to answer for...

But my patience was rewarded: on the dot of seven the cutest little waiter came and opened the door... Blonde, thirty or so, beautiful brown eyes like a squirrel's, an irresistible smile, the little white apron tied nice and tight around his waist... I nearly thanked the corpse across the street who'd kicked me out...

As if I were his only customer, the waiter looked after me as if I were the King of England. It was all, "How are you this evening?" and, "Have a seat here." As La Vaillancourt says whenever she sees some guy she likes: "That's it, I'm in love!" If he thought I was a Belgian or an Arab he didn't let it show, ever after I'd told him in my best Parisian accent: "Thank you so very much, you're terribly kind!"

Still smiling, he held out the menu.

"This evening, the chef recommends the duck with prunes."

I'd begun to salivate like a baby and I actually had to cover my mouth with my napkin: he could have recommended rat tails cooked in dishwater and I'd have kissed his feet! Then all at once my woman-of-the-world side surfaced and I said, after a cascade of laughter that surprised even me:

"Why don't you construct a menu, I trust you..."

He frowned while I was speaking and I realized that I'd used the wrong expression. You don't *construct* a menu, you *compose* it.

I blushed, I cleared my throat and I didn't open my mouth again throughout the meal—except to eat, of course.

And I want you to know, I stuffed my face like it was going out of style!

The simple, family fare at this restaurant had it all over the pretentious, fancy creations I'd tucked into during the crossing: to hell with their "temptations of St. Anthony with two scoops of green," their "dreams of a young girl" or "breasts of Venus"; and hurray for asparagus in vinaigrette, duck with prunes and *tarte Tatin!*

My oh my, *tarte Tatin!* Listen to this: a big hot apple pie with chunks of fruit that were nearly burnt, served with good thick country cream, the kind that not even Alex, my sister Madeleine's husband, can find where they live in the depths of the country! Yellow cream so good it gives you indigestion!

All washed down with a red wine I don't even know the name of but that went directly and delightfully to my head.

While I was eating with such gusto (I must have been a sight to see because the waiter kept giving me loving looks) customers were arriving, reserved and unassuming, and by the time I asked for the *facture* (which brought another smile from the waiter), the restaurant was nearly full. Looks like the French have nothing better to do at night than eat supper late.

The *addition* (which is what I should have asked for) finally arrived. These people have a peculiar way of writing their letters and numbers. I couldn't understand half of it, especially the total, so I asked Roger, which is the waiter's name, to explain it. I hope you've realized that even if I'd understood every word, I'd still have asked him…

Do you know what? In restaurants here you have to pay a cover charge, otherwise they don't give you a knife or fork or even a plate! They're more and more bizarre! I even looked around discreetly to see if anybody was eating with their hands right on the table! Mind you, I was just a bit tipsy…

Roger had recognized my accent, even though I'd disguised it as best I could, and he listened to me as if what was coming out of my mouth was music… I'll tell you one thing, my woman-of-the-world accent was tossed overboard—and fast! Roger even confided to me very softly that he'd met a soldier from Trois-Rivières at the end of the war…

So on top of it all, he's family! Fantastic! That little restaurant hasn't seen the last of me, that's for sure!

Especially because Roger said he'd given me a double portion of bread. I'd eaten a hundred grams instead of the fifty stipulated by law since this morning.

I left there satiated and sloshed, my heart thumping, and feeling as light as a feather. And if my calculations were correct, it had cost next to nothing. A buck and a quarter, I think. Though I'm not sure I counted right. But so what!

As you know, I don't often drink wine; two glasses and everything starts spinning. Beer, sure, I can take it fairly well because it makes me happy, but wine deadens me. All I want to do is go to bed and bemoan my sorry fate, or sing to the point of exhaustion some sad, depressing song about unhappy love.

I'd drunk a whole bottle but I still had all my faculties. I was sloshed but in a good mood and not the least bit sleepy. Now I admit, I'd done hardly anything but sleep since I got to Paris. So I was drunk, but fresh as a daisy. I felt wonderful, a little as if I was floating but not very high. Just an inch or two above the ground. A heavy balloon, good and full, but one that *feels* light.

Knowing absolutely nothing about Paris I decided to just wander, thinking that surely fate would guide me towards some stunning wonders…

I resolutely turned my back on the Sacré-Coeur, maybe because I knew that it stands on a hill and I didn't feel like tackling the famous staircases that children are always climbing up and hurtling down in French movies, squealing like dogs being tormented, or maybe it was simply because I'd seen it from my window and now I felt like being surprised by discovering unexpectedly at some street corner a famous monument that would leap out at me with no warning and turn my heart upside down.

Surprised I was, and right away.

From my bed where I'd slept so well, I'd thought several times that I'd heard a train whistle and the characteristic sound of metal wheels at a level crossing. Now I know why: my apartment is behind a railway station! Immediately after rue Stephenson on the right, you see in the distance the glass wall of an enormous station: the Gare du Nord, as I discovered later, but which at that point I'd thought was the Gare Saint-Lazare, where I'd arrived. Abruptly, the rue Doudeauville becomes a viaduct and straddles dozens and dozens of railway tracks, close together and bright and shiny as new metal. You know how us fatties tend to get vertigo... But I still stopped in the middle of the viaduct (does wine make you brave?) even though I felt a little wobbly, and I watched a train pass just beneath me. The white smoke came all the way up to the viaduct; I got a good grip on the wire mesh that reinforces the guardrail. Another scene from the movies came to me—like Annie Ducaux on the Orient Express or Eric von Stroheim pushing somebody under a train...

To the north of rue Doudeauville, practically under my feet, was a little station that was empty. The train sped right past it. I'm sure it was the wine that made me think that it looked very sad. Another convoy was arriving in the opposite direction, going much more slowly because it was entering the station. I ran so I'd be above it and I watched the roofs of the cars go by. Like a child. What can I say, it's true that travel broadens the minds of the young, but coming down with a case of youth when you're over forty...

I crossed rue Doudeauville to watch the train go inside the glass wall. I thought about all the nobodies like me who come to Paris, naïvely thinking that they'll conquer her—and I smiled; I was relieved to know I'm not the only sucker in this crazy big city. I stood there for five long minutes, wishing them good luck, then I continued along my way.

Rue Doudeauville stops abruptly at a main thoroughfare called Marx-Dormoy. I don't think much ever happened there because the name doesn't ring any bells. A lot of stores, all closed. A gloomy little neighbourhood; more anonymous than my street in any case. And always those same grey, peeling house fronts. I decided to stop looking up... Few passersby, and all in a hurry to get home. Clutching their little ration of bread, like a priceless treasure. How sad.

It seemed to me that my explorations of the great tentacular city were ending abruptly! I turned left, thinking I'd spotted a terrace at the next corner.

A few silent couples sitting over a beer. A red-faced old lady drinking her glass of red wine and checking to see that no one was watching her, as if she was afraid of being caught in the act. On the other side of rue Marx-Dormoy and rue Ordener, a tiny square with a tiny merry-go-round that was shut down. I sat on a straw-bottomed chair that made me think of the streetcar seats back home and I felt so homesick all of a sudden, I nearly jumped. The sound of the streetcars, their smells, the straw that tickles your legs... I could hear you saying to your little boy: "Did you hear what the streetcar was saying? Ta-pocketa, ta-pocketa, ta-pocketa..."

I wanted something to happen, right then, before I started sobbing, but there I was in the middle of nowhere, in an empty part of town, and I didn't know where to go to find the action!

When the waiter came and asked what I wanted to drink, in my best Parisian accent and with a casualness I didn't feel, I asked him:

"Which way to the Eiffel Tower?"

He thought that was a good one and I was still totally ignorant. Without even touching his damn mineral water, I took off in the direction I'd come from, assuming that the neighbourhoods around railway stations always have something interesting to offer.

Not much happened at the beginning of my walk. Crossing rue Doudeauville again, I glanced in the direction of the Sacré-Coeur. I felt like going to bed. It wears you out, always dropping from seventh heaven to the third sub-basement, even if you're rested. I was hot. But fortunately a little breeze had come up while I was pacing the sidewalk of boring old rue Marx-Dormoy. Ahead of me, the street took a sharp turn, and I didn't know what to expect. I thought that if nothing happened in the next fifteen minutes, I'd go back to the apartment like a good boy and wait to see when handsome Roger got off work.

And all at once, with no warning, I was in the middle of the weirdest crowd: foreigners, and when I say foreigners I mean people of every colour, not foreigners like me who can go unnoticed: Arabs, I think they were, in long striped robes; tall, shiny Blacks wearing turbans; Whites too, of course, but craggy, curly-haired, even smaller than the French who aren't very tall. A happy crowd in the Square de la Chapelle, bustling around a colourful outdoor market that was giving off not just food smells but also the scents of spices and exotic ingredients, strong, piquant smells that made me sneeze.

Above it all, the dirty grey metal framework of the overhead Métro. When a car went by—ugly green and clattering like an overage train, no one but me looked up. After the peace and quiet of rue Marx-Dormoy, this lively market came as a surprise. I was afraid to cross boulevard de la Chapelle: car horns kept blowing as pedestrians waded into the street without looking to see where they were going; dozens of dogs were racing around and I've always hated dogs; I was constantly being pushed and shoved by men and women who were lugging crates and shouting things like: "Move along, move along!" or "Watch out for the crates!" I crossed almost in spite of myself, carried along by a wave of children who kept colliding with me and yelling because I was in their way.

The market was closing; below the Métro bicycles, trucks, cars, even carts kept colliding in a concert of insults that I couldn't understand. To my amazement, all the vendors in this market seemed to be French, while their customers were foreigners. So the drivers were heaping abuse on each other in French, but a French that was gravelly and abrupt, hasty and full of foreign words punctuated by more familiar expressions, like "Come on!" or "Say, tell me...," the sole islands of clarity in this sea of incomprehensible jargon. And they claim that *we've* got an accent!

It was still light out, enough to see the garbage scattered around under the overhead Métro: mashed leaves of lettuce, rotten fruit, crates of spoiled vegetables that smelled vaguely disgusting. As I was crossing the second part of boulevard de la Chapelle, which was much calmer, I noticed a street sign that read "rue du Faubourg Saint-Denis" and I stopped dead. This sounded familiar. I looked around. Boulevard de la Chapelle... rue du Faubourg Saint-Denis... If you'd been there we could have tried to place it together... A movie? A book?

I left the market, relieved. I'd been looking for action, but not that kind.

I walked along the tracks that went to the Gare du Nord; the glass wall opened on my right and I could make out the travellers, restless, anxious, running along the platforms, exhausted from long hours of uncomfortable travelling or impatient to be off. When a train left or pulled in, everything disappeared into the white smoke. I kept hearing whistles. The setting sun played on the glass walls and courting birds crisscrossed the empty sky. It was very beautiful.

I emerged onto rue de Dunkerque at twenty past eight. I know because I could see the time on a huge clock on the front of the station. And I stood there stunned. I was at an intersection but instead of two streets crossing like we have in Montréal, there were four or five, big and little, coming from every direction. I was in the middle of a many-pointed star and I stood there paralyzed, with absolutely no idea where to go. I don't have a very good sense of direction, as you know, and even back home

I tend to get lost when I've been into the sauce... So imagine, after a whole bottle of red wine, even if it was mild! I thought that if I crossed three or four streets on the right, I'd end up on rue du Faubourg Saint-Denis, so I took my courage in both hands. Needless to say, I made a fool of myself... First I went a good distance along rue La Fayette, till I realized that it wasn't the right one, then I crossed an enormous boulevard called Magenta (which also sounded familiar) until finally I had to own up to it: I was lost, already. Idiot! Even though the front of the Gare du Nord was behind me, so I must have been going in the right direction! I thought that rue du Faubourg Saint-Denis might have changed its name (apparently that happens all the time in Paris) and I continued along rue La Fayette up to rue de Chabrol where once again, three or four streets came together. Now I had no idea what was going on. I spun around like an obese top, with my nose in the air as I tried to read the street names.

I went up to a Métro station. Poissonnière. Another familiar name... I stuck my nose against a map of the city at the station exit.

Good luck!

I couldn't find a single solitary thing! It was a hopelessly tangled spiderweb! Greek! A thousand-piece Big Ben puzzle put together wrong!

I could see myself starving to death in the streets of Paris, looking for a forgettable little bit of a street called Doudeauville... There's nothing like making yourself laugh when you're on the verge of hysteria. I stopped a passerby and asked him as politely as I could to show me the way to the rue du Faubourg Saint-Denis. His answer was so idiotic, I thought he was going to jump on me.

"It's over there! At the end of rue de Chabrol! You have your back to it!"

I felt I should apologize for living... But I just said, "Thank you, Monsieur," like a schoolboy who's just been punished by the wicked Brother Superior. And I'd travelled the whole length of rue de Chabrol without once turning my head, eyes focussed on the distance where I thought I could make out a big boulevard that I hoped was boulevard Magenta. Yes! I'm not so dumb after all! And on the right, the rue du Faubourg Saint-Denis! My first great victory! I could have kissed the sidewalk!

The street went down towards what looked to me like a black wall with a gate in it that completely blocked the view. I thought that maybe the city stopped there and that once again, I'd gone in the wrong direction. But before turning around I decided to take a closer look at that carved wall that from a distance looked wet as if it had been rained on forever.

The rue du Faubourg Saint-Denis was full of life: another market was closing, but different from the one I'd just crossed. This one stood right on the street as if, back home, we'd decided to sell vegetables on the sidewalk of Fabre Street... The houses seemed to be swallowing up the stalls they'd been disgorging all day long and I couldn't help feeling sorry for the poor people who had to sleep surrounded by the smells of cheese and fish. But I suppose that eventually they'd stop smelling anything, just as I'm surprised whenever a customer comments on the good smell of leather in the shoe store... The merchants were clearly happier than those at la Chapelle; you could hear bawdy songs, and the insults they traded were friendlier.

The men were quite good-looking in general. Many of them red-faced in their workers' blues (you know, those uniforms they always wear in movies if they work in garages or shops... and they're royal blue, not blue-grey as we'd thought), they're prompt to smile and quick to wink. They greet women with ironic deference and the women reply with that natural off-handedness that I want so much to learn. Which produces a concert of: "How's the little lady this morning?" followed by a "Very well, Monsieur Marcel, thank you for asking!" and other superficial but charming civilities and, most of all, filled with innuendo. Or maybe it's just my imagination... Because the French hear so often that they're the world's best lovers, maybe they believe it... But we'd have to check on that...

The air was filled with that same smell of something beginning to rot and the *clochards*, disgusting, stinking, had started rummaging in the garbage, holding their bottles of wine (that must be what they call a *litre,)* spouting a never-ending stream of insults and curses. I stopped at the corner of rue du Paradis to look at one. He was particularly horrible. A repulsive bump was growing on his neck, which his greasy hair couldn't hide completely and a beard several months old hung onto his winter coat (in June!). Whatever he found he stuffed into a greasy potato sack, muttering about some guy called Léon Blum whose guts he hated. He said among other things: "Dirty Jew—we got rid of you but I'm still eating garbage! Piece of filth!" Dirty Jew? I thought the war had put an end to remarks like that!

He realized that I was watching him and I nearly melted on the spot. He staggered up to me and started to harangue the passersby: "Look at this big ox that's spying on me! Who are you anyway? Was it Léon the Jew that sent you? You can tell your Léon to kiss my ass! And you too, you filthy bourgeois who's got fat on the sweat of the poor!" I was very frightened at first, then I thought about *La Charlotte prie Notre-Dame* that the whole family listened to at Christmas, bawling... and that kept me from taking him seriously. Isn't that terrible? I had the impression he was reciting a speech, very realistic but still a speech, written by someone else, that he'd memorized so he could disturb me or insult me. He kept it up while I sped across rue du Paradis, with my tail between my legs because I'd realized, on account of his smell, that he was serious and really was mad at me.

My heart was pounding when I started back towards the wall that was slowly disappearing as night fell.

The streets around here have funny names too: rue des Petites-Écuries, rue du Château-d'Eau, Passage du Désir right next to rue de la Fidélité (I'm not making this up!)... It's a change from all our saints who come from who knows where and our nobodies who none of us has ever heard of! Do you know who Monsieur Sanguinet was? Or Monsieur Drolet? Or Gilford?

At the corner of rue de l'Échiquier, I came across something I thought had disappeared ages ago: a public bath! Not a municipal swimming pool either, but a bath where you go to get washed! Right across the street, on the other side of rue du Faubourg Saint-Denis, there was a nice gaudy sign with fancy lettering that clearly announced: Municipal Baths, Paris Health Department. In the colours of the French flag. I felt relieved. They have other ways of washing besides parish by parish!

I was going to continue along my way when I noticed a monsieur of a certain age (more or less the same as mine) who was staring at me in a way that left no doubt as to his intentions... Believe me, I'd recognize that look out of a thousand; you get a jolt of warmth at the back of your neck that travels down your spine and radiates into your solar plexus... A great shudder went through me and I pretended to cough. The monsieur was lingering at the door to the baths, in fact he seemed to be just leaving. He was dressed impeccably, which clashed a little with the general slovenliness around him, and in his left hand he was holding a pair of buttery kid gloves, visible proof of good taste and good breeding (In Morgan's ads the male models *never* wear their gloves; they hold them in their left hand, like some accessory that's superfluous as far as dressing is concerned but essential for one's appearance). A bourgeois out for a good time who was slumming it among the cabbage cores and turnip peels?

Anyway, he showed me what was what in a very obvious way—in Montréal he'd have been arrested on the spot! Then after one last provocative look, he skipped into a little alley, an extension of rue de l'Échiquier that's called rue de Metz.

He kept turning around every ten paces. I decided to follow him. "We'll see what we'll see," as my mother used to say. But I was only doing it for fun, I swear! I was in no shape for a trip to seventh heaven with a stranger I'd run into at the door to a municipal bath-house even though it indicated cleanliness—a pretty rare commodity in this town...

Rue de Metz opened quite abruptly onto a very big street, boulevard de Strasbourg, which at this time of day was crowded with fairly peaceful folks: poppas out for a stroll with mommas and babies, carefree young couples, and madames, all stiff, walking their horrible, hysterical, hairy mops that bark at everything that moves and crap wherever they want as if the whole world was their toilet. In fact I slipped on a fresh turd and had to scrape it off my shoe on the edge of the sidewalk, cursing. On top of that, it made me lose my prospect! I was mad as hell! I felt like taking the first dog I saw and tying a knot in it! It would be able to eat what it wanted but nothing would come out the other end!

I was about to turn around when I spotted a theatre across the street. The Théâtre Antoine. My first Paris theatre! I raced across boulevard de Strasbourg like a madman. I was so worked up I didn't even notice that I'd nearly gotten myself killed. The play that was on was a comedy, *La Femme de mon ami,* by Yves Mirande and Henri Géroule (Antoinette and Germaine Giroux are doing it at the Arcade next season), with Jacques Henri-Duval and Henri Vilbert. I can't say it sounded terribly exciting but it was a quarter to nine and the show started at nine... I went into the lobby. A small sign to the right of the cash drew my attention: it said that at intermission, a great couturier whose name I didn't recognize would present his summer collection in front of the curtain.

Have you ever heard of such a thing?

A fashion show in the middle of a play! I wonder if it's like that everywhere... Do they sell cough drops at the Comédie Française just before the death of Marguerite Gautier, or laundry soap after the carnage in *Hamlet?*

I decided to take a look—for once the intermission seemed more interesting than the show!

But at the back of the house, on a red-velvet-covered platform where you could see the word *contrôle* in gold letters, my guy from the baths, in a plain suit and a black tie, had just taken a seat. Madames were holding their tickets out to him and he was writing something on them without ever looking at the women, as if they were garbage. He only deigned to speak to the men and with them he seemed to be totally servile and obsequious. I thought to myself, his body may be clean but his tongue must be brown, and my crush evaporated.

I turned my back on the fashion show, Henri Vilbert and the Théâtre Antoine and hurried back to rue du Faubourg Saint-Denis for fear of getting lost.

(I *was* lost but I knew where!)

It wasn't a wall, it was just a stone gate darkened by time in the middle of a noisy square filled with a mixed crowd that was always looking out for something. Actually everyone was looking at everyone else but it wasn't flirtation in the air, it was an atmosphere of minor lewd offences, something like the Main but more dangerous. I didn't feel safe; I crossed the first part of the square quickly, so I could cut through the gate instead of going around it.

A disgusting smell of urine both fresh and stale nearly made me gag when I walked under the carved porch; the stench was so powerful, I had to hold my nose. In fact a *clochard* was relieving himself in one corner and I practically ran past him.

At this hour traffic was fairly heavy. I had to weave my way through the many square cars whose drivers were quick to use their horns, swallowing along the way some clear insults that hit their target, as if the drivers knew me personally. When I got to the other side of the square I turned towards the gate one last time. It must have been part of a wall that once surrounded Paris but I couldn't picture where the inside of the city had been and where the outside: had I just entered Vieux-Paris or just left it? I decided to ask one of the passersby, even though they didn't strike me as very friendly. I waited for some agreeable-looking person I could ask. It was a long wait; the sinister-looking faces that went by didn't inspire confidence.

The Porte Saint-Denis (that was the name of the gate) changed colour too as the night began settling in. Its ribs became less precise, the friezes covering it not so ugly. I tried to imagine the wall that it used to be part of, the comings and goings of which it used to be the heart, the peasants, the carts, the animals that met up with each other there. Once again I was struck by a sense of déjà vu, but I couldn't really grasp it. Something kept running around the edge of my memory and it infuriated me that I couldn't figure out what it was.

Now there was a smell of frying. Very strong. Peddlers were scattered all over the square, selling sausages mainly, and crêpes that they'd spread with jam and then fold in four. No rationing cards here, no coloured coupons. If I closed my eyes I could have imagined I was in Dominion Square.

A young man who didn't look too shady approached me; I asked him as simply as possible:

"Could you tell me where Vieux Paris is—on this side of the gate or the other?"

He looked at me as if I'd just stepped out of a box of Cracker Jack.

"Are you Canadian? I like Canadians, they were all over Paris two years ago!"

He showed me the street that continued to descend.

"It's easy, le Vieux-Paris is on rue de Tracy, fourth on your left. You can't miss it, there's a neon sign! Regards to Canada!"

Ask a silly question and you get a silly answer... He must have thought I was asking about a restaurant. I didn't feel like launching into complicated explanations, and anyway he was already walking away with his hands in his pockets, eyes focussed on the women's backsides as he passed.

So I went onto the street that appeared in front of me, which was called just Saint-Denis, no "Faubourg." And then I figured it out. All by myself. In the olden days the Faubourg Saint-Denis must have been outside of Paris. So I'd just entered the old city. I was going in the right direction. Even if I didn't know exactly what I was looking for.

It was no different though from what I'd just passed through since rue Doudeauville. Except for the atmosphere.

Rue Saint-Denis was fairly well lit but strangely calm. A lot of men walking around, sometimes in groups but mainly on their own, but none of them talking; they'd hug the walls as they turned street corners, their shoulders slightly hunched, hands stuffed in their pockets as if to protect their money. I thought that maybe the neighbourhood was dangerous so I did the same. You should have seen me... With a fedora I'd have looked like an obese Humphrey Bogart on the trail of some gangster who'd stolen his Lauren Bacall.

I didn't realize what the neighbourhood was till I got to the corner.

I'll tell you, the Main with its fairly discreet hookers might as well give up!

First I spotted some girls leaning against the walls or under the porches on rue Saint-Denis; it reminded me of rue de Provence last night, but tackier. These girls hadn't bothered to dress up like neat and tidy little secretaries: believe me, they didn't hide what they were! But once again, the cliché sprang to your eyes: the prostitutes on rue Saint-Denis seemed to be practically in uniform, their outfits were so close to what we might think of as the clothing habits of a French hooker: very short black satin skirt, slit all the way up of course, plain or fishnet nylons, black-and-white or red-and-white striped sweaters, scarf around the neck, purse slung across the chest, cigarette dangling. Only the size changes, everything else is pretty well the same. And as I went along the street, the same concert as yesterday followed me: "Want to come up, handsome?" "I'll do whatever you want," "We'll have a good time…" I found their repertoire limited but entertaining because, once again, it didn't look altogether real.

But at the corner of rue Blondel, something strange attracted my attention.

It was a tiny little street, very dark and even narrower than our lanes back home, I think. Barely seven or eight paces wide… but *packed full* of prostitutes! They covered the entire sidewalk, vigilant, jeering, brash or downright hostile, while the men were pacing the street in an amazing silence. The girls talked, the men didn't. Small hotel signs blinked on and off, pink or orange, giving the street an amber tint that was flattering to all the girls, from the puny and skinny to the soft, shiny fatties, but none of them spring chickens as far as I could tell.

I took a few steps along rue Blondel in the middle of these wild-eyed men who avoided looking at each other but were practically eating up the merchandise they'd rent for a quarter of an hour, who were daring to insult them and mock them. And it seemed to me that it was us, the men, who were on display!

Over it all, the stench of unwashed armpits, stale underwear and cheap makeup and perfume made you gag.

Then the clichés flew away and all at once everything looked all too real: the customers' contemptuous way of looking at merchandise that was no longer very fresh and probably cheaper than elsewhere, the obvious fatigue and bitterness on the faces of the women who had to come to these amber-lit passages to hide their blemishes. The sadness that drifted over this market of human flesh was solid, palpable, devastating.

You know me, I don't have even a hint of a missionary's soul, yet I wished I could do something for those women, even though I felt ridiculous for thinking that way. Feeling helpless has always infuriated me.

I emerged from rue Blondel as from some dank place where you've felt faint because you couldn't breathe.

The girls on rue Saint-Denis must have thought I'd satisfied myself because they stopped approaching me. I only heard one: "Feeling better now, big boy?" from a fairly pretty girl who didn't yet have to hide herself on a side street.

The next streets too—rue Lemoine, rue de Tracy—were packed with silent shadows and provocative silhouettes, all caressed by the same yellow light.

Still, Le Vieux-Paris, a little brasserie at the corner of rue de Tracy, made me smile.

I was relieved to cross rue Réaumur which was hectic, even tumultuous, after the heavy silence of rue Blondel.

It was the first time in my life that I'd crossed a city where smells are so important. Mind you, I haven't travelled very much. But I don't think Montréal has any particular smell, or Québec City, and in New York last week all I smelled was the dusty dampness that came through the air vents in the subway and the fantastic aroma of chestnuts roasting at the corners of the streets.

Here though every block has its own smell that sweeps over you and stays with you till you've found another one, stronger and often so different that you feel vaguely sick to your stomach, the way you might feel in a restaurant if you've finished your dessert and a waiter walks by carrying a dish of snails with garlic.

Every possible odour has gone past my nose since this morning: spices, coffee, soap, bread (even though I didn't eat much),. dairy products, vegetables, especially cabbage and leeks, duck with prunes, and *rillettes*, to say nothing of the body odours hidden or not by perfumes that are more or less effective, whereas in Montréal I wouldn't be able to recognize more than a few very particular smells that I like or that excite me: Samarcette when we've just made love and he's smoking one last cigarette before going to sleep; the french fry wagon that goes past my window in the summer that I can't resist; the offerings left behind by horses that merry flocks of sparrows peck at; the tomato ketchup you and Albertine make in September that sends all of Fabre Street into raptures; Germaine Giroux's neck when I give her a kiss after a show; and you—yes, you—during the July heatwaves when you sit out on the balcony in the evening after you've dabbed some Chénard's Tulipe Noire behind your ears. But that's all. I don't think anything smells all the time the way it does here, neither neighbourhoods nor streets nor stores, as if back home our sense of smell was something to be afraid of.

But then again, maybe we have smells we aren't aware of. We'd have to ask a Frenchman who's just arrived in town...

I'm writing about this because as I was crossing rue Rambuteau I was submerged by so many of those powerful odours that have been following me since I left rue Doudeauville, joined now by the repulsive smells of henhouse and pigsty. Against a background of fish and vegetables, it's quite a brew.

I stopped to take a look on either side. On the left, the boulevard went on discharging its overflow of nocturnal strollers; on the right, trucks emerged from rue Rambuteau, making a terrible racket on the bumpy pavement; and in the distance I could decipher some huge black metal buildings with glass roofs, a little like the two train stations I've seen since yesterday, surrounded by a lively, milling crowd making its way through the stalls, the crates, the cartons, the boxes of all shapes and sizes, and the animal cages from which you could hear snorts, squeals, coos: les Halles!

Another market that was closing, but this one was immense, colossal! The third in a row—the fourth if you count the sex market, which never closes. Even though they have to take out a booklet of coupons every time they want to buy something, people don't seem to complain too much!

There were plenty of bistros open on rue Saint-Denis and on the side streets. Big men in leather aprons were going in and out, greeting everybody. They all shouted the same: "M'sieurs-dames!" when they arrived and when they left and no one ever answered them. A little pink pig was tied to a table leg and quivering with fright as the drinkers looked on, amused. Sometimes, when the door of a bistro opened abruptly, a smell of grilled *boudin* buried everything else and I thought I was back at my Auntie Mona's, who used to eat *boudin* and sausages all year long and died of it one Christmas Eve, in the middle of dinner.

Above the big metal structures, the sky was now coloured a violent pink. The sun had just set and one by one, the streetlamps were coming on. I continued along my way, constantly turning my head to identify the smells, craning my neck and closing my eyes. I must have looked like a cat in heat or a calf that's lost its mother.

At the Square des Innocents (Why "square?" That's not a French word!), a metal fountain painted green, depicting madames holding up a kind of rounded big top was surrounded by chatty women with empty baskets or cloth or string shopping bags. I drank some water from my hand and listened to them complain: "My husband's run out of tickets for wine! You ought to see the look on his face!" "Good thing the Dutch potatoes are in or my soup would have been very thin!" "It's the rich who eat up everything, as usual!" "Do you think they have food tickets in the 16th arrondissement?" Some of them eyed me and nudged one another because I was lingering there. I gave them my most dazzling smile and said, very loud: "M'sieurs-dames!" and left them to their gossip.

I arrived at the Place du Châtelet on the stroke of nine. On my left rose a kind of tower, black with soot, an odd construction covered with irregular arabesques and grimacing gargoyles that I thought was very ugly. It looked like a botched attempt to make a church steeple that had been left on the ground because nobody wanted it. I even thought I might be looking at the first traces of war that I'd seen since I arrived here, that there used to be a church next to this tower that had been destroyed by a bomb which had left standing nothing but an ugly steeple in the middle of a tiny park. I crossed the grand boulevard that now was called Sébastopol... No, it was just a tower. Funny-looking and taken over by an aggressive bunch of nasty pigeons fighting over scraps of stale bread that an old madame was taking from a paper bag, shouting: "Cheep cheep, cheep cheep..." You know how terrified I am of birds. When I saw those hideous creatures with patches of three or four different shades of grey battling over a mouthful of moldy bread, I turned right around, my hand on my heart, and went back to the Place du Châtelet.

Pigeons everywhere! On the statues, the newsstand, the windows of buildings, perched on roofs or asleep under public benches, in pairs on the sidewalk, shameless, the males pursuing their females like pimps following their whores, the females, often with the feathers around the neck missing, practically grabbing us by the legs to ask for help. My heart was in my boots! I actually wondered how I'd get across the square without passing out.

I decided not to look too carefully where I set my feet and to try and appreciate the true value of this magnificent square that opened onto the Seine and a stunningly beautiful sky.

The Théâtre Sarah-Bernhardt was closed. I walked past it slowly, I even pressed my nose against the door in an attempt to get a look inside. I thought I could make out some old photos on the walls. (I thought about Sarah Bernhardt's last visit to Montréal. I was a teenager. My uncle Josaphat had taken me to see her at Dominion Square. What a disappointment! An old woman with dyed, frizzy hair, in a cast, limping, decked out like a rag doll, who recited poetry, stretching out every syllable as if she was being tortured and who everybody thought was brilliant no matter what she did—and she did whatever she felt like. When she came out with her famous: "Such warmth under all that cold," I felt like yelling: "Such a ham under all that paint!" Though she should have awed me too, the uncultivated young provincial whom the Great Artiste had come to shower with her genius. But it seemed to me that she was laughing at us and I could have whacked her. My uncle Josaphat cried his eyes out and when I asked him if he was crying because Sarah Bernhardt limped like Gramma, he gave me a slap upside my head. But I think I was right.) Across the street at the Châtelet, the cradle of operetta, there was a Sold Out sign for *Valses de Vienne*, which I'd promised myself I'd see. We'd heard so much about the stage machinery, the shows with twenty or thirty tableaus that followed one another as if it were the most ordinary thing in the world, finales with a chorus line of a hundred, the horses, hens, pigs (after all, Les Halles is practically next door...) and now I'll be able to check it out!

I crossed the Quai de Gesvres feeling very emotional. I was going to see the Seine I'd heard so much about in so many songs, I was going to walk across it to see—and this I was sure of—the treasures of the Île de la Cité!

The Pont du Change was blocked by a demonstration of bakers chanting at the tops of their lungs inane and incredibly vulgar slogans along the lines of: "Up your ass, Auriol!" Lucky man! "We've had enough, Auriol!" or "Auriol to the glue factory!" Whatever they felt like, and loud!

From this jubilant crowd that was obviously excited by something other than its stupid slogans came a fairground atmosphere that was nearly out of control and about to turn into a riot.

But the road to the Île de la Cité was closed! I felt like tearing up the streamers and banners and stomping on the demonstrators so I could get across. Then I thought that I was reacting like a real tourist for whom a country's problems are just snags in his own visit and who gets annoyed, wrongly most likely, at anything that gets in his way. After all, those bakers may be right. But damn it all, couldn't they have waited till tomorrow?

So I walked west along the Quai Mégisserie, just across from the Conciergerie which I'd have recognized anywhere because my other idol, Marie-Antoinette, had been imprisoned there. I leaned against the stone wall. It feels strange to see a place where things *really* happened. Marie-Antoinette must have looked out one of those windows; she may even have waved her arm as a sign of distress, called for help in her Austrian accent. (In the movies, Marie-Antoinette never has an accent, but in life she must have sounded like Marlene Dietrich). That was where she left from when she went to have her head sliced off, poor woman. I ran my hand over my neck. How horrible!

A narrow, pointed spire, a real steeple this time, I think, protruded from the roof of the Conciergerie, drawing a vertical line of light against the blue of early evening. Was it the Sainte-Chapelle?

On the quai just beneath me were moored barges large and small, which hoists unloaded almost without a sound. Mainly vegetables, mountains of them, were being transferred, lowered, counted—yes, counted—and piled onto trucks that set off for Les Halles as soon as they were loaded.

Women all hunched over were making their way through it, avoiding the trucks, sometimes pushing aside the longshoremen, picking up lumps of coal which they dropped into potato sacks fastened to their waists.

I don't know if we'd see such things back home if we went to the Pied-du-Courant. Maybe. I know that my mother used to do it, just after she was married. She'd follow the railway tracks in the port to pick up her coal, piece by piece, while my father strutted around on St. Jacques Street in the midst of the judges and lawyers who laughed at him. My father was a tavern orator, you know. Gabriel must have inherited it—and me too!

I continued along, slightly depressed. The effect of the wine was starting to wear off and that vision of my mother bent over to pick up fuel to keep us warm had me very upset.

The Samaritaine department store (the Dupuis Frères of Paris) was a big letdown. From the outside, at least, because of course at this time of day it was closed. That is, the building itself is impressive, with its resemblance to a grand hotel and its enormous neon sign overlooking the Seine, but the windows I looked at were just boring. No fantasy, not much decoration, just dummies dressed any old way, frozen in unnatural postures in cardboard settings that were totally ridiculous. I expected a riot of colours, a daring summer collection that would astonish me and made me envious, but all I saw were brown and grey. Beautiful, but classic and too tame. A kind of poor man's Coco Chanel. Anyway, I'd look like a tower in them myself!

I went back across the Quai Mégisserie as if I were dragging a ball and chain on both ankles. I had no energy. Not just for marvelling at things but even for simply moving.

When I realized that I was right in front of the Pont-Neuf though, my depression and fatigue flew away and I crossed the first arm of the Seine almost at a run. I stopped at the statue of Henri IV that was worn away by pigeon shit and bad weather; it was a very ugly pale green as if some clown with an upset stomach had painted it one night and it hadn't been cleaned since then because it didn't matter. Behind me was the Vert-Galant itself, its nose pointing into the Seine and just across from it—the Quai de l'Horloge and the Quai des Orfèvres that meet to form the entrance to the Place Dauphine.

Maigret!

I was sure I'd see him emerge from the Quai des Orfèvres, wave at me and go into a café for his inevitable beer and blow his nose because of his inevitable cold, with one of his assistants, Janvier or Lapointe or the forensic scientist, Dr. Paul on his heels, reading the results of an autopsy to him from a bound file.

I walked around Place Dauphine, which was cool and peaceful, rustling with birds and filled with his presence, his heavy silhouette, always grouchy when he crosses rue de Harlay in the rain (in Simenon's novels it's always raining), a scarf around his throat in winter, carrying an umbrella most of the rest of the year—at least that's how I see him. I heard him swear, I saw him hail a cab after he'd walked around Place Dauphine in search of a clue that would help him solve the murder of a dancing girl from Pigalle or a croupier from the provinces on holiday in Paris. I stood on the steps of the Palais de Justice for a long time, waiting for him to appear. And I saw him. More than once. I know I did.

Back on the Pont-Neuf, I took a seat on one of the benches lining the stone balconies built on the pillars of the bridge that jut out in a half-moon above the water. The stone was still warm. A barge was travelling very slowly under the bridge superstructure, coughing. More coal. Tons of it.

In the distance, towards the east, Notre Dame—the real thing, not a picture, blackened by time and very dimly lit but still majestic—stood out against a background of stars; I watched the sky turn from rose to lilac, from lilac to grey. It was as if it was being switched off. I couldn't really see, I only guessed at the top of the Eiffel Tower which stood higher than the houses on my left, the little red light at the summit blinking to warn airplanes that a giant was standing watch in the heart of the city. I ran my hand slowly over the warm stone, thinking: "I'm really here, I absolutely have to appreciate what's happening to me..." I opened my eyes wide, I could see everything, but it was as if the meaning of what was going on before my eyes didn't make it all the way to my brain. Once again, I felt as if I was just a spectator at what was happening to me because I'd never been prepared to be the actor. I was squeezed into the rounded part of the balcony, one arm over the guardrail, trying to feel moved—unsuccessfully, because what I was seeing was too beautiful for me. As if I didn't deserve it. I was at the very edge of emotion but I couldn't take the plunge. It was like an unsuccessful masturbation, exhausting and humiliating.

If I'd had a postcard depicting that landscape in front of me, I'd probably have wept in frustration; in the presence of the thing itself I was bewildered and helpless.

I'd been moved earlier when I imagined Maigret but I couldn't manage it in front of the genuine Paris landscape as it was lit up in the night now being born.

I chalked it up to all the sensations, emotions and shocks I'd been subjected to since yesterday, and I told myself I'd be better off going to sleep, I'd seen enough for today. You've told me that you'd had the impression you were dreaming during the second half of your wedding day because you couldn't take in anymore. That came back to me while I stood gazing at the front of the Louvre, feeling nothing, and then I told myself: "For her sake I'll try and experience the second part of my own wedding day as I should!"

Two lovers came and sat on the same balcony and I don't think they even realized I was there.

Back home, what they did would have been denounced, shouted down from the pulpit, they'd have been banished from the Catholic Church forever, driven out with holy water and Hail Marys. But it was so beautiful.

That too is forbidden to me.

I pictured myself with Samarcette in that same position and I was overcome with anguish. What I feel for Samarcette isn't love. I think you know that. He's always been just a convenience for me. For the health of the spirit as well as the body. He was there, at the Palace, easy to pick up, which is fairly rare in Montréal, and I got into a relationship with him that was relatively easy and comfortable, that just droned on. I make him laugh, he amuses me. We have the same tastes and we hang out with the same nobodies. We talk on and on about the movies and plays that we see, about the books I persuade him to read and the yellow press that he's addicted to. Each of us is the other's lady's companion. Our lovemaking is okay, sometimes even vigorous and thrilling, but something's lacking, the spark of passion, the heart bowled over by happiness, the senses that are fired up when you lose control like those two young people beside me, who were practically abusing each other on that stone bench in the middle of the Seine.

I moved away as discreetly as I could after a brassiere was flung over the apron of the bridge. For a few seconds I imagined a man's BVDs following the same trajectory, mine or another man's—a partner to be discarded after use, like a dirty handkerchief—and I was surprised by a semi-erection as I was leaving the Pont-Neuf.

On the Quai des Grands-Augustins, a public urinal you could smell a hundred feet away stood in the middle of the sidewalk. Those famous *pissotières* I'd heard so many horror stories about: the slices of bread that lunatics put there in the morning and pick up soaked with urine at the end of the day; the mortal traps laid there by gangsters who are much too handsome; the pitiful orgies of groups for whom the ammonia fumes act as a drug.

In fact, a few discreet silhouettes were already stirring around the metal structure with its small square openings for ventilation. I approached, more fascinated than interested.

Several wrecks and one god. The wrecks were orbiting around the god, who let them gaze upon him as he leaned against the curved wall of the *pissotière*, at once encouraging and contemptuous, cock-teaser and wet blanket. He had his hands in his pockets and his head high, and he stood there perfectly still. Among the wrecks were two or three former gods who'd seen better days; they were admiring and envious and they dared to go farther than the others—without being rejected outright, but without being really encouraged to pursue their tributes either.

I spent a long time watching, leaning against the window of an art gallery (I pity the salesmen who work there!) Everything was happening in a damp, heavy silence that smelled of frustrated desire. Wrecks entered the *pissotière* in the hope that the god would follow them. He never did, he only shifted his eyes in search of adoring gazes or gestures that were downright obscene and made him smile.

Sometimes the wrecks went on to satisfy each other and you'd hear pitiful cries of release that could break your heart. Pity is the feeling I hate more than anything else. The god would offer an ironic look and I could have slapped that oh so handsome face, that wonderful mouth that had never given pleasure to anyone, I was sure of it. That god, focussed entirely on himself, will be coming here to exhibit himself until the first ravages put in their appearance, at first discreet and invisible in the shadow of the Quai des Grands-Augustins, then increasingly obvious as time goes by, till he too is obliged to join the rank of the wrecks because some fresher goods will have taken his place, whom he'll fawn on in vain while he thinks back bitterly to the time when he was the one people fought over without winning his favour, only a look of contempt.

But I was wrong. A second god arrived, went up to the first one, said something in his ear. They both smiled, made some vague gestures.

I left before the show got underway.

The lovers' game on the Pont-Neuf had excited me; the circus on the Quai des Grands-Augustins made me lose my hard-on. (I apologize for the words but you agreed that I should tell you everything. Anyway, you can skip the parts you don't want to read.)

Not a taxi in sight. Only a few square cars now and then that slowed down when they drew level with the *pissotière*, lights off and gleaming under the streetlamps.

I headed for a street that's also called Dauphine, because in the distance I'd noticed an excited group at the door to some establishment, a theatre or a club, I couldn't tell. I figured they'd be able to tell me where to call a taxi if the neighbourhood was too deserted to drive around in search of fares.

As I got closer to them I could hear bits of jazz, an energetic trumpet in particular, coming out the little door where the happy group was standing.

It was an amazing assortment of types that don't go together: pale teenagers dressed in loose black clothes, turtle-neck sweaters that were obviously secondhand and not properly cared for, berets on the girls whose hair was long and straight (and often greasy), some guys with short hair that made them look nearly military, others with very long hair who seemed proud of it and kept fiddling with it, constantly shaking their heads as they spoke; some proper-looking people in proper little suits, more discreet and not so talkative, as if they were stunned to be there; women in long gowns, boisterous and casual, talking shrilly to everybody, laughing constantly, accompanied by magnificent specimens of wildly elegant men, who called to one another from one end of the line to the other with no concern for the people around them. There was an atmosphere of intoxication all around them, still new and fairly well controlled; it was barely ten p.m. and the night, the real night that gets underway after midnight and ends in the small hours of the morning with the coup de grâce of the one drink too many, was still far away.

I was thirsty, I was hot, I just wanted to collapse over a cold beer. Before I joined the line, I read the poster that was dimly lit by a dying fluorescent light. It was a perfectly simple photo of a young red-haired woman and a square-faced man, both as solemn as judges but with amused, nearly mocking expressions, above which you could read in awkward letters: *LE TABOU: Anne-Marie Cazalis Presents Boris Vian and His Orchestra.*

I glanced inside the partly open door. A stone staircase went down to the basement. Was it one of those Paris *caves?*

All at once the door was flung open and a couple of young fools emerged, clapping their hands and trying to imitate musical instruments with their mouths. Satisfied "Ah!s" rose from the waiting crowd.

Now that the door was open the music was very clear. I thought about the little dumps where they play jazz down on Peel Street, where me and my gang don't dare to go because drugs circulate freely and the Black Americans who perform there are too quick to get into a brawl. I was on my way back to my place in line when the redhead in the photo came out, shouting:

"There's two seats, but I warn you, they aren't very good!"

Everyone started yelling at once. I'd never seen anything like it. Some arms went up, others pushed, heads moved, feet got stepped on, there was pushing and shoving... In less than three seconds Anne-Marie Cazalis was bombarded; money was flung at her, her arm was grabbed, people yelled at her. She was smiling in the midst of the cries and she selected her customers the way someone else might choose French pastries, saying:

"You and you, come along..."

The chosen, pink with pleasure, walked past the others, who yelled at them, and at the owner of the bar. When the door was shut again, this time all the way, a sigh of disappointment travelled through the ranks of the rejected. Figuring that I didn't have a chance of getting inside, I turned my back on Le Tabou.

But a window was thrown open above us, very high, someone shouted: "Is your circus over, you savages? I can't sleep! *I* have to work tomorrow!" and a sheet of cold water poured onto us, followed by a wooden bucket that brushed against the head of a madame in a satin gown who passed out on the spot from fright. Luckily, I was spared, I just got a few drops of water on one shirt-sleeve, but others were soaked from head to toe and cursing like the damned. More windows opened, more insults landed on our heads. The clients of Le Tabou scattered onto the street, shaking themselves like wet dogs, raving and waving their fists at the poor people who wanted to sleep in peace, whose usually quiet neighbourhood was being invaded.

In the midst of the general brouhaha I heard a familiar voice: "Yes, it's him! It's my friend the Canadian!"

The Princess Clavet-Daudun! That's all I needed!

"You're the last person I'd've expected to see here! You know Le Tabou? And yet where you come from, they know nothing of the *rive gauche*, I've just been there... Hmmm? But of course, you're an artiste..."

She was poured into a champagne taffeta gown with square shoulders, her hairdo was slightly crooked and her breath was scented with every kind of spicy food that smells bad. She'd grabbed my arm, staggering and slightly damp. Her night was no longer very young. She'd left her "princess" title at the bottom of a glass somewhere.

"Jean-Loup! It's the Canadian I was talking about this afternoon! You know, the one who dressed up like a *dame-pipi* at the *Liberté* ball. Hmm?"

They were all looking at me and laughing. I wished that the sidewalk would swallow me up. I felt as if I were dreaming. I must have looked like a halfwit!

A handsome monsieur in a pin-striped suit, with a grizzled mustache but bald as an egg, came up to me with his hand extended. I hate it when handshakes don't come off as they should and I admit that this one was particularly unsuccessful. I was limp, terrified, humiliated.

The princess had put her arm around my waist (which wasn't easy!) and pushed me towards a group of newcomers who were laughing at the people who'd got sprayed.

"This is my Canadian! What a stroke of luck, finding him like this! You're an actor, go on now, say something! I've been describing your accent to my friends since yesterday but I can't imitate it! Hmm? You'll see, the rest of you, it's quite improbable! You won't understand a word but it's hilarious!"

I could have killed her! After torturing her for hours—skillfully, ingeniously and patiently.

She went on as if she'd just pointed out some trinket in a window.

"No, look, here's a better idea! We'll ring the bell at Anne-Marie's, I know her well, we'll all go down, you'll go on stage and do your little Canadian act for us. I'm sure Boris will be flabbergasted, with his love of accents! Hmmm?"

I hadn't said a word but the whole street knew that I had an accent you could cut with a knife!

I broke away from her as best I could and took off like a beaten dog. And I didn't even do her the favour of telling her to screw off, that would only have made her happy!

I've been spared nothing today! And I mean *nothing*! I was so furious I was staggering, like a drunk. I was dizzy, my heart was racing, my legs were like jelly. I don't know why but I felt as if I'd just narrowly escaped being raped!

I like putting on a show, it's one of the things I enjoy most, but I refuse to perform like a monkey for a bunch of drunken Frenchmen who want a folklore fix! Even though I'm beginning to realize that it's the only way I could make an impression here! In Montréal, the Duchess of Langeais; here, a visiting uncle from Canada!

I walked for a long time, getting lost in little streets that were very pretty but that ordinarily I wouldn't have bothered looking at. At one point I saw a grand boulevard on my left, just as I was about to turn onto rue de l'Échaudé (and I certainly felt scalded), that looked as if it turned back towards the Seine.

A warm wind had come up, enervating and water-logged. A storm was all I needed to make my happiness complete...

An old church, black and squat and half-hidden by trees, drew my attention. It wasn't brightly lit and the white that remained on its walls was taking on a warm yellow tone. I walked around it because the front didn't open onto boulevard Saint-Germain.

That church must have been there forever; the stones of the bell-tower have had time to crumble under the effects of the weather. It almost seemed badly built, the stones are so uneven, rubbed down and rounded. I would have liked to look around. Churches back home are fairly flashy, but this one was quite discreet, surrounded by trees, and God knows I'd have liked to go somewhere calm for a few minutes. It was closed, of course.

At the corner of the little square and the boulevard was a newsstand that never closed. An old fellow, wearing a cap despite the heat, was slumped on a tiny chair next to an oil lamp that sat on a stool, his head nodding gently and a cigarette butt stuck to his lower lip.

For a hundred francs (around fifteen cents in our money) I bought the May 24 issue of *France Illustration* (back home, we always get it four or five months late—if we get it) and a map of Paris. I was thinking it was about time that I got to know where I was coming from and where I was going in this damn city!

A terrace was open on the other side of the square. A large one, with metal tables and straw-bottomed chairs. But a wild bunch of young people had taken it over, shouting that they were committing gratuitous, existential acts. I read something somewhere about those nut cases dressed in black who want to turn everything upside down... I continued on my way, thinking they were very unlikely to look kindly on a fat, gasping tourist unfolding a map of Paris on a table that was too small as he tried to figure out where he was. The gratuitous, existential acts that might suggest to them didn't really tempt me.

I found another terrace, this one relatively calm, a little further on. It's strange to sit down on the street like that, to have a drink and read. You think that passersby are going to stop and look over your shoulder. I leafed through the *France Illustration* while waiting for my beer. There was an article about the show I nearly went to see at the Théâtre Antoine. It doesn't sound all that hot.

I was facing a group of people more or less my age who were talking loudly and seriously about a play they'd just seen, called *Les Bonnes*. From what they were saying it didn't sound like a barrel of laughs... Two servant girls who kill their mistress... The one who seemed to be the head of the group, whose name was Jean-Paul as far as I could tell, claimed that the director had staged the play the wrong way. I'd like to know how you can do that! What's written is written, isn't it? The actors can't come on stage and say the opposite of what they have to say! What a weird idea! Those people just liked the sound of their own voices! Especially because the director in question wasn't just anybody, it was Louis Jouvet!

The woman, Simone, who was very beautiful and looked breathtakingly intelligent, listened to the man for a long time before replying, but when she did it was very short and irrefutable. She seemed to enjoy taking the wind out of his sails. She was wearing a turban, something like Germaine Giroux, that emphasized the straight line of her beautiful forehead. When all's said and done I think I'd rather resemble her than a broad like the Princess Clavet-Daudun. But I haven't got the brains. Even though she's the same age as me. But she can't have been born in Montréal to an alcoholic father and a mother who died of boredom. Besides, I don't think you dress up the way I do to talk about literature over a scotch, but to make others laugh, and to laugh hard enough yourself to make yourself sick.

The third one, Albert, who was well on the way to being drunk, kept bringing the conversation back to his own success. He looked very sure of himself and didn't always listen to what the others were saying. At one point the woman actually told him: "Please, Albert, stop bringing up your triumphs! We know all about them. And you're well aware that I've just had a particularly difficult winter!" They must be celebrities of some kind. Stage actors maybe... Though I got a very good look at the woman and I didn't recognize her. Maybe she's a member of the Comédie-Française who's only played supporting roles in the movies... The one called Albert looked like Pierre Brasseur and his voice even sounded similar, but his name was Albert...

As for Jean-Paul, he didn't look in the least like an actor. For a second I'd thought of asking for his autograph, but I was too embarrassed. I wasn't really sure they were actors and I couldn't very well risk saying that I'd liked them in the movies, maybe they were just operetta singers! Or musicians.

The beer tasted fine. Not like good old Black Horse of course, but the smell was nearly the same, so comforting when you're depressed, and that little tingle in your nose that promises a temporary calming of the great storms. It felt softer in the mouth, it almost went down better. I realized at the first sip how thirsty I was and I didn't stop until my glass was empty. When I'd finished I had a little foam mustache that I licked before wiping my lip.

I ordered another one.

The group of famous nobodies had been enlarged by a girl with long black hair that everybody called Toutoune and an Arab whose name I didn't catch. They were talking about Le Tabou where they wanted to finish their evening.

Good luck!

I slowly unfolded the map of Paris. Maps have always seemed ridiculous to me. When I was a child (and already obese) I couldn't understand how the same size paper could contain the map of the world or the map of a city. In my child's logic I expected maps of the world to be bigger than the others, and of course I was thinking about that as I spread mine on the table and smiled at my own naïveté. Both then and now. Who but me would set off to conquer one of the greatest cities in the world without documenting myself, imagining that I'd understand everything and master everything in one fell swoop, as if I was getting off at Drummondville or La Tuque. But I don't think I'm all that naïve. Only careless.

At first I couldn't understand a thing I saw: a big maroon circle with a blue line through it that curved to the left and was striped with little white veins that ran off in every direction and had the most incredible names: boulevard des Filles-du-Calvaire; Place des Abbesses; Porte de Pantin; rue Le-Vau; rue des Petits-Champs and rue Croix-des-Petits-Champs, which intersect ("Where do you live?" "At the corner of Petits-Champs and Croix-des-Petits-Champs!"), the Cour Juin and rue Juillet... I think there are so many streets in Paris, they call them whatever comes into their heads. But when they christened the rue du Chat-qui-Pêche, they must have been drunk as skunks! Imagine naming a street for a fishing cat!

When my second beer arrived I asked the waiter to set the glass down anywhere on his city. Simone at the next table smiled. And needless to say, the waiter asked if I was Canadian. I answered in a Québec City accent: "You got my number, kiddo, I'm from Québec City!" Simone laughed out loud and Toutoune gawked at me. Someone in the group who hadn't spoken yet and whose name I didn't know muttered between his teeth: "I detest the Canadian accent." Tears sprang to my eyes and I snapped right back: "Don't I have the right to live?" The other men who hadn't been following what was going on turned to look at me. Simone reached out and patted my hand. "Pay no attention to him, Monsieur, he's drunk." Before I went back to my map I replied: "Me too, but I don't insult people!" The man shrugged and made a mocking sound with his mouth. If I'd had fingernails I'd have shredded his face.

I sipped my beer. The glass had left a big wet circle on the map. And it was while I was trying to wipe away the water with the flat of my hand that I found the route I'd taken.

I had sliced Paris in two, like an onion or a piece of fruit. I'd started at the far north and headed due south, by way of the kernel of the fruit—the Île de la Cité. Without realizing it, I'd penetrated Paris the way a worm makes its way inside an apple, from the peel to the core.

And naturally I felt like an intruder, an undesirable who hasn't been invited but who settles into your place all the same, as if everything was due him. Something like a mixture of embarrassment and fear had my stomach in a knot. My head was spinning. I looked, all around, at boulevard Saint-Germain, the terrace of the Café de Flore, the passersby, all dolled up or grubby, Simone and Jean-Paul and Albert and Toutoune and the others... and I felt so... I felt so *out of place*. And unworthy! Not unworthy to be part of what I was seeing, just to be there! And furious too, because I couldn't just tell myself: "A worm in an apple doesn't feel guilty! It moves in and has a feast!" I'm sick and tired of feeling like I have to preach myself a sermon every time something a little out of the ordinary happens in my life, but what can I do? I have guilt branded on my soul.

Simone was watching me. I felt like telling her everything. The way I tell you. But I had the impression that she understood, at least in part, what I was feeling, maybe because of the panic she could see in my eyes. Lost-looking foreigners must be the same all over the world.

In the end, she was the one who finally asked:

"Have you found what you were looking for?"

"Yes, I was looking for rue Doudeauville, in the 18th arrondissement of Paris. And I'd like to take the Métro home but I don't know how..."

"Oh, that's very simple..."

She got up and bent over my map. Her finger immediately found the right Métro station.

"Here, it's this one, Château-Rouge. Get the Métro there, across the street, next to the newsstand, take the train in the direction of Porte de Clignancourt, and get off at Château-Rouge. It's direct."

She stayed beside the table for a moment, then asked:

"Do you need some help?"

I waited a few seconds too before I replied. I wished I could stay in her field of vision for a very long time. Her gaze felt nourishing. Finally I said:

"Yes. But the help I need is on the other side of the Atlantic."

"Do you miss your home?"

"What I really miss is my friends..."

I got up, apologizing, left a hundred francs on the map of Paris that had beer all over it and took off like a thief.

As soon as I'd pushed open the door of the Saint-Germain-des-Prés Métro station, the smell of dust and urine, dry and stifling, nearly made me turn around and walk out. I stood there in the corridor, grimacing in the warm air for a while before I decided to keep going. I went up to the ticket seller's glass cage.

"I'd like to go to Château-Rouge, please..."

He approached the glass that had little holes in it, probably to protect him from people's bad breath.

"I beg your pardon."

"I'd like a ticket to go in the direction of Porte de Clignancourt... I'm getting off at Château-Rouge."

I was too tired now to try faking a French accent.

A big grin appeared on the ticket seller's grey face that had dark circles under the eyes.

"Are you Canadian? Why are you going to Château-Rouge at this hour of the night? That's not for you! Why not go to Pigalle like everybody else? Get off at Barbès and change there for Pigalle! First or second?"

"First or second what?"

"Class. First or second class?"

I couldn't believe my ears! Here too! Does it even extend to the toilets? Is there a first class on the sidewalks, in the restaurants? Did I drink my beer in a section I wasn't entitled to?

"Give me a second class, third class even if you've got one, that's good enough for me! And I'm not Canadian. I'm a bilingual Zulu!"

Clutching my ticket, I went down the dark staircase that led to the platforms, thinking about the French movies we've seen recently, that showed Parisians hiding out in the Métro during the war.

I met a gang of young fools dressed in black who smelled very strongly of neglected armpit. I wouldn't have wanted to share an elevator with them! Unless I had a gas mask!

Something vaguely resembling a human being was waiting at the barrier that gave access to the platform: a man still young, but from whom all life had been removed long ago. He was holding a ticket punch and he'd grab your ticket without looking at you and punch it, his eyes never leaving the cement floor. Completely absent. How many hours a day did he spend there, surrounded by everybody's smells, punching little pieces of paper? Despite the heat he had a scarf around his neck. The perpetual draft must be a constant danger for him.

A Métro train pulled in; I ran. Not many people were waiting there in the station made of white imitation bricks that had long since turned yellow. It was very impressive, that train enclosed in a tunnel. Something like Santa Claus's little train at Eaton's, but bigger, uglier, and much, much noisier. A door stopped right in front of me... But nothing happened. It stayed shut. For a moment I thought you might have to slip your ticket somewhere so I looked at the other cars. You have to open the doors yourself! First there's a latch you have to lift, then you pull as hard as you can to shove the door into the wall of the car. I had just enough time to climb aboard before a whistle bleated and all the doors shut at the same time, with the most horrible sound like clacking jaws.

I've always hated tunnels. And that day I got more than my fill. Thirteen stations! The train tosses you around, it turns, stops without warning then jerks to a start, it shakes you up so badly that your head has trouble following the rest of your body... I spent five days on a boat with practically no ill effect, but it didn't take five stations of the Paris Métro to make me sick to my stomach! Between Châtelet and Les Halles, I thought I was going to stay there. The train turned left so suddenly, I had to grab hold of the back of the seat. I put my hand over my mouth. The duck with prunes and the tarte Tatin rose to my throat at the same time. I tried to take deep breaths through my nose the way you showed me but the smell was so bad, my stomach rebelled even more. And that was when I realized that *I* was the one who stank! I kept my elbows tight against my body and didn't move, for fear that one of the other passengers would notice.

With a tremendous effort I managed to get to the Château-Rouge station. I'm sure I was as white as a sheet and drenched with sweat when I emerged. I was at the corner of boulevard Barbès and rue Poulet, close to home. Home?

Now that I knew where to find rue Doudeauville on the map, I went up to the big panel that stood near the exit from the Métro station to check whether I should take rue Poulet right away or continue along boulevard Barbès before turning right. I put my index finger on the Château-Rouge station. The sense of déjà vu that had been following me since morning because of the vaguely familiar street names came back all at once and I remembered that when I started this diary, I said that I was going to look for Gervaise and Lucien de Rubempré.

I was so surprised at my discovery that I stood there without moving for a long moment, my index finger on the map, before I could react.

Gervaise! *L'Assommoir*!

For the past twenty-four hours I'd been living in a novel by Zola!

They were all there, practically next door: rue des Poissonniers, rue Myrha, rue de la Goutte-d'or, rue Polonceau, rue Labat. I live in the very heart of the section of Paris where *L'Assommoir* takes place, between rue Marcadet and boulevard Rochechouart!

Remember how we adored that book a few years ago, because the characters were so much like our family: Gervaise herself, who limped like my mother; Coupeau and Lantier, who represented all the men on Papa's side; Nana, who'd turned out badly like cousin Berthe and who made us think of what could happen to Thérèse if we didn't hold her back; and the others, friends and neighbours, to whom we could give dozens of names.

We hid when we read *L'Assommoir* because it was on the Index, you in your bedroom, pretending you had the flu to avoid the wrath of Albertine, me during my lunch hour at the back of a restaurant on St. Catherine Street, over a bowl of cooling soup tor a congealing hot chicken sandwich. We described it to each other afterwards, moved by the misfortunes of Gervaise but criticizing her anyway because she hadn't been braver at the end of her life. We practically hated Zola for letting her die under a staircase like a bum, but we know pathetic individuals like her who let themselves go after suffering tragedies that overwhelmed them. In the end, we felt as if we knew each of the characters personally, wishing we could talk to them and warn them about what lay in store because we knew what their tragic destinies would be. Do you remember Gervaise's vertigo over the hole on boulevard Magenta that was under construction? I was there! And the wedding procession that comes down from Montmartre towards the heart of the city? That's the very route I took today! I crossed boulevard de La Chapelle where one night Gervaise—the pitiful, limping drunk whom everyone laughed at—tried to sell her body.

And do you know what I did? I'm sure you do because you'd have done the same thing. I ran through the whole neighbourhood, looking for Gervaise! I knew that she'd never existed and that in any case it all took place in the nineteenth century, but just as with Maigret earlier, I was sure I'd find her! Zola's descriptions were so precise that I thought I recognized the old houses: the laundry on rue de la Goutte-d'Or, the *assommoir* itself, a gin joint on rue des Poissonniers, the washhouse where Gervaise and fat Virginie had fought...

I knew that I looked like a fool. As soon as I recognized a street name I'd step onto it resolutely, studying every house front, looking out of the corner of my eye for a hobbling figure, sometimes young and perky, with a song on her lips and a little girl dogging her footsteps, sometimes obese and staggering, dirty and inarticulate. I watched as Lantier fell off the sloping roof of a house that was under construction; the numerous drinking binges whose stench and echoes reached the street; the nuptial procession with the bride lagging behind because she couldn't walk as fast as the others.

I strolled around like that in Gervaise's footsteps for a good hour, then I came back to rue Doudeauville, exhausted, gasping and drunk with emotion.

A few months ago I loved Gabrielle Roy's *The Tin Flute* just as passionately, yet it never occurred to me to wander around Saint-Henri in search of the Lacasse family! So why was the neighbourhood of Goutte-d'Or so thrilling? Because it's somewhere else? Because I run into Florentine Lacasse every day while Gervaise, even though she resembles us, is part of someone else's culture and I can take pity on her fate without feeling guilty about her existence? Because Montréal belongs to me whereas Paris, so far away, was a fantasy described in dozens of books that made me dream? Because you and I prefer dreams to life?

I climbed up the damp stairs of my new dwelling four at a time. I couldn't stand still so I began pacing the little apartment, from fireplace to bed, from bed to fireplace. I wanted to understand! My head was a confusion of thoughts that I couldn't sort out. I opened one of the windows that look onto rue Doudeauville. The bell-tower of the Sacré-Coeur was no longer lit up but it still formed a paler splotch against the black of the night. Everything was incredibly beautiful but something was missing. And I realized that I was quite simply dying to talk to you. Directly. Not through this damn diary that isn't really doing me any good and that you'll read too late: to you in person. I've pictured you leaning against me, breathing the night air, maybe singing in your beautiful voice, "Le Temps des cerises" to Paris that's half-asleep. I'm dying of loneliness! For you and my gang! What I want is to be able to laugh about my day or be ecstatic about it with Samarcette, La Vaillancourt, La Rollande Saint-Germain; to be at the Palace under the fake coconut tree that smells of dust, surrounded by the floozies and the drunks, with young Maurice who gets on everybody's nerves and Thérèse who's starting to make men drool—and still wake up here tomorrow morning to continue my quest. But with the family! I wish I could have dragged along my gang, my relatives, my neighbourhood, my city so I could share it! Share it, do you understand? I was born into a gang and I can't live, or even more, understand on my own! What's the good of living an adventure if you don't know what it means? With you, whom I love so much, with you whom I love, I'd understand; on my own, I know now, I can't do it. You've only lent me your eyes, while I wanted to ferry you with me all over Paris in search of— what can I call it? Of happiness? In any case, the happiness of discovery.

I'll never feel comfortable with solitude. I need an audience. Now. Right away. So I can explain myself to myself.

And the only audience I know is at the other end of the world. I realize that it's absolutely impossible for me to wait months before appearing before you. Alone in an adventure that's too great for me I'd die of loneliness, of fear and frustration.

It's six a.m. Paris is waking. The garbage-men have just passed. An infernal commotion that shook up the whole neighbourhood. The sky is all white now after shifting through every possible shade of pink and orange. The other side of last night. The new beginning.

I wrote all night, feverishly as you can tell, going wherever my pen led me, without censoring myself or worrying too much about how it would all come out.

I'm going to pack my bag, go to the Gare Saint-Lazare and take the first train leaving Paris for Le Havre. I couldn't spend another day like yesterday so I'd rather retreat on tiptoe, as discreetly as I can. On the boat, the *Liberté* or another one, I'll invent a fantastic journey for myself that I'll touch up so I can offer it to everybody when I'm back in Montréal. Everybody but you; to you, I'll offer this piece of myself to read that you and I will be the only ones to know.

The Duchess of Langeais is inside me, in my imagination, and she'll only be believable if I flesh her out. To hell with Antoinette Beaugrand and her "Kulture," to hell with the phony Princess Clavet-Daudun and her nights in Saint-Germain-des-Prés. Plateau Mont-Royal is waiting for me, the Main too maybe, ready to be taken in by the first fine storyteller who comes along. It's not the experience that matters, it's the well-organized lie, and I'm going to organize the finest ones for you…

I'll end this hodgepodge diary here. I won't need it anymore. As of now I'll improvise out loud. No more writing.

Good luck!

P.S. I'll have spent ten days on the boat and thirty-six hours in Paris... Isn't that sad?

Insert

Scheherazade IV

Hosanna didn't close the blue notebook right away. He left it open on his knees, the pages yellow from the summer humidity and the winter dryness of overheated apartments. The last pages in particular had been hard to read: the paper was crumbling, the ink blurred as if someone had deliberately wet them. Finally, Cuirette took Édouard's diary with his own hands, the soft hands of a big ox who hasn't done a day's work in his life. Hosanna didn't interfere, or didn't notice. "Wow, she was some liar, the Duchess, eh Hosanna? Always saying she'd spent months and months in Paris... She'd talk about meeting stars and famous writers, about how she hung out with people in high society, her outfits that made le Tout-Paris laugh, like she said... I believed every word... How about you?" Hosanna took a while to answer. And when he did it was in a soft, even voice, as if what he was saying was perfectly obvious. "Didn't you ever notice, Cuirette, how every year her trip got longer? How she kept piling on more and more names, how new facts kept cropping up out of the blue, thirty years later... The Duchess used to say naïvely: 'Oh, that's right, I never told you about that...!' And then she'd cook up some story and stick it in between a couple of others we already knew by heart... Me too, Cuirette, I believed her at first. Longer, even... I'd listen to her stories without asking any questions, like everybody else... Then one day..." Hosanna turned to face Cuirette, smiling. His eyes shone, the way they did when he was about to cry. "When she started talking about Brigitte Bardot, saying she'd known her when she was just starting out, that was when I caught on. In 1947 Brigitte Bardot was a child, like me... I was shocked at first... but then I started admiring how incredibly good she was at inventing and persuading. She made you swallow stories about three generations of actors and singers and you never realized it!" "It's true! And you never said a word!" "No. The rest of you were dreaming, too. And her stories were so much more wonderful than anything that might have really happened to her..." Hosanna took back the diary, held it against him with his chin resting on it. "She was the real Scheherazade, Cuirette. And it went on for thirty years. Eleven thousand and one nights!" Then all at once he broke down. Hosanna was bent double over Édouard's diary, moaning like a little animal that's being tortured. "I miss her... I miss her... I miss her..."

Coda

To fat individuals, one in a rocking chair, the other on a straight-backed chair, were whispering on the balcony of the house on Fabre Street. Behind them the door to the apartment was shut despite the heat. Nothing was moving. There was no night wind to dishevel the treetops that were motionless, frozen there as if they were listening or waiting for the slightest breeze, the smallest breath of life that would drive away the stifling humidity that had swept over Montréal a few days earlier.

"Why are you coming to see me so late?"

"Nobody knows I'm back."

"You'll have to let them see you one of these days."

"Not yet—I'm not ready."

"But on the phone you said you'd come back to see your friends and family…"

"That's you."

Édouard held out his notebook to the fat woman.

"I can't stay long. Read this. I wrote down a phone number where you can get me. Amherst 2261. It's a hotel."

"You're staying in a hotel! But that's so expensive!"

"I've got plenty of money left. Don't worry about it."

"I hate whispering like this, Édouard… We're like criminals. I hope you haven't got anything to hide!"

"Of course not. I'm just not ready to face the family. I'll come off as a failure again, a good-for-nothing spendthrift…"

The fat woman had set the notebook on her lap. Now she stroked it with the flat of her hand.

"Is your whole trip in there?"

"We'll talk about that when you finish reading. But I don't think I'm going to live that long. I've been like a vegetable since I came back. I spend all day in bed, I don't read, I don't do anything—I don't even think."

Édouard felt a hand that he hadn't seen alight on his wrist.

"Was Paris wonderful?"

"Yes. Too wonderful."

"Why *too?*"

"Too much for just me."

"But Édouard, I was there with you."

"No, that's just it. It didn't work. You'd've had to be there for real... I needed you not to be just in my head..."

He hesitated briefly then came out with it:

"Do you know how much I love you?"

The hand withdrew and moved to the fat woman's heart.

"No."

"I know you're my sister-in-law and I'm... well, I'm different... But I love you all the same. Love isn't just two... two bodies rubbing together, you know."

Édouard was speaking louder now. His last remark had rung out over Fabre Street as it slept. He clapped his hand over his mouth like a child who's just done something wrong.

"I can't answer that, Édouard."

"I'm not asking you to, I'm just telling you, that's all. I know it's hopeless, for me as well as for you, but it was there and it had to come out."

They sat there in silence for a long moment. Édouard even thought his sister-in-law had dozed off. But from the way that her shoulders were rising too rapidly he realized she was crying.

"I'm sorry. I know you adore my brother. I'd like just a piece, just a little speck of that love."

The fat woman got to her feet, giving her chair a good push as she always did.

"You have that already. Don't ask for more, Édouard. I'll call you when I've read it."

He took her hand, but abruptly, as if he were grabbing hold of one last hope.

"I hope you'll understand... How helpless I felt... How Paris overwhelmed me... How the loneliness made me panic..."

"Go to bed now, it's late... Try and sleep."

The fat woman went inside, very gently pushing the door which had a tendency to creak. Édouard was alone on the balcony, overwhelmed and shocked by his confessions. He changed seats very cautiously to avoid making a sound and started to rock in the fat woman's chair.

"All alone over there. All alone here. But when I resurface, just watch me! You'll have never seen a guy on his own surrounded by so many friends!"

On his right, in the window that for so long had been that of his mother, Victoire's, bedroom, a little boy, with his eyes closed and his head swaying from left to right, was pretending to play the piano on the white window-sill.

Outremont, January-August 1984

The Chronicles of the Plateau Mont Royal:

The Fat Woman Next Door is Pregnant

Thérèse and Pierette and the Little Hanging Angel

The Duchess and the Commoner

News from Édouard

The First Quarter of the Moon

A Thing of Beauty